William Clark Russell

List ye Landsmen!

Vol. 2

William Clark Russell

List ye Landsmen!
Vol. 2

ISBN/EAN: 9783337347369

Printed in Europe, USA, Canada, Australia, Japan

Cover: Foto ©Andreas Hilbeck / pixelio.de

More available books at **www.hansebooks.com**

LIST, YE LANDSMEN!

A Romance of Incident.

BY

W. CLARK RUSSELL,

AUTHOR OF "THE WRECK OF THE 'GROSVENOR,'" "AN OCEAN TRAGEDY,"
"THE FROZEN PIRATE," ETC. ETC.

In Three Volumes.

VOL. II.

CASSELL & COMPANY, LIMITED:
LONDON, PARIS & MELBOURNE.
1893.

CONTENTS.

LIST, YE LANDSMEN!

CHAPTER XIV.

I SEND MY LETTER.

AT sunrise nothing was to be seen of the schooner, though a seaman was sent on to the main-royal-yard with a telescope, where he swept the sea in all directions.

We crossed the equator before noon, and drove into the South Atlantic, with a pleasant breeze of wind out of the east. A day or two of such sailing would send us clear of the zone of calms and catspaws, and then, with the south-east trade wind strong on the larboard bow, the yards braced forward, the blue seas breaking in foam from the sides, we might hope for a smart run south-west, with weather enough to follow to bring that wonderful island of Greaves within reach of a few days of us, instead of a few months of us, as it had been and still was.

I considered very seriously whether I should

repeat to the captain my brief conversation with Yan
Bol—that chat, I mean, which I have related at the
end of the last chapter. For my own part, I could
not comfortably settle my views of Yan Bol, yet I saw
nothing to object to in the man. Nothing could I
recollect him saying of a kind to excite misgiving.
Though he was acting as second mate, he associated with
the seamen as one of them, slept and ate with them
in their forecastle, and yet had their respect. This I
observed and thought well of. He was a bold and
hearty seaman—a practical sailor. Of navigation he
knew nothing; indeed, he once owned that he could
never understand how it happened that the progress
of a ship altered time; the reason, he said, had been
explained to him on several occasions, but it was all
the same—it was a mystery, "und it vhas fonderful dot
any man vhas born mit brains to understand him."

And yet I could not arrive at any conclusion to
satisfy me. "Am I influenced almost unconsciously
against him," thought I, "by his Dutch airs and
graces? Am I moved to an inward, secret dislike by
a certain freedom of speech and accost, by a sort
of familiarity I have noticed amongst Germans, and
thought particularly detestable in Germans? though
I had heretofore found such Dutchmen as I had
encountered too stodgy and stolid, too insipid and
inexpressive, too torpid in mind and laborious in perception to be readily capable of vexing one by that kind

of freedom and easiness of address and bearing which makes you thirsty to kick the beast whose burden it is. No, I could not trace my doubts of Yan Bol to my dislike of his behaviour to me. Indeed, I could not trace any doubts at all. And yet I never thought of him quite comfortably. If Greaves's dollar-ship was no vision of his slumbers, if Greaves's chests of milled silver were veritably aboard *La Perfecta Casada* in the cave he had described, then we should be a rich brig when we set sail from the island; we should need an honest crew to carry us safely home. Was Yan Bol honest? If a doubt of him arose, he was the one man of the whole ship's company whom it would be Greaves's policy to get rid of as soon as possible, because he was the one man of all our little ship's company the most capable, should he take the trouble to exert himself, of obtaining an ascendancy over his mates, and of directing them for good or ill as he decided.

These being my thoughts, I resolved to repeat to Greaves the questions which Bol had put to me touching the money in the island ship. He listened to me anxiously and attentively.

"I hope that man will not go wrong," said he, when I had concluded; "I like him."

"He is a good man in the forecastle sense of the word," I answered.

"I like him," he repeated. "He controls his

b 2

mates ; he is the sort of man to keep them straight if
he chooses, and I am almost resolved to make him
choose, by promising him a handsomer share than
his bond states—not at the expense of the crew—no ;
but by drawing on my own and the ship's share.
Tulp must do what I want when I plan for the
interests of all."

"That is a hammer to drive the nail home," said
I. "For this has to be considered, captain : your cases
of dollars will be handed over the side. The men are
not fools ; they will count them and roughly calculate
the value of every case. As we sail home there will
be much talk forwards. The amount of money on
board will, of course, be exaggerated. Bol will say, ' I
am second mate and boatswain, and my share is
to come out of sixty-one thousand dollars, eleven
sharing. How much does the Englishman get, the
stranger that did not sail with us from Amsterdam,
who is merely a shipwrecked man, and not one of
us ?' He will wish to know how much, and he may
breed trouble if he does not learn how much. On
the other hand, if he gets the truth and compares it
with *his* share ——"

" All this has been in my head. I will confirm him
in such honesty as he has by a written undertaking
to pay him more dollars." He added, after thinking
a little while, "I wish he had not asked you those
questions. But the fellow may doubt my story. All

hands may doubt it." He gazed at me significantly for a moment, and continued : "He might have hoped to get you to tell him something that he could repeat to the others, and that would hearten 'em. Should he question you again, encourage him to talk."

"Very good, sir."

"You are not to know the value of the freight of dollars."

"I will know nothing when I converse with him."

"But I shall want you to persuade him that my yarn is true," said he with a faint smile, but with a gleam in his eyes which neutralised that weak expression of good-humour.

The relations between the master and the mate—between the captain and the lieutenant—instantly made themselves felt by me. I looked him in the face awaiting instructions.

"You will be able to convince him that my yarn is true," said he.

"He has all the reasons which I have for believing it."

"Do you believe it ?"

"Why, yes! Mynheer Tulp's promotion of this voyage is all the proof that one wants."

He cast his eyes upon the deck, and a light smile twitched his lips. When he next spoke it was to ask me some question that had no relation to the subject we had been conversing upon.

After this I created opportunities for Yan Bol to question me. I lingered when he came on deck to relieve me. I sought to coax him into asking about the ship in the cavern, by loitering in his company instead of at once going below, and by speaking of the voyage, of the Galapagos Islands, of the uncharted island to which we were bound; but his mind appeared to have suddenly and completely turned round; what was before an eager, was now a blank countenance; indeed, he would look at me suspiciously when I talked of the voyage and the dollarship, as though I had a stratagem in my head which must oblige him to mind his eye. Thereupon I ceased to trouble myself to attempt to convince Yan Bol that the captain's story was true, and that our errand was as real as a silver dollar itself is; and it was as well, perhaps, that this Dutchman found me no occasion to tax my wits by the invention of proofs for what I could by no means prove to myself. I did not like Greaves' looks when he talked of his dollarship; I did not understand his half-smiles at such times; I was puzzled by the dreamy expression of his eye, and by the light that had kindled in his gaze when he asked me, with an unspoken doubt behind his words, to convince Yan Bol that his story was true, in order that the crew might be satisfied.

It was a few days after my chat with him about the Dutch boatswain's questions that he asked me if

I had succeeded in satisfying the fellow that there was a vessel, with a lazarette full of dollars, locked up in an island off the Western American coast ? I told him that the man had bouted ship and was on the other tack now; that he shifted his helm when I approached him, exhibited no further curiosity, but, on the contrary, shrank from the subject as though it vexed him. He made, or seemed to make, little of this. But that same evening, when I was sitting at supper with him, he said—

"Yan Bol will go to the devil for me now. I talked with him for an hour this afternoon, whilst you were below. He was frank. I like him none the less for being frank. He is a bit jealous of you. Mind ye, he said not one word against you, Fielding, not a syllable—though at the first syllable I should have brought him up, all standing ! But the spirit of jealousy was strong in his remarks; it smelt in his words like a dram in a man's breath. 'Tis natural. You are an Englishman—he is a durned Dutchman. You came aboard through the cabin window, and his countryman, Van Laar, goes out as you walk in. But a plague upon forecastle passions ! He was frank, as I have said, and told me that he had some doubts of the truth of my story, and that the rest of the men had not yet made up their minds about it. 'And what the deuce,' said I, 'is it to you or to the men whether my story be true or false ? You were

engaged for the voyage. It was a question of wages
with you, and your wages will be paid.' 'Dot vhas
right,' said this Dutchman. But I talked of the
Casuda, nevertheless, described her in the cave, gave
him, in short, the story of my discovery that it might
go the rounds forward; and then I told him that
I had made up my mind to increase his share of the
booty; his share of the sixty one thousand dollars, I
said, was to be according to his rating, which was the
highest next yours; but I added that if he chose to
work with a will and aid me and you to the utmost
to carry this brig in safety to the Downs, I would give
him a written undertaking to pay him a percentage
on the whole value of the property, which sum would
be over and above what he would receive in money as
wages and as his share in the sixty-one thousand
dollars."

"What did he say to that, sir?"

"He smiled, he thanked me, he let fall several
Dutch words, swore that I was the finest captain that
he had ever sailed under, and that his earnings out of
this voyage would set him up for life in his native
town. He was a fairly trustworthy fellow before. He
is as honest now as is to be reasonably expected of
human flesh. I am satisfied; and you need give
yourself no further trouble, Fielding, to convince him
that my story is true."

"Well," thought I, "this, no doubt, is as it should be,"

though it seemed to me that Greaves was making too
much of Yan Bol, too much of his own anxieties—
indeed, sinking the skipper in the adventurer, and a
little heedless of Nelson's axiom that at sea much
must be left to chance. "If," thought I, "he is cocksure
that his ship and her dollars are where he says he
beheld them, then how can it matter to him one jot
whether his crew believe in his story or not?" But
conjecture and speculations of this sort were to no
purpose. In a few weeks the problem would be
solved : either the money would be aboard or we
should have found the ship broken up and everything
gone out of her to the bottom—to such bottom as she
rested upon, twenty or thirty feet maybe, but as un-
searchable to us without diving equipment as the floor
of the mid-Atlantic; or we should have discovered
that there was no ship and no island, and that ours
had been the expedition of a dream. "And still no
matter," I would think. "There are wages to be
pocketed in the end, and I can only be worse off *then*
by being so many months older than I was when I
was fished up out of the Channel by the people of the
brig."

The letter I had written to my uncle, Captain
Round, when I agreed to sail in the *Black Watch*
in the room of Van Laar, I had not yet been able to
send. I forgot all about that letter when I went
aboard Tarbrick's ship to arrange for the reception

of the Dutch mate, and I had not witnessed in the little *Rebecca*, with her two of a crew, a very likely opportunity for communicating with Uncle Joe. But when we were somewhere about six degrees south we fell in with a large snow homeward bound. She was from round the Horn, and proceeding direct to the Thames. I had several selfish as well as respectable and honourable motives for desiring to send the news of my being alive to my uncle, not to mention the pleasure it would give him and my aunt and cousin to learn that I was alive. I was down in his will for what you might call a trifle, but such a trifle as would prove very acceptable to me should it come to my having to continue the sea life for a living. There were other reasons why I desired that my uncle should know that I was alive, but let the one I have given suffice.

Our meeting with that snow was rendered memorable by a phenomenal caprice of wind. It was blowing a light breeze off our starboard bow. The hour was about two, the sky was like a sheet of pale blue silver, here and there shaded with curls and plumes and streamers of high-floating yellow-coloured cloud. There was wind enough to keep the ocean trembling, but at intervals, and at fairly regular intervals, there ran north and south a number of glassy swathes, oil-calm paths from the remotest of the northern airy reaches to the most distant of the recesses of the south. It was my watch below when we sighted the sail. I had dined. It was soul-consumingly hot in the cabin, and I came on deck to smoke a pipe and lounge amid the brine-sweet draughts of air, and in the pleasant shadows cast upon the white and glaring planks by the quietly breathing sails. Greaves was below. Presently Yan Bol, who was in charge of the brig, approached me. I had watched him staring at the approaching vessel through the ship's telescope, his vast chest rising and falling under his extended arms, which, clothed as he went—in pilot cloth, though the sun made him no shadow—looked as big as the thighs of an ordinary man. He approached me and said—

"Mr. Fielding, didt you belief in impossibilities?"

"No, Bol, I don't; do you?"

"By de tunder of Cott, den, I shall for effermore after dis, onless, indeedt, I have lost der eyes I schipped mit at Amsterdam."

"What's the matter?" said I.

"Coom dis way, Mr. Fielding, und you see for yourself."

He crossed the deck. I followed him. He put the telescope into my hands and levelled a square fat forefinger at the sail that was now at no great distance. I viewed the vessel through the glass, but saw nothing remarkable. She was a motherly tub of a ship, with big topsails and short topgallant masts, and a cask-like roll in the sway of her whole fabric as the silver-blue undulations took her.

"Well, what is there to see?"

"Tunder of God!" cried he in Dutch. "Lok, Mr. Fielding, how her yards vhas braced."

And now, indeed, I beheld what Jack might fairly call a miraculous sight. The wind, as I have said, was off our starboard bow, and we were, therefore, braced up on what is termed the starboard tack; but the stranger that was coming along was also braced up on the starboard tack, showing that she, like ourselves, had the wind on her starboard bow. For what did our two postures signify? This—that the wind with us was directly west-south-west, whilst the wind with the stranger was directly east-north-east. Here, then, were two vessels within a couple of miles of each other, so heading that one would pass the other within a biscuit-toss: here, I say, were two vessels steering in exactly opposite directions, but each braced up on the same tack, and each with the wind off the same bow!

"May der toyfell seize me if I like him!" exclaimed Bol, looking aloft at our canvas and then around the sea.

The sailors at work about the deck stared aloft and then at the approaching ship. They bit hard upon the tobacco in their cheeks. One of the Dutchmen called to an English seaman in the fore-rigging—

" Dis vhas der ocean of Kingdom Coom. Der angels vhas not far off when efery ship hov a vindt for himself."

The English sailor, with an uneasy motion of his body, swang off the rigging to spit clear into the sea.

"Arter this, mate," he called down to the Dutchman, "I shall give up drinking water when I gets ashore."

I looked into the cabin skylight, and, seeing Greaves at the table, begged him to step on deck and behold a strange sight. By this time both vessels had hoisted their ensigns, and each flag blew in an opposite direction.

" I have heard of this sort of thing," said Greaves, " but never before saw it. Lord, now, if every ship could have a wind of her own, as we and yonder craft have ! There would be no weather-gauge then—no complicated dodging for advantageous positions. Ha ! Look at that, now. She has taken our wind !"

The sails of the approaching vessel fell and trembled. A minute later, the yards were slowly swung, and the canvas shone like white satin as it swelled to the same breeze that was breathing off our bow.

" I should be glad to send my letter home by that ship," said I.

" It may be managed," he exclaimed, " and without

bothering to back yards or lower a boat. Get your letter."

I ran to my berth and returned with the letter, which Greaves posted for me on the passing ship in the following manner :—

He sent me to procure a piece of canvas, a small number of musket-balls, some twine, and an end of ratlin stuff. He put the balls and my letter into the canvas, and, with the twine, bound the cloth into a small, heavy parcel, to which he secured the end of the piece of ratlin stuff; then, giving directions to the man at the helm to starboard, so as to close the stranger, he sprang upon the rail and waited for the two vessels to draw together.

" Oh, the snow ahoy !" he shouted.

" Hillo !" responded a man who stood on the quarter of the vessel.

" Where are you bound to ?"

" London."

" Will you take a letter for me ?"

The man motioned assent, and looked aloft, as though about to order his topsail to be backed.

" I will chuck the letter aboard," said Greaves, swinging the parcel by its line, that the man might guess what he intended to do. " Stand by to receive it !"

Again the fellow, who was probably the captain, motioned; and then, waiting until the two craft were abreast, Greaves, with a dexterous swing of his arm, sent the parcel flying through the air. It fell on the deck of the passing vessel just abaft her mainmast. The fellow who had answered Greaves's hail, running forward, picked it up, and held it high in his hand that we might see he had it. After this there was no opportunity for further communication; for scarce were the two vessels abreast when they were on each other's quarter, rapidly sliding a widening interval betwixt their sterns.

The snow was the *Lady Godiva.* I read her name under her counter. But her being bound to London, now that my letter was aboard, was information enough about her to answer my turn.

From this date down to the period of our arrival off the west coast of South America my clear recollection of every particular of this voyage yields me little that is good enough to record. Incidents so far had not been lacking, but south of the equator our sea-life grew as dull as ever the vocation can be at its dullest. Heavens! how incommunicably tedious is the mechanic round of shipboard days! Wonderful to me is it that sailors in those times, when a single passage kept them afloat for months, remained human. And less than human some of them were, I am bound to say. Think of their lodging—a small, black hole in the bows of the ship, dimly lighted by a lamp fed with slush skimmed from the coppers in the galley;

no fire in bitter weather, no air in hot; every straining timber sweating brine into the dark interior, till
the floor in a head-sea was awash; till every blanket
was like a newly-wrung-out swab; till there was not
a dry rag in the hole of a living-room to enable the
poor devils to shift themselves withal. Think of their
food—salted meat, out of which they could have sawn
and chiselled blocks for reeving-gear to hoist their
sails with; biscuit that crawled on the innumerable
legs of vermin, alive but unintelligent, for it came not
to your whistle nor did it elude your grasp; tea from
which the thirstiest of the fiery-eyed rats in the fore-
peak are known to have recoiled with lamentable
squeaks and dying shrieks of disappointment. Think
of their labour—the scrubbing, the tarring, the greas-
ing, the furling and reefing and stitching, the kicks,
the blows, the curses which accompanied the toil.
Think of their pleasures—an inch of sooty pipe to
suck, an ancient story to nod over, a song at long
intervals.

Alas, poor Jack! What is it that carries thee to
sea in the first instance? The love of freedom? Hie
thee to the nearest jail: there is more freedom
in it; better food, kinder words. The desire to see
the world? What dost see unless thou runnest
from thy ship? for in harbour all day long thou art
sweating in the hold and stamping round and round
to the music of pawls; and when the night comes

and thou goest ashore, if thou hast a shot in thy
locker thou gettest drunk, and with whirling brains
and blistered lips art thrust rather than conveyed to
thy toil in the morning by the constable whom thy
skipper hath sent in search of thee. And so much,
therefore, Jack, dost thou see of foreign parts. But
whatever may have been the cause that sent thee to
sea, my lad, this will I affirm : that when once thou
art afloat, there is nothing clothed in flesh, with an
immortal spirit to be saved or damned, more de-
serving of pity.

But though we were a dull, we were a comfortable
little ship. I never heard of any falling out amongst
the crew. They worked well together. The common
hope of the dollar that lay on t'other side the Horn
was strong in them. It kept them well-meaning. It
was clear they all had full confidence in the captain's
yarn, and their spirits danced with anticipation of the
money they would jingle when they got home—the
money in wages and share per man. This I used to
think.

They made much of their dog-watches when the
weather was fine. One of the Dutchmen played on
the flute; one of the Englishmen had a fiddle.
The fellows would save their nooutide grog for a
dog-watch, and make merry. Yan Bol sang as a bull
roars, but his singing was vastly enjoyed. Never did
any mariner better dance the sailor's hornpipe than

c

the English sailor, Thomas Teach. He went through
it grim and unsmiling, but his postures were full
of that sort of elegance which is the gift of old Ocean
to such men as Teach. It is old Ocean alone that can
animate the limbs with the careless beauty of motion
that Teach's arms and legs displayed when he danced
the hornpipe.

And there was a sailor named Harry Call. He
had served in American ships, and knew the negro
character, and when he blacked his face he was good
entertainment. Greaves liked his fooling so well that
he would call him aft, send for the men, order Jimmy
to mix a can of grog, and Call with his spare voice
and negro pleasantries would agreeably kill an hour.

My own life was as pleasant as a seafaring life can
very well be. Greaves had much to talk about. He
had looked into books. He had travelled widely and
observed closely. He was a person of much good-
nature. In truth, a more genial, informing man I
could not have prayed for as a shipmate. Yet I
would take notice of a certain haziness on one side of
his mind. He loved metaphysical speculations, and
would wriggle out of a homely topic to start a religious discussion. I humoured him for some time,
but religion being one of those subjects that I did not
much care to talk about, I soon ceased to argue, and
then all the talking was his. He entertained some
odd notions for a sailor—believed that every man had

a good and a bad angel, that when a man died his spirit slept with his dust. "Otherwise," he asked, "what is to bring the parts together again, inform them with mind, and render the whole sensible of what is happening?" I found that he had a leaning towards the Roman Catholic faith. I asked him if he was married. He answered "No." I then inquired why Van Laar had threatened to take the bed from under him and his wife. "To vex me," said he.

He would be talking of religion and metaphysics, of dreams and a future life, of the state of his soul a million years ago, and of the inhabitants of certain of the stars, when I would be thinking of his ship in the cave and the dollars aboard of her. But as our voyage progressed, as we drove southwards towards the Horn, he found little or nothing to say about his ship in the cave. You would have said he was done with the subject. He had so little to say, indeed, that I would wonder at times whether the purpose of this expedition was not slipping out of his memory, as a dream, that is vital and brilliant on one's awaking from it, fades ere nightfall, and is effaced by the vision of another slumber. "It will be a confounded disappointment should it prove false after all," I would think; for, spite of my misgivings, which sometimes I would nourish and sometimes spurn, I, during those tedious days and weeks running into months, I, in many a lonely watch on deck, in many a waking hour

c 2

in my hammock, had built my little castles in the air,
had furnished them handsomely for one of my degree,
had gazed at them with fondness as they glittered in
the light of my hope. Six thousand pounds! The
money was a bigger pile in those day than it is now;
to be so easily earned too! Why, in imagination
I had bought me a little house, I had married a wife,
I was gardening often in mine own little estate, and
every quarter I was receiving dividend warrants; and
there was good ale in my cellar, and no stint at meal-
times; and I was a happy young man, in imagination,
sitting, as I did, on the apex of that pyramid of
promised dollars, whence I commanded a boundless
prospect for a mariner's eye. And now if it was all to
end in a hoaxing dream! Bless me! Whilst I was
on this side of the Horn, how I pined for t'other side,
how I thrashed the old brig through it in my watch
on deck! With what ardour of expectancy did I
every day sit down to work out the sights!

CHAPTER XV.

THE WHITE WATER.

THE *Black Watch* had sailed through the Downs in the middle of September, and on the morning of December 12, 1814, she was upon the meridian of Cape Horn, and in about fifty-seven degrees south latitude. This passage, for so swift a keel, was a long one. It was owing to diabolical weather between the degrees of forty and fifty south.

Greaves and I would sometimes say that the devil was afloat in a craft of his own within that belt of ten degrees. Head-winds more maddening to the most angelic soul, calms more provocative of impious and affrighting language, it is not in the imagination of the most seasoned mariner to conceive.

But enough. We were off the Horn at last. Our bowsprit would be heading north presently, and, when our ship's forefoot cut this meridian again, the little fabric would (but would she ?) be deeper in the water (by what division of a strake ?) with a cargo of minted silver !

In 1814 much was made of the passage of the
Horn.   The doubling of that bleak, inhospitable,
deep-seated rock was accepted, on the whole, as
a considerable adventure.   The old traditions of
mountain-high seas and gales of cyclonic fury sur-
vived.   The traffic down there was small; the
colonies of New Holland were still raw in their
making; and ships bound for Europe from that
distant continent chose the mild but tedious passage
of the South African headland.

The old dread has vanished.   Experience has
footed prejudice out of time.   In furious weather the
ocean off the Horn is as terrible as the North Atlantic,
as the Southern Ocean, as any vast breast of water
is in furious weather; and that is the long and short
of it.   Oh, yes; off the Horn you get some monstrous
seas, it is true.   I have known what it is to be running
off the Horn before a westerly gale and to be afraid—
seasoned as I then was—*to look astern!*   But there
is a safety in the mighty swing of those wide Andean
heaps of brine which the sharper-edged surge of the
smaller ocean does not yield.

The old freebooters and the early navigators are
responsible for the evil reputation of the Horn.   They
returned from the wonders of foreign sight-seeing,
from the joys of plunder and the delights of discovery, with their hearts full of astonishment and
their mouths full of lies.   There is Shelvocke's

description of the Horn : it is heartrending reading even in these days. The ice forms upon the page as you read ; the atmosphere darkens with snow. And what, on the testimony of such a record, did Wapping think of that distant, ice-girt, howling navigation, with its enchanted islands, and bergs whose spires seemed to pink the moon ? What did Wapping think, when there was never a man in every company of a thousand jackets who had rounded the Horn and could tell of it ?

We, passing the Horn on December 12, found the southern hemisphere's midsummer there. We met, for the most part, with bright skies, a cheerful sun, not wanting in warmth, coming soon and going late, and a noble field of swelling blue seas. One iceberg we sighted. It was infinitely remote—a point of pearl on the sea-line.

"She vhas like a babe's milk-tooth," said Yan Bol, pointing to it.

There was a fancy of milk in the whiteness of it ; but, when I brought my eyes from the distant berg to Bol's face, I said unto myself—"What should *that* man know of a babe's milk-tooth ? "

Two disappointments await those who round the Horn with expectations bred of the reading of books. First, the weather. Often is it as placid as any quiet day that sleeps over the Straits of Dover, when the sky is streaked with the lingering smoke of vanished

steamers and the white cliffs of France hang in the
air.   No ; the weather off the Horn is not the ever-
lasting saddle of the Storm Fiend.   The seas are not
always boiling, the hurricanes of wind are not always
black with frost, heavy with snow, man-killing with
ice-darts.

Next, the constellation called the Southern Cross.
It hangs over you when you are off the Horn; often
have I looked up at it, and never have I thought it
beautiful.   The smallest of the gems of the English
skies is a richer jewel than the Southern Cross.   A
singular superstition is this widespread faith in the
beauty of the Crux of the ancient mariner.   The
stars are unequally set ; one is disproportionately
small.

But now came a morning when we struck a
meridian that enabled us to shift our helm for a
northern passage, and then we had the whole length
of the mighty seaboard of South America to climb.
We were in the South Pacific at last.   The island was
hard upon three thousand miles distant ; but it was
over the bows—it was ahead !   We had turned the
stormy corner, and the verification of Greaves's yarn
could be thought of as something that was about to
happen soon.

Day by day we climbéd the parallels and all went
well.   Certain stars sank behind the edge of the sea
astern of us, and as we sailed northward many particular

stars which were familiar to our northern eyes rose over the bows and wheeled in little arcs. We made some westing that we might give the land a wide berth; for whether Great Britain was or was not at war with Spain, the Spaniards of that vast seaboard were scarcely less jealously and passionately tenacious, in those days of their dominion in the South Sea and under the Line to beyond Panama, than they were in the preceding century; and though we could not positively affirm that there was anything to be afraid of, anything curiously and sneakingly dangerous to be shunned (if it were not Commodore Porter, whose ship the *Essex* was believed to be prowling hereabouts at this time), yet Greaves was determined to provide his bad angel with the slenderest possible opportunity for delaying or arresting the voyage to the island.

So we kept well out to the west, and fine sailing it was. For days we hardly touched a brace; the steady wind, growing daily warmer, sweetly blew the little brig along. It was the South Pacific Ocean. Many reports are there of the various tempers of that sea, but, for my part, northwards of the parallel of forty degrees I have ever found it a gentle breast of ocean. Long and lazy was the blue swell brimming to our counter, drowsy the flap of the sunny canvas, soft the cradled motion of the ship. Once again the silver flying-fish glanced from the slope of the violet knolls. The wet, black fin of a shark hung steadfast in our

wake. What a world of waters it was! Never the
gleam of a ship's canvas for days and days to break
the boundless continuity of the distant sea-line. The
men relaxed their labours, Yan Bol took no notice,
and I, who was never a "hazer," was willing
that they should lounge through their toil of the
hours in a climate so enervating that one yearned to
sling a hammock in some cool corner of the deck, to
lie in it all day, to smoke and doze whilst the imagination glided away on the stream of the rippling music
made by the broken waters and passed into the fairy
harbours of dreams.

"By this time to-morrow," said Greaves to me one
evening, "if this breeze holds and our reckoning is
true, and the island has not been exploded by a
volcano or an earthquake, you will be having a good
view of the ship in the cave—no, I am wrong, a good
view of her you will not obtain from the sea, but you
will be having a good view of the cave in which she
lies, and I shall be very much surprised if you are not
mightily impressed by the magnitude and beauty of
that great hole or split in the rock, and by the inde-
scribable complicated atmosphere or shadow within,
caused, as I long ago explained to you, by the inter-
lacery of the ship's gear and spars, visible and indeterminable."

"Visible and indeterminable! Captain, you put it
as though it were some mystery of religion."

"Do you object, Fielding," said he, "to sailors—I mean quarter-deck sailors—expressing themselves as educated men would, nay, as average gentlemen would? Are you for keeping the quarter-deck sailor down to Smollett's platform of Hatchway and Trunnion? Must we swear, must we drink, must we behave when ashore like lascivious baboons and at sea like Newgate felons, who have burst through the iron bars and are sailing away for their lives, merely to justify the landgoing notion that the best of all sailors are the most brutal of all beasts?"

"I beg your pardon," said I. "I meant nothing."

"Visible and indeterminable. Are they not good words? Do they not exactly express what I want to convey to your mind? How der toyfell would you have me talk?"

He looked at me, and I looked at him. He then burst into a laugh, and we stepped the deck for a little while in silence. The time was something after half-past seven. The sun was gone, and night had descended upon the sea. It was a tropic night. The dark sky was full of splendid brilliants. A mild air blew from the westward, and the brig, with her two spires of canvas lifting pale to the stars, dreamily floated over the black water that here and there shone with a little cloud of sea-fire, as though some luminous jelly-fish was riding past, whilst here and there it caught and feathered back the flash of some large star, whose silver in a dead calm would have made an almost moon-like wake. Galloon marched by our side. Jimmy, forward with a pipe in his mouth, lay leaning over the windlass-end gazing aft, seemingly at the shadowy form of the dog, as though he hoped to coax the brute that way by persistent staring and wishing. The men, in twos and threes, trudged the forecastle. So still was the evening, so seldom the flap of canvas, so unvexing to the hearing the summer sound of the water lightly washing into the furrow of bubbles and foam-bells astern, that the voices of the men fell distinctly upon the ear; by hearkening one might have caught the syllables of their speech.

It had gone forward—taken there by Yan Bol, or whispered by the lad, Jimmy, who by listening to the captain and me as we discoursed at the cabin table at meals, would be able to pick up news enough to repeat; it had gone forward, I say, that, the weather holding as it was, and all continuing well, by some hour next day we should be having the island on the bow or beam, perhaps hove-to off it, or with an anchor down. Expectation was strong in the men's voices. It was the very night for their flute or fiddle, for "Tom Tough," or "Britons, strike home!" or for some boisterous Dutch song in Yan Bol's thunder, for Call's lamp-blacked Jack Puddingisms, for Teach's hornpipe for general caper-cutting, in a word, with a can of grog betwixt the knight-heads, and the fumes of mundungus strong in the back-draughts. But the humour of the sailors this night was to walk up and down the deck in twos and threes, and to talk of to-morrow and of dollars.

"If *La Perfecta Casada*—a fine sounding name, by the way, captain," said I; "what is the English of it ?"

" The Perfect Wife."

"The Spaniards," said I, "choose strange names for their ships. They have many *Holy Virgins* and *Purest Marias* at sea. I knew a Spanish ship that was called the *Holy Ghost*. Figure an English ship so called. She meets another English vessel, and hails her : 'Ship ahoy !' 'Hallo !' 'What ship's that ?' 'The *Holy Ghost*.' There is a looseness in this sort of naming that is not very pleasing to Protestant prejudice. I asked the mate of the *Holy Ghost*, 'Why is your ship thus named ?' 'That she may not sink,' he answered. 'Hell lies downwards. If the *Holy Ghost* goes anywhere, 'tis upwards.'"

" You are in a talkative humour this evening."

" Well, it is like being homeward bound when the end of the outward passage is within hail."

"What were you going to say about the *Casada?*"

" I have never clearly gathered—supposing her to be still lying in that cave where you saw her——"

"She is still lying in that cave where I saw her," he interrupted, repeating my words in a strong voice.

"I have never clearly gathered," I continued, "whether it is your intention to tranship her cargo— I mean the cocoa and wool?"

"I cannot make up my mind whether or not to meddle with those commodities," said he, "and so because I have not been able to form an intention, you have not been able to gather one from our conversation. The weather will advise me. Then I shall want to know the condition of the cargo. The wool, cocoa, and hides in the hair may not be worth lifting out of a hold that has been aground in a cave since 1810. But there are a thousand quintals of tin, and there are some casks of tortoiseshell—we shall see, we shall see."

"Mynheer Tulp," said I, "will, no doubt, be able to find room for all that you can carry home."

"Room and a market. But I am here for dollars. I believe I shall not meddle with the other stuff. We'll tranship as fast as the boats can ply, and then away."

I made no answer, being occupied at that instant with admiring the effect of a flash of lightning in the south-west—a clear and lovely blaze of violet which threw out the horizon in a black, firm indigo line.

I went below with Greaves at eight o'clock to drink a glass of cold grog before turning in. Greaves had brought the chart of this part of the American coast out of his cabin, and we sat together conversing and looking at it. At intervals I was sensible of the burly figure of Yan Bol pausing near the open sky-light, under which we sat, to peer down and to listen. But there was nothing Greaves desired to withhold from the crew, nothing he was not willing that any man of them should overhear, if it were not, perhaps, the value of the money on board the *Casada;* though even their overhearing of this must be a matter of indifference, since they were bound to form an opinion of their own of the contents of the cases of dollars when they came to handle them.

Greaves had marked down upon the chart the position of the island in accordance with his observations when he hove-to off it and sighted the ship in the cave on his way to Guayaquil. The position of the brig by dead reckoning since noon brought us, at this hour of eight, within twenty leagues of the spot, and, therefore, supposing Greaves's observations to have been correct, and supposing that the weak wind that was flapping us onwards continued to blow throughout the night, we had good reason to hope that the bright morning light would give us a view of the tall heap of cinder cliffs before another twelve hours should have gone round.

Greaves was making certain calculations with a pencil on a sheet of paper, and I, with a pair of compasses, was measuring the distance of the island from the main land, when we were startled by the roaring voice of Yan Bol, whose full face was thrust into the open skylight.

"For der love of Cott, captain, goom on deck und see vhat vhas wrong!   Der sea vhas on fire.   Quick! or ve vhas all burnt up."

"What does he say?" cried Greaves, who had been unable to promptly disengage his attention from his calculations.

"He says that the sea is on fire, and that we shall all be burnt up," I exclaimed, picking up my cap; and, in a moment, we were both on deck.

"Der sea vhas on fire!" thundered Yan Bol as we stepped through the hatch.

I looked ahead over the bows of the brig, and the sea all that way was splendid and terrible with light. I call it light, but light it was *not*, unless that be light which is made by snow in darkness.   It was a wonderful whiteness that seemed a sort of fire.   It blended the junction of sea and sky into a wide and ghastly glare, and the light of the white water rolled upwards into the sky as the clearly defined edge of the milky surface advanced, as you see a blue edge of breeze sweeping over a silver surface of dead calm.   The sea where the brig was sailing was black, as it had been before we went below, and in the deep, soft, indigo dusk over our mastheads the stars were shining; but the sparkling of the luminaries languished over our fore yardarms, and it was easy to guess that, if the coming whiteness spread, the sky and all that was shining in it would be hidden.

"Captain," cried Bol, " vhat, in der good anchel's name, vhas she ? "

"A star has fallen," answered Greaves, "and is shining at the bottom of the sea."

" A star? Vhat, a star from der sky ? "

" Where do stars grow ? " said Greaves.

" Do you mean a shooting star, captain ? " cried Bol.

" Yan Bol," said Greaves, nudging me as we stood side by side, " you have much to learn. Do not you know that the stars are often falling ? They drop into other worlds than ours. Sometimes they plump into our earth, fizz into the sea, and lie on the ooze, shining for a while and making queer lights upon the water like that yonder."

Bol breathed deeply. He could read, indeed ; but he was as ignorant, prejudiced, and grossly super-stitious as most forecastle hands in his day—fitter for the faiths of a Finn than a Hollander. He stared at the advancing whiteness, and seemed not to know what to make of the captain's discourse.

" Yes," continued Greaves, " they are frequently falling. They are the stars which were loosed in the pavement of heaven when the angels fell. There should be many more stars than there are. Un-happily, when Lucifer was hurled over the battlements

d

he swept away a number of stars with his tail and loosened many more, and it is those which drop."

" Der toyfell ! " muttered Bol. " Von lifs und larns."

" It is a wonderful sight," said I, gazing with astonishment, not wholly unmixed, at the mighty sheet of whiteness that was coming along.

Already on high the verge of the startling milky reflection was over our fore royal-masthead. You might look straight up now and see no stars. The line of the flaring whiteness upon the sea was a little more than a mile distant. The wind blew softly, and before it the brig floated onwards, meeting the coming whiteness with an occasional flap of canvas that fell upon the ear like a note of alarm from aloft.

" Did you never before see the white water, Fielding ? " exclaimed Greaves.

" Never, sir."

" I have sailed through it three times," said he. " Once off Natal, once in Indian and once in China seas. I did not know it was to be met with on this side the world; but everything is probable and possible at sea. I tell you what, Bol," he exclaimed, calling across to the Dutchman, who had gone to the side to stare, and was holding on to a shroud, or back-stay, with his big body painted black as ink against

the whiteness that was coming along, " I believe
I am mistaken, after all. It is not a star; it is an
insect."

" I likes to handle dot insect. I likes her in der
forecastle to read by und light mine pipe by," said Bol,
with a coarse, heavy, uneasy laugh, that sounded like
the bray of an ass.

" It is a sub-globular insect," said Greaves, nudging
me again, " compressed vertically, convex above,
concave beneath, wrapped in a transparent coriaceous
envelope, containing a white, gelatinous substance.
Repeat that to the men, Bol—will you ?—should the
whiteness make them uneasy. Very few sailors," said
he, addressing me, and talking without appearing in
the least degree sensible of the wonderful and alarm-
ing milk-white light that was now almost upon us,
" take the trouble to scientifically examine what passes
under their noses. What, for example, is more often
under a sailor's nose than bilge-water ? An Irish·
skipper once asked me what bilge-water was. I told
him that it was sulphuretted hydrogen, hydro-sul-
phate of ammonia, oxide of iron, and compounds of
lead and zinc. " Jasus," said he, " and is that how you
spell shtink in English ? "

As he spoke, the brig, with a long-drawn flap up
aloft, smote the sharply defined white line, and in an
instant was bathed in the unearthly light. We had
not been able to see each other's faces before. Now

the very expression of countenance was visible. The whole body of the brig was revealed as though by the light of the moon, and the ghastliness of the light lay in its making no shadow. The seamen stood staring and gaping: withered, they seemed, into a posture of utter lifelessness. But no shadows lay at their feet, no shadow stretched from the foot of the mast; I looked down; the planks lay plain, the seams clear, but I made no shadow. Nor did this magic light mirror itself. I glanced at the polished brass piece aft, but no star of reflection burnt in it, no gleam lay upon the cabin skylight. It was light and yet it was not light, and the wonder of it, and, perhaps, the fearfulness of it, to me, who had never beheld such a sight before, lay in *that*.

And now, by this time, the whole sea was as though covered with snow or milk as far as we could extend the gaze. The sky reflected the light, and the stars were eclipsed, but the reflection on high had not the glare of the ocean surface. I went to the side and peered over; the brig seemed to be thrusting through an ocean of quicksilver. The water broke thickly and sluggishly in small heaps from the bows, and the patches, as they came eddying aft, were like clots of cream. The sensation induced by the progress of the vessel was as though she were forcing her way through a dense jelly. The slight heave of the sea was flattened; there was not the least visible motion

in this surface of whiteness ; the brig stood upright on
it, and the swing of the trucks would not have spanned
the diameter of the moon. There was no fire in the
water, no coruscation of sea-glow, no green gleam of
phosphor. To the very recesses of the horizon went
sheeting this marvellous breast of milk-white softness, that, though it was not luminous, yet flung an
illumination as of the radiance of a faint aurora bore-
alis upon the heavens.

" This is a beautiful sight ! " exclaimed Greaves.

" It will be a memorable one," I answered.

" I have never before," said he, " seen the white
water so white, but the like of this phenomenon which
I witnessed off the coast of Natal was heightened and
beautified by a strange light in the heavens to the
northward. It was a delicate, rosy light. I should
have imagined it was the moon rising had not the
moon been up."

" Do I understand," said I, " that this sublime
light is produced by a marine insect ? "

" By nothing more nor less—so 'tis said. It is the
marine insect that will sometimes give you an ocean
of blood, and sometimes an ocean of exquisite violet,
and sometimes, as I have heard, though it is something rare to witness, an ocean of ink."

" An insect ! " I exclaimed. " And how many go
to this show ? "

" Oh, for a shipload of infidels now ! " cried he.

" D'ye see them looking up to God after gazing, white as the water itself, at the ocean ? "

By this time the watch below had turned out, aroused, no doubt, by one of the sailors on duty. The men in a body had gradually worked their way from the forecastle to the gangway. They were all as plainly to be viewed as by the sickly light of a foggy day. No man spoke; not for minute after minute did the grunt or growl of any one of their hurricane throats reach my ears. The wild vast scene of whiteness terrified them. The impression produced was the deeper because this was the night before the day that was to heave Greaves's island out of the sea for our sight to feast on. For let it be remembered at least that the adventure we were on was highly romantic; the plain, illiterate Jacks would find something almost magical, something a little out of nature, according to their scuttle-butt and harness-cask views of life, in Greaves's discovery of an uncharted island, with a ship full of dollars in a hole in it. Also in these seas stood the Galapagos, islands of mystery and darkness whose dusky rocks had not width enough of front to receive from the chisel or the knife the records of the bloody and diabolic tragedies of which they had been the theatre.

A man stepped out of the group; he coughed hoarsely and spat. His hand went to his forehead, and he scraped the sea-bow of those times.

"Capt'n, I beg your honour's pardon," he said; "us men would like to know what sea this here is?"

"The South Pacific—always the South Pacific," answered Greaves.

"Will your honour tell us what's the meaning of this here chalkiness?"

"My lads, some clumsy son of a gun has capsized a milk-can. Look for his ship, my hearts; she can't be far off."

Some of the men stupidly gazed seawards.

"Vhas der island vashed by dis milkiness, captain?" exclaimed Wirtz.

"It stands in the bluest sea in the world," answered Greaves.

"This here's a sight," said Travers, "that may be all blooming fine to read about, but tain't lucky, to my ways of thinking. Give me natur, says I."

He did not use the word, *blooming*. This elegant expression was not to be heard in those days; but let it stand.

"Has none of you ever seen such a sight as this before?" called Greaves.

After a pause, "Ne'er a man," answered Teach.

"Then gaze your eyes full! drink your hearts full! Never again may you behold the like of this field of glory. Look thirstily! look till ye burst with the beauty that'll come into you by looking! Fear not, my sons—we shall be out of it all too soon. Gaze,

my livelies, and silver your souls with this brightness
as it silvers your cheeks. Bol, out whistle and pipe
grog, that we may watch with enjoyment."

Bol blew. Jimmy, with Galloon at his heels, arrived with the can; the tot measure was dipped into
the black liquor, lifted and emptied, and the dram
seemed to give every man heart enough to look about
him with common curiosity. One of the fellows
fetched a bucket, dropped it over the side, and hauled
it up full. I drew close. It was as though a pail of
cream had been handed aboard.

I put my finger into the whiteness. It was as
thin as salt water, nothing gluey or cheesy about it,
though from the bows the whiteness rolled away from
the rending slide of the cutwater as thickly and
obstinately as melted ore, and astern there was no
wake; it might have been oil.

For an hour we sailed through this sea of cream
and under a dimmer sky of white. Bald and ghostly
was that passage rendered by the shadowlessness
of our decks. The sails swelled dark against the
paleness; so clear was the tracing of the fabric of
mast and canvas against the sky, that the course of
so delicate a rope as the royal backstay could be
traced to the head of the mast, and you saw the jewel
block at each topsail and topgallant yard-arm, clean
cut as a pear on a bough against a sunset. Greaves
came to a stand opposite me and looked me in the face.

" You make me think of my dreams of the dead," said he ; "the dead are always pale when they come to me in dreams. Most people who dream of the dead, dream of them as they remember them in life. There is light in the eye, and colour on the cheek. They always rise before me pale from their coffins."

" Inspiriting talk, captain," said I, "at such a moment ! But I hope I look no more like a dead man than the rest of us."

" If I were an artist," said he, " I would give many guineas out of my earnings for the chance of beholding such a light as this ; this is the sort of light through which I would paint the Phantom Ship sailing. Figure that wondrous ghost out upon those white waters, the pallid faces of her men, to whom death is denied, looking over her side at the white sky, every timber in her glowing with the jewellery of rottenness—you know what I mean—the green phosphoric sparkling of decay. Cannot you see her out yonder, dully gleaming with dim green crawlings of fire as she steals noiselessly through this frothy softness, the hush of living death upon her, the silence of catalepsy ? But what is the name of the painter, I should like to know, who is going to give us this light upon canvas ? Oh, tell me his name, Fielding, that I may offer him all the ducats I hope to be in sight of to-morrow for his secret."

" Less my whack."

"Less yours. But mine, plus Tulp's. Damn Tulp; I'll drink his health." He called to Jimmy: "Two glasses of brandy and water, three finger-nips, James."

The liquor was brought, we chinked glasses, and down went the doses, to the benefit of *one* of us certainly; for I had not liked his talk of my looking like a dead man, and his fancies of the Phantom Ship with her crawlings of fire and cheese-like faces overhanging the side. Jack, if you are reading this, bear with me. I was a sailor, and, as a sailor, *you* will know that I would not relish such talk at such a time.

On a sudden the wind slightly freshened, with a melancholy cry, across the white water, and, as if by magic, the sea ahead opened black, with a few stars hovering over it. Some minutes later, the northern edge of the milky surface came streaming to our bows, and swept past us as though 'twas the edge of a mighty white sheet dragged by giant hands down in the south over the surface of the ocean. I watched the marvellous appearance receding astern, the sky unveiling its stars, as the whiteness dimmed away, till it was pure nature once again, the heavens shining, the swell coming into the ocean with its long and lazy lift of the brig, the pleasant hiss of foam under the bow, and a little dance of jewels in the furrow astern.

It was my watch below, and I went to my cabin.

CHAPTER XVI.

GREAVES'S ISLAND.

I PULLED off my coat and lay down. Eleven o'clock was struck on deck before I closed my eyes. I was much excited. The prospect of the dawn disclosing the island kept me restless. Was there an island in this part of these seas for the dawn to disclose? and, if an island existed, would there be a cave in it, and would that cave contain a large Spanish ship, with five hundred and fifty thousand dollars stowed away in cases in her lazarette?

I reviewed Greaves's behaviour. He had been cool, I thought, seeing that this was the eve of the day that was to bring us off the island and put the dollars within reach of our oars. He had joked at the overwhelming apparition of the white water; he had talked of worms and fallen stars; he had treated a magnificent phenomenon without reverence; and, in one way or another, he had acted as though to-morrow were to be charged with no more than what to-day had held. These and the like reflections kept me awake. Shortly after six bells had been struck I fell asleep.

At midnight Bol aroused me to take his place, and I went on deck to keep watch until four o'clock. It was a quiet, rippling night; the moist breath of old Ocean gushed pleasantly over the larboard quarter, and the brig slipped softly forwards, clothed with studding-sails. Several shadowy figures of the crew moved about the deck; their motions were restless; they'd go to the side, bend over, and peer ahead. At any other time it was just the night for a quiet snooze about the decks, with a coil of rope for a pillow, and the stars right overhead to watch until they winked one asleep. But the men were too restless to "plank it" this night. They guessed the island to be some-where away out yonder in the dusk. They might hope at any moment for an order from the quarter-deck to back the main topsail yard. They were under the spell of the almighty dollar!

Bol hung near, waiting for me to arrive.

" Anything in sight, Bol ? "

" Not'ing, Mr. Fielding," he answered out of the depth of his lungs ; " but dere vhas time. She vhas not to-morrow yet."

" No more white water ? "

" No, by tunder, Mr. Fielding. Enough vhas as goodt as a feast. I like der captain's notion of a star.

She vhas a fine idea. Der verm vhas silly. How shall
a verm shine in vater? Vill not der vater put her
light out?"

I was in no humour to talk to him about phosphorus.

"You had better go forward and get some rest,"
said I. "Should daylight give us the island, there
will be plenty to do for all hands."

He grunted and moved forward, but not to turn
in. His unwieldy shape joined other flitting forms,
and I heard his deep voice rumbling first on one bow
and then on t'other as he crossed the deck.

Greaves made his appearance three or four times
during this middle watch. He did not stay. He
would come up to me and say—

"Well, what do you see?"

"I see nothing."

"All the same, it's in sight, but you're not a cat,
Fielding. Mind your helm. The difference of a
quarter of a point might sink the island for us by
daybreak."

He would then go to the binnacle and stand looking upon the card, address the helmsman, and after
running his eyes over the canvas and stepping to the
side, not to peer ahead like the men, but to judge of
the rate of sailing by the passage of the sea-fire
through the deep shadow made by the hull, disappear
through the companion-way.

It was very dark at four o'clock in the morning, at which hour my watch ended. When eight bells were struck, I went into the head and sunk my sight into the obscurity forward, running my gaze from beam to beam; for though it was very black there were stars sparely shining over the sea-line, and by the obliteration of a handful of them might I guess the presence of land; but I saw nothing. I went aft and found Bol near the wheel and Greaves in the act of stepping through the hatchway. Eight bells had not long been chimed, and the larboard watch had not yet gone below.

"Whilst all hands are on deck, reduce sail, Mr. Fielding," said Greaves. "Take in your studding-sails and ease her down to the main topgallant sail."

"Ay, ay, sir."

Nothing more was said. Yan Bol went forward, I remained aft, whence I delivered the necessary orders. The heavier canvas was rolled up by all hands; the watch was then called—that is to say, the larboard watch were sent below. Daybreak was still an hour off. I said to myself, "If the island is hereabouts, there will be plenty to do when daylight comes. Let me sleep whilst I can;" and for the second time that night I withdrew to my cabin and lay down, "all standing," ready for a call.

I slept well, and was awakened by a beating

upon the door. The voice of the lad Jimmy called out—

"It's eight bells, sir."

"Any news of the island?" I cried.

I received no reply; in fact, the lad had run on deck the instant he had called the time to me. The berth was full of light, and the glass of the scuttle was a trembling, brilliant, silver-blue disc, with the ocean splendour flowing to it. I stepped on deck, and the moment my head was clear of the companion-way I beheld the island. It stood at a distance of about seven miles upon the lee or starboard bow. Greaves was pacing the deck with his hands locked behind him and his head thoughtfully bent. Yan Bol stood in the gangway, and all hands were forward breakfasting in the open; they grasped pannikins of steaming tea; they sawed with jack-knives at cubes of beef, blue with brine, locked by their hairy thumbs to biscuit, which served for trenchers; the muscles of their leather cheeks moved slowly as they chawed, chawed, chawed, cow-like, and cow-like still they moved their eyes slowly in their sockets to direct them at the island over the bow.

The morning was a wide field of day, a full heaven of tropic splendour, with a light breeze off the larboard beam blowing you knew not whence, for there was never a cloud for the wind to come out of. They had made all plain sail on the brig; she was floating

forward, spars erect, under royals; the studding-sails
were stowed and the booms rigged in.

I stood staring for some moments with my mind
in a state of confusion. *There* was the island! The
mass of it standing upon the light blue glory of water
north-east was a hard rebuke to my scepticism. Yet—
shall I say it—not the most mercenary of the munch-
ing Jacks in the bows could have felt a keener delight
at the sight of that island than I. It signified dollars
and independence to my ardent hopes. I had thought
much upon my share—the six thousand pounds—
dreamt of the money often, had builded many fancies
tall and radiant upon Greaves's bond, and sometimes
had I believed that Greaves's story was true, and sometimes had I believed that Greaves's story was a dream,
and therefore a lie. And now there was the island,
down away over the starboard bow, a lump of shadow
against the blue, to verify Greaves's assurance of an
island being thereabouts anyhow, and, on the merits
of that verification, to warrant all the rest of the
wonder of cave, of ship, and of a lazarette full of
dollars!

For a few moments only I stood staring. Thought
hath wondrous velocity, and in a few moments much
will pass through the mind. I stepped up to Greaves
as his walk brought him to me. I should have
wished to give him my hand, but the etiquette of the
quarter-deck forbade that.

"Captain," said I, in a low voice, full, nevertheless, of cordiality and enthusiasm, "I warmly congratulate you."

"And yourself," said he, drily.

"And myself," said I, "and all hands, including Mynheer Tulp."

"Seeing is believing," said he, still drily. I looked at the island. "And yet," continued he, "though that land be there, the ship and her cargo may be nothing more than a dream."

He had seen a little deeper into me than I had supposed. Finding him sarcastic, I held my peace, and the better to cover my silence stooped to caress Galloon. He changed his voice and manner.

"My observations," said he, "of the latitude and longitude of that island were perfectly correct, you see."

"Perfectly correct, indeed," I echoed. "It is strange that so big a rock should remain uncharted."

"Nothing is strange at sea—in this sea particularly. The Spaniards are always for making their journeys by one road. Anything lying off that road they miss, unless they happen to be blown on to it, when one of two things happens: they perish, or they petition the Madonna and escape. If they escape, they have no more to tell about the rock or coast from which they narrowly came off with their

e

lives than if they had perished. Why is that island
uncharted by the Spaniards? Is it because no mariner
amongst them has fallen in with it? Oh, they are
lazy rogues all—they are lazy rogues all; timid, fearful
navigators, execrable hydrographers."

"It is odd that no Englishman should have fallen
in with it."

"That is as it happens to be."

I fetched the glass, and steadied it upon the
rail, and looked. The island stood up large and livid,
tawny in patches, a huge cinderous heap. The hue
and even the appearance of it somewhat reminded
me of Ascension viewed at a distance. One or two
parts were robed with green. There was a tremble
and flash of surf at the extremities, and I guessed
that when the sea ran high it would break very
fiercely and dangerously against all weather-front-
ing corners of that lonely rock. Greaves came
and stood beside me. I was conscious of his presence, and talked to him with my eye at the telescope.

"In what part of the island is the cave situated,
sir?"

"Do you observe a lump of land swelling above
the edge of the cliff to the left?"

"Yes."

"That lump or round is the summit of the front
of the rock in which lies the cave. We are opening

it from the southward. I opened it, when I fell in with that land, from the westward."

"It is a volcanic pile," said I. "I observe points of rocks like chimneys. They may have smoked once upon a time."

He took the glass from me, leisurely inspected the island, and walked the deck in his earlier thoughtful posture, head bowed, hands locked behind him. I understood what was in his mind, and held off; he would have nothing to say until the wreck of the Spaniard stood before him in its dusky tomb. He mastered his anxiety, but would now and again pause and direct at the island a look that, with its accompanying play of face, expression of lip, suggestion of posture, told more of what was passing in him than had he talked for an hour.

He ordered the boy Jimmy to put breakfast on the skylight; and we ate, standing or walking, but exchanging very few words. Thus slipped the time away, and so slipped we through the water. The brig bowed as she went; a long breathing swell followed her astern, and the sails came into the mast as she rose with the heave of the dark-blue brine. The sailors lay over the forecastle-head, waiting for the approach of the island and for orders. Now and again one would point and one would speak, but expectation lay as a weight upon their minds. It subdued them. For there was the island, to be sure, and

e 2

the cave, no doubt, was round the corner, and in that cave might be the ship. But the dollars, the dollars! Ah! Lay they there still, massive, good tender as the guinea, plentiful as roe in the herring, noble coins to tassel a handkerchief with, to clink out the sweetest music in the world with to the accompaniment of deck-blistered feet marching across the gangway to the wharf, to the joys of the alley boarding-house, to the delights of the runner's parlour—lay they there still in the mouldering hold within the cave?

So did I interpret the thoughts of the sailors, and I would have bet the last dollar of my share upon the accuracy of my construction of their several countenances and attitudes.

" Let her go off," said the captain.

The man at the helm put the wheel over by two or three spokes.

" Steady!" exclaimed Greaves. He viewed the island through the glass. " We are opening the reef," said he; and, taking the telescope from him, I instantly discerned the sallow line of a projection of rock, with a dazzle of sunshine coming and going along the base of the formation as the swell rose and sank there.

Deep silence fell upon the brig. All hands of us—nay, my beloved Galloon and the very brig herself—seemed to know that in a few minutes the cave would lie open before us.

And a few minutes disclosed it. I viewed the picture as though I had beheld it before, so clearly had Greaves painted it in his description, so familiar had it grown by frequent meditation. Almost abreast of us now, within a mile, lay a very perfect little natural harbour. The reefs swept out from either hand the island. They looked like piers. They needed but a lighthouse to have passed, at a glance, for roughly constructed artificial piers. Within their embrace lay a wide, smooth surface of dark blue water. A flat, livid front of rock overlooked, on the left, this placid expanse. Low down on the right of this rock ran a herbless and treeless beach, without scintillation as of sand or gleam as of coral—a dead ground of foreshore, mouse-coloured; a sort of pumice, with a small shelving to the wash of the water. But I had no eyes for that beach then, nor for any other portion of the island saving the vast, sullen, gloomy fissure which denoted the entrance of the cave right amidships of the tall face of flat rock.

Greaves let fall the glass from his eye. He swung it with an odd gesture of irritable triumph.

"Back the main-topsail, Mr. Fielding."

I instantly delivered the necessary orders for heaving the ship to. The men sprang out of the bows and rushed to the braces and clew-garnets as though to a summons which signified life or death to them. The brig's way was arrested. She came with her head to

the south-west, bringing the island upon her starboard
quarter. All the time, whilst I sung out orders and
whilst the men were hauling upon the braces, Greaves
stood at the rail, his eye glued to the glass that was
pointed at the cavern. He turned his head when
the noise about our decks had ceased, and, observing
me standing at a little distance regarding him, he
beckoned.

" Look for yourself," said he.

I brought the tube to bear upon the cave, and, for
some moments, saw nothing but the darkness of the
interior. A singular appearance of darkness it was,
burnished to the gleam of a raven's wing by the silver-
blue atmosphere, by the azure glory floating off the surface of the natural harbour through which I viewed it.
But after a little I seemed to make out a sort of
intricacy of pale lines in that gloom. Well, *pale* I
will not call them. They were of a lighter hue than
the dusk out of which they stole to the eye. Then,
knowing very well that that complication of shadow
signified the spars, yards, and rigging of a large ship,
I seemed to distinguish the form of the fabric ; could
almost swear to her bowsprit, to the tops, to the side
she showed, to the crosses of the lower masts and fore
and main yards.

" What do you see ? " said Greaves.

" A ship," said I.

" Oh, you have no doubt ? "

"I should have plenty of doubt," said I, "if you had not told me how to name, how to define that bewildering muddle of shadow."

"Give me the glass!" cried he suddenly, with a change and vehemence of voice that made the abrupt note of it wild as madness itself to my ears.

I started, gave him the glass, and watched him.

"My God!" he cried, "I fear we are too late."

"Captain," called Bol from the gangway, "dere vhas people valking on der beach."

The telescope fell with a crash from Greaves's hand. He gazed at me with an ashen face. "It was my *only* fear!" he cried. "Are we too late?"

"I see three people," said I, after looking awhile. "One of them is a woman."

"Are you sure of that?" he shouted.

"One of them is a woman," I repeated. "Two men and one woman. I see no more. One of the men is waving his hat, and now the woman is waving something white—a handkerchief. They are castaways."

Greaves snatched the glass from me.

"You are right, I believe," he exclaimed, after looking. "What should a woman be doing in a salvage or wrecking job? Yes; they are flourishing to us. I did not before observe that one was a woman. Get a boat manned, Mr. Fielding, and bring them aboard. I am mad till I learn what their business is there, who they are, what has brought them to *this* of all the hundred rocks of the Pacific."

"Which boat shall I take, sir?"

"The cutter. Let the crew go armed. Those two fellows and the woman may prove a piratical decoy, for all you know. Mind your eye as you enter the reefs, and hold on your oars to parley. There may be a big gang in ambush round the corner at the extremity of the flat there."

I have elsewhere told you that we carried three boats—a little one, which we termed a jolly-boat, stowed in a big one amidships; and abreast of these boats lay a third boat in chocks. This boat, whose capacity rose to a lading of from twenty to five-and-twenty people, we termed the cutter. Tackles were swiftly carried aloft. Whilst this was being done the fellows who were to man her armed themselves with cutlasses and pistols. The boat was then swayed over the side, six men and myself entered her, and we headed for the island.

We gained the entrance of the natural harbour, and I bade the men pause on their oars whilst I looked and considered. I gave no attention to the singular aspect of the island, nor to the wondrous revelation of the ship in the vast cave. I could think of nothing but the three people on the beach. Were they decoys, as Greaves had suggested? Was there a crowd of formidable ruffians somewhere in hiding close at hand, but ready for a rush when the moment should arrive? I gazed carefully around, but saw nothing resembling a boat. We might be quite sure that there was no vessel in the neighbourhood; the island was small— we had sailed half round it before heaving to. It was impossible to imagine that any craft with masts could be lying off the north side of the island without our having caught sight of her as we approached. But then it might matter nothing that no vessel should be in sight. Likely as not the ship in the cave had been discovered and explored, in which case the discoverer had acted as Greaves had—sailed away for a port to re-embark in a properly equipped expedition; a number of men had been thrown ashore to work at the caverned Spaniard whilst the vessel to which they belonged went away to put the horizon betwixt her and the rock, lest, by hovering and lingering close to, she should invite the attention of anything that passed.

These were my thoughts as I stood up in the stern-sheets staring around. But the woman? Truly, methought, had Greaves conjectured that fellows engaged on such an errand as this of clearing the Spaniard's hold, would not burden themselves with a woman ashore, at all events. No noise came from the island. A low note of the thunder of surf hummed from the north side, a great number of sea-birds were wheeling about in the air over that northern part, at too great a distance for their cries to reach us.

"Give way," said I.

We pulled into the middle of the harbour, halted afresh, and now we had a good view of the three people, who, throughout this time of our tardy approach, continued to flourish to us, but without calling. The two men were apparently forecastle hands — foreigners. They wore grass hats, wide-brimmed, sombrero fashion ; their clothes were loose blue shirts or blouses and blue trousers ; they were barefooted ; they were both of them hairy and dark, one of them of the colour of coffee. Their hair lay upon their backs in a snaky shower, and I caught a glance of earrings as they moved their heads.

The woman I could not very clearly make out. Her gown was of some pearl-coloured stuff—it had a look of shot silk, but I dare not attempt any descriptions in this way. She wore a large white hat with a white veil coiled round the crown of it ready for dropping over the face. Some sort of mantilla she had on. She was a tall and graceful figure of a woman, and as she stood a little apart from the men, I observed the grace of a dancer in her attitudes of entreaty, in her gesticulations to us to approach.

We pulled closer in to the beach upon which those three were standing. One of the men cried out to us, the other clasped his hands, and the woman stood motionlessly gazing.

" What language is that ? " said I.

None of my men could tell me. The man continued to exclaim, gesticulating very eagerly and wildly. I listened and thought he spoke in French.

" Are you French ? " I sung out.

" Spaniards, señor, Spaniards," he answered, in Spanish.

" Do you speak English ? "

He cried back that he understood a little English.

" Are there others, besides yourselves, on this island ? "

He answered " No."

" What are you doing here ? "

" We are shipwrecked," he answered, but in an accent I cannot imitate ; the spelling would be meaningless to eye and brain.

" How long have you been here ? "

He held up his right hand, the thumb pressed into the palm, that his four fingers might answer my question.

Here the woman exclaimed in Spanish. Her voice was clear, sweet, and rich. It came to the ear like music from the beach. There seemed no harshness of shipwreck, no weakness of privation or despair in it. She spoke with her face directed to the boat, but I could not understand one word she uttered.

"Do you wish to be taken off this island?" I cried.

"Yes, señor, yes," shouted the man who had answered throughout. "We starve here—we die here if you do not take us off."

I again looked very carefully about, fearful still lest some deadly trick was intended, but could see no signs of anything elsewhere on the island living or stirring. All was motionless; nothing came along with the wind but the sound of the creaming of waters, the throb and hum of surf at a distance.

"Back in, men," said I.

We got the boat stern-on to the beach. It was like a lake for the quiet lipping of the water there. The men held their places on the thwarts, ready at the instant of a cry to give way.

"Come, madam," said I to the lady.

She approached, comprehending my gesture. I took her by the hands and helped her to spring over the stern; then seated her. The two men jumped in, and we shoved off. I looked back and around as we pulled away for the opening betwixt the reefs. Nothing stirred.

The woman had very fine features. Her eyes were large, dark, and full of fire; her complexion was a very delicate pale olive; her mouth small and firm.

Indeed, her mouth wanted but a corresponding and helping expression of sweetness and of tenderness in the other lineaments to be a lovely feature. She was clearly a lady. Her hands were small—models of hands to the finger-tips ; her hair was extraordinarily thick, plentiful beyond anything I ever saw in a woman, and of a rich dead blackness. She wore a pair of long gold ear-rings, bulb-shaped, with a ball at each extremity in which sparkled a little star of diamonds. Some rings, too, she had—one on the forefinger of her right hand was a cross, formed of a sort of dark stone set upon gold, probably a signet ring. No other jewellery did she carry. Her clothes were of some rich stuff, but I could not give a name to the material: a magically contrived combination of dyes, swiftly blending and alternating with every move, and cheating the eye kaleidoscopically—the product of some Asiatic loom, an art that may have ceased as an art, and that has been extinguished by the neglect of taste. So much for my observations of this Spanish lady whilst we were making for the brig.

I found nothing remarkable in the two seamen. One had a pinched look; he was hollow in the eyes, and an expression of fear lay on his face. In appearance they answered to the beachcomber of the present day. They were hairy, dirty, and wild. A small silver crucifix gleamed in the moss upon the chest of the fellow who spoke English.

I had time to ask a few questions. The men swung upon their oars with a will, and the brig lay scarcely a mile distant. I inquired of the lady if she spoke English. She bent her fine eyes very wistfully upon me, and shook her head on the Spanish sailor explaining what I had said. I again inquired of the fellow who understood my speech if there were others upon the island, and he answered, with energy and with passion, that there had been but three, as though he understood me to refer to his shipwreck. I asked if they had found water on the island. He answered " Yes," and pointed to some cliffs past the beach, where stood a small grove of trees, and vegetation resembling guinea grass, along with a thickness of green bushes coming down the slope.

But now we were alongside the brig. I helped the lady up the side, the two Spanish seamen followed. Greaves called down an order for the boat to keep alongside, and for two hands to remain in her. He then approached us, holding his hat whilst he bowed to the lady, who returned his salutation with a slow, very stately, elegant gesture, irreconcilable with the horrors from which she was newly rescued, and with the distress and apprehension in which she must continue until she reached her home, wherever *that* might be.

" She is Spanish, sir," said I, " and understands not a syllable of our tongue."

He called to Jimmy to bring a chair from the cabin, and placed it for her in some square of shadow cast by the canvas. The crew of the brig, saving the two men over the side, were collected in the bows, and talked eagerly, and often looked our way and then at the island. Yan Bol, pipe in mouth, towered among the men.

CHAPTER XVII.

THE SHIP IN THE CAVE.

GREAVES read Spanish, but spoke it ill. He was a North-countryman, and was without musical accents for soft or swelling or vowelled tongues. On seating the lady, he looked at her and pronounced some words in her speech. My ear told me they were barbarous. They might have been Welsh or Erse.

"This man," said I, pointing to one of the Spanish seamen who stood near, "understands English."

Greaves was about to address the sailor; he broke off, and beckoned to Bol. The lumbering Dutchman came pitching aft like one of the bum-bowed boats of his own country over a swell.

"Station a man on the fore-royal yard, Bol," said Greaves, "to instantly report anything that may heave into view."

"Ay, ay, sir."

The Dutchman went forward again, and a minute later the sailor, named Meehan, ran patting aloft.

"Fielding, should a sail be reported when I am

ashore," said Greaves, speaking as though the lady and the Spanish seamen were not present, "fill on your topsail and stand away under easy canvas in a direction opposite to what the stranger may be taking. Keep your eye on her, and haul in again for the island as she settles away. Nothing must observe us hanging about here until we have got what we have come to take. I do not think it likely that anything will heave into view. I give you these directions whilst they are present to my mind."

I replied in the customary affirmative of the sea.

"Now for our friends," he exclaimed; "I will give them ten minutes to make sure of them." He looked at his watch, and turned to the Spanish sailors. "Which of you speaks English?"

"Me—Antonio. I speak a little English," answered the sailor.

"Have you enough English to make me understand how it comes to pass that you are on this island? You may use a few Spanish words."

The Spaniard told this story. Their ship was *La Diana.* They had sailed from Acapulco—the date of their departure escapes me. The ship was bound to Cadiz. She was a rich ship, and a vessel of six hundred tons. A few passengers went in the cabin, and her company of working hands, from captain to boy, numbered thirty-eight souls. They steered straight south down the meridian of 100° W., and all went

f

well till they were in about 3° S. of the equator,
when a hurricane struck the ship. Neither I nor
Greaves could clearly understand from the man's
recital what then happened. The memory of suffering
and horror worked him into passion. He talked in
Spanish, forgot that he was speaking to us, addressed
the lady, who frequently sighed and moaned and
lifted her eyes to heaven, whilst the other Spanish
sailor, holding his clenched fists a little forward of
his hips, shook them, nodding his head with a miser-
able, convulsed grin of temper, and horror, and tears.

We gathered that the ship's masts were swept out
of her, that most of the seamen made off in the boats,
that the captain ordered Antonio and his companion,
whose name was Jorge, together with other seamen,
to enter a boat to receive the passengers. This we
understood. Then it seemed that though Jorge and
Antonio got into the boat that lay lifting and beating
alongside, threatening to scatter in staves at every
moment, others of the crew did not follow. A
lady was handed down—" the Señorita Aurora de la
Cueva," said Antonio, with a nod of his head in the
direction of the young lady—and scarcely had the
two fellows grasped her when the boat's line parted
and the fabric blew away.

What followed was just the old-world, well-worn
story of a couple of days and a couple of nights of
suffering in an open boat. Often has this form of

misery been described ; and a changeless condition of ocean life it must ever be, let the marine transformations of the coming ages be what they may. They fell in with Greaves's island. A heave of swell was running from the west; the two fellows were half-dead with thirst and with the fear of dying. Spineless creatures they looked. If *they* were examples of the fellows who fought us at St. Vincent and Trafalgar, what was there in the victories of our beef-fed pig-tails to brag about ? They aimed for a head of reef to spring ashore, dragging the lady with them, heedless of their boat, the wretches thinking only of a drink of water, and the boat went to pieces whilst they staggered inland.

Here Antonio swore horribly in Spanish. He smote his hands together, squinted fiercely at Jorge, and abused him with a torrent of words. The other hung his head and occasionally shrugged his shoulders. The lady kept her fine eyes fastened upon me. Her face worked slightly in sympathy with the speech of Antonio when he spoke in Spanish, and occasionally she sighed and moaned low ; but her eyes rarely left my face. Never before had I been honoured by the intent regard of eyes so liquid, so beautiful, so full of fire, eyes whose lightest glance, when all was well with the owner, could hardly fail to be impassioned.

" Who is this lady ? " said Greaves, breaking in upon Antonio.

f 2

The man again pronounced her name.

Greaves said, " She was a passenger ? "

" With her mother, my capitan. Both were proceeding to Cadiz for Madrid."

" With her mother ! Then she is separated from her mother by the shipwreck ? "

" The boat would have received the mother, but the line parted."

" Did the people you left behind perish, think you ? "

Antonio replied with a shrug.

" You have been four days on the island, I understand, and there is water in abundance ? "

" There is good water among those trees," said the Spaniard, pointing.

" And what food have you met with ? "

He succeeded, with much difficulty, in making us understand that they had lived upon terrapin, crabs, and iguanas.

" Did you get fire for dressing your food ? "

Antonio put his hand in his pocket and produced a little burning-glass.

" Fielding," said Greaves, " I am going ashore. Look to the brig and see to the lady. Take her below ; let Jimmy put meat and wine upon the table. There's a spare berth for her, and by-and-by we will make her comfortable and keep her so till we can dispose of her. I wish she were not here, though." He made

a face. " Go along forward, Antonio, with your companion. D'ye see that big man there ? His name is
Yan Bol. Ask him to feed you. Hold ! "

Antonio and his mate faced about.

" Did you go on board the ship in the cave ? "

" What ship, señor ? "

" There is a ship in that cave," said Greaves, pointing. " Did you go on board of her ? "

The man placed the sharp of his hand against his
brow and looked at the island.

" I know no ship—I know no cave, señor,"
said he.

"Go forward and ask that big Dutchman to feed
you," exclaimed Greaves.

" When you think of it," he continued, addressing
me as the men walked forward, "they would not be
able to see the cave when on the island. It is clear
that they did not notice the ship when they landed
on the reef: they were too thirsty, poor devils."

" And how could they board the ship without a
boat, sir ? " said I.

" True," he answered. " I see too much, Fielding.
I put on glasses and they magnify my meat, but they
don't cheat my appetite. See to the lady."

He called to Bol to put a couple of lanterns into
the boat and to send the crew of the cutter aft, and
walked to the gangway. In a few minutes he was
making for the island.

" Hail the masthead, Bol," cried I, "and ascertain if all is clear round the horizon."

The answer fell from the lofty height in thin syllables—there was nothing in sight. I beckoned to the lad Jimmy, who was standing by the caboose, and bade him furnish the cabin table with the best meal he could put upon it and to look alive. I then turned to the lady, and, with my hat in my hand, exclaimed—

" Will you let me take you below ? "

She viewed me anxiously. Her fine eyes made a passion of even a trifling emotion in her. She did not understand, and so I had to fall to Robinson Crusoe's old trick of gesticulating. Heavens, how doth ignorance of another's tongue seal the lips ! You are as one who walks dumb through many lands. Had this poor lady had power of speech in English, or could I have understood her Spanish, how would she have given vent to her full breast ! I could see in her lips, in her eyes, in the movement of her features, how grievously was her heart in labour. Yes ; in her face worked the anguish of enforced silence. I pointed to the cabin, made signs of eating, extended my hand to take hers, on which she rose, gave me a low bow, put her hand in mine, and I led her through the companion-way.

Jimmy had not yet arrived with the meal. Still holding her hand, to deliver myself from the absurdity of gesticulating, I conducted her to a berth on the starboard side in the fore part of the living-room, opened the door, and sought, with a flourish of my fist, to make her understand that it was at her disposal.

"*Yrá ó hará muy bien*" (It will do very well), said she.

I afterwards understood this to be her remark; *then* it was darker than Hebrew. In fact, I thought she referred to the emptiness of the berth. The bunk was without bedding; and that bare bunk and a little, naked, unequipped semicircle of wooden washstand, screwed into the bulkhead, formed all the visible furniture of the interior.

I knew a few words in French, and tried her with a "Parlez-vous Français, señorita?"

"Nó, caballero," she answered.

I made a step into the berth, and motioned toward the bunk and the washstand, in the hope that she would be able to collect from my contortions that her comfort would be presently seen to. She inclined her head and slightly smiled, and the flash of her teeth was like sunshine betwixt her lips. Again I presented my hand, and she gave me hers; and I led her into the cabin where Jimmy was now busy. Galloon sat upon his chair watching the lad lay the cloth. He pricked his ears and growled at the Spanish lady. I shook my fist at him, and his eyes languished, though his ears remained pricked. The lady exclaimed in Spanish, and fearlessly walked round to the dog and

patted him. Galloon wagged his tail, but his ears
remained elevated, as though one end of him was in
doubt whilst the other end was satisfied. I again
noticed the beauty of the lady's hand as she laid it on
the dog, and the sparkle of the rings upon her fingers.
Jimmy breathed fast and grinned much, and could
scarcely proceed in his work for staring. I abused
him for a lazy cub, and bade him bear a hand.

The meal was spread. I motioned the lady into
the chair occupied by Greaves, with further gesticulations desired her to help herself, and poured out
a bumper of claret, of which wine Greaves had laid in
a handsome stock, whether at Tulp's cost or not I
could not say. I was greatly impressed by the self-
control and dignity of this lady Aurora, as I understood one of her names to be. Hungry I could not
question she was. Tempted, I might also feel sure
she would be, by the food before her after four days
of such living as the island beach and the grove of
trees provided. Yet she helped herself to but a little
at a time, first crossing herself with great devotion
before lifting her fork, then eating with the well-bred
leisureliness you would have looked to see in her
at her mother's table. But the silence grew moment-
arily more oppressive.

"Jimmy," said I, "go forward and bring that
Spanish sailor Antonio aft with you, unless he's still
eating."

At the expiration of five minutes Antonio followed Jimmy into the cabin.

"Have you had plenty to eat?" said I.

His ear-rings danced whilst he nodded—he wore ear-rings like those you see on a French fishwife—his bloodstained, dark eyes searched the cabin.

"A very good ship—very kind men," said he. "When do you sail, señor?"

"I have not sent for you to question me," said I.. "I desire you to interpret my speech to this lady. Tell her——" and, in few, I bade him inform her that instructions would be given for her cabin to be comfortably equipped, and that whatever the brig could supply was at her service.

She smiled and bowed to me on this being interpreted, and then addressed Antonio, who, however, found himself at a loss, and was obliged to act to make me understand. He feigned to wash his face, and unnecessarily passed his fingers through the length of his hair, and then, finding words, made me understand that the lady was weary, that she had slept but little, and then on the hard ground, and that she would be thankful to lie down and sleep. Thereupon I told Jimmy to convey my bedding to her bunk, also to place one or two toilet conveniences of my own in her cabin; and, after waiting to see my instructions carried out, I bowed low and sprang on deck, with my mind full of the dollars ashore, wondering likewise what Greaves's report would be, whether the dollars were still in the ship's hold, and when he meant to go to work to discharge the vessel of her silver.

My first look was at the weather. It was boundless azure down to the lens-like brim of the sea—not a feather-sized wing of cloud—and a light air of wind with just enough of weight in it to hold the backed topsail steady to the mast. I looked at the island; the boat had entered the cave, and was lost in the shadow. I picked up the glass, and levelled it; the dark lines of rigging and spar were faintly discernible, but the boat was deep in the dusk, and not to be seen. It was the ugliest rock of island I had ever viewed, swart, sterile—save where the trees stood—gloomy, menacing with its suggestion of arrested fires. A few terrapin, or land tortoises, crawled upon the beach. Many birds, most of them white as shapes of marble, wheeled and hovered over the further extremity of the land, with frequent stoopings and dartings, like our gulls over a herring shoal. I swept every foot of the visible surface of land with a telescope, but witnessed no signs of life of any sort. Nevertheless, the two long arms of the reef strangely civilised the beach and the face of cliff where the cave was, by their likeness to artificial piers. They formed a very perfect, spacious harbour, in which, during a heedless moment or two, I caught myself looking for a cluster of rowboats, for some group of shipping, for cranes and capstans, for men walking, as though, forsooth, I gazed at the piers of a dock!

How it had come to pass that a big ship of seven or eight hundred tons should have backed and neatly threaded an eye of cave, and fixed herself within, Greaves had doubtless correctly explained. The commander of her had stumbled upon this island in thick weather; or he may have found the island aboard of him on a sudden in a black night. He had a reason for bringing up in the shelter of that harbour, and when his anchors were down it came on to blow dead inshore. The ship dragged. Her stern made a straight course for the opening in the cave. Would they seek to give her a sheer to divert her from that entry? No. For there might be safety in that cave, but outside it was certain destruction. To touch was to go to pieces against such a steep-to front of cliff as that. But many are the conundrums submitted by the ocean, and victoriously insoluble are they for the most part. You may theorise as you will. Nothing is certain but this—

"There was a ship!"

Whilst I waited for the return of Greaves, I called to Bol to get a cast of the deep-sea lead. There was no bottom at eighty fathoms. I had expected from the appearance of the island to find a great depth of water to the very wash of the surf. No need, therefore, to bother with our ground tackle. And so much the better! Nothing like having your ship under control when the land is aboard. With an offing of a mile it would be easy to "ratch" clear of any point of the island, even should it come on to blow with hurricane power; then it would be up-helm and a brief run for it, and a heave-to till the weather mended.

The two Spanish sailors sat, Lascar fashion, against the caboose. They sucked alternately at a short pipe which one of them had probably borrowed. When the lead-line was coiled away, Yan Bol rolled up to me and said, in his voice of thunder, but very civilly—

"Dot vhas a scare."

"What was a scare?" said I.

He levelled a massive forefinger at the two Spaniards. I nodded. "Der captain vhas some time ·gone," said he. "I hope no man vhas before her."

"And that's my hope."

"How many cases of dollars might der be, Mr. Fielding?"

"I don't know."

He looked as if he did not believe me, and said, "Vell, der more der better for Mynheer Tulp und oders." He paused upon this word, *oders*. I gazed at the island. "Der more der better, certainly," continued he, "yet dey vhas not so plentiful but dot efery dollar might be shipped before dark. Tell me dey vhas plentiful some more dan dot, and, by Cott, Mr. Fielding, der crew's share vhas as a flea upon der dog dot scratch her."

" My name is Fielding, not Greaves, Yan Bol," said I.

" Oh, yaw, dot vhas right. But I likes to tink aloud sometimes, Mr. Fielding."

" Are not you satisfied ? " cried I, suddenly rounding upon him and looking him full in the face.

" Perfectly satisfied, Mr. Fielding."

" Then why, by that devil who always seems to be busy in ships' forecastles, come you to me now with your growlings and your questions and your dots, and your Cotts and your dollars, Yan Bol ? "

" Growlings—questions ! I likes to know vhen we get der dollars on boardt und make sail, dot vhas all."

" Strike a light with your eyes and keep a look-out for yourself, and hail the fore-royal yard, will ye, and receive the man's report."

He went forward, and his roar swept straight aloft like a blast from the mouth of a cannon. There was nothing in sight at sea, the man called down. I looked towards the island, and saw the boat at that moment stealing out of the cave. I mused on Bol while the boat swept across the satin-calm surface of the natural harbour, the oars swinging like lines of flame in the men's hands. Was Bol going to give trouble ? It was late in the day to ask that question. It would be impossible to rid the ship of him on this side the Horn, and by the time it came to t'other side——

The boat arrived, and Greaves rose in the stern sheets; he rose, but he was supported too. A sailor grasped him by either arm, and he was helped with difficulty over the side of the brig. I was at the gangway to receive him, and assisted by seizing his hands as the men helped him to climb. He was pale as milk, and his mouth was drawn with pain.

"What is the matter ?" I asked.

"I have had a fall," he said, speaking with a laboured breath. "I tripped and drove my whole weight against the sharp edge of a case in the lazarette of the ship yonder. I wish I may not have broken a rib. Help me, Fielding."

I took him by the arm, and Jimmy, who stood near, grasped him in obedience to my gesture by the other arm, and together we got him into the cabin and to his berth. He asked for brandy-and-water, and drank a tumblerful, and then requested me to help him to strip, that he might see if he had broken any bones. He had hurt himself over the right hip, and the skin was somewhat darkened there, but the ribs were unbroken. He felt over himself anxiously, occasionally groaning, and said—

"No, my good angel be praised, the bones are

sound. I am in torment from the pain of the blow. That must be it, and it will pass—it will pass."

" I would recommend you to lie perfectly still."

" No; I must be on deck. I can sit and keep watch and look about me whilst you go ashore."

I helped him to dress, and he seemed unable to speak for pain whilst he put his arms and body in motion. He then asked for another glass of brandy-and-water, and sat, saying he would rest and talk to me for ten minutes.

" Are you in pain when you are still ? " said I.

" No. I was too eager, and consequently careless, pressed forward, tripped, and should have set fire to the ship had I swooned, for I was alone, and the fall flung the lighted lantern from me, and the candle lay naked and burning among the cases."

" Lord, how suddenly will a trifle become a frightful thing at sea ! " said I.

" Where is the Spanish lady, Fielding ? "

" In her berth, and perhaps asleep, sir."

" Well," said he, after a pause, " the dollars are there."

" I am glad to hear it, sir," said I, feeling the blood in my cheek, for I own that the news worked as a sort of transport in me.

" This cursed accident will hinder me from superintending the unlading of the vessel. You must undertake that job."

"You can trust me, captain."

"Up to the hilt I do. Open that drawer and hand me the pocket-book you'll see." His extending his hand to receive the book made him wince. "There are a hundred and forty cases," said he. "You will take slings and tackles to hoist the cases out and lower them over the side into the boat. Be careful not to overload your boat. The money may be safely transhipped in three journeys: so divide one hundred and forty by three and your quotient is your lading for each trip."

"Ay, ay, sir."

"Be careful with your fire. I split open some of the boxes, as I told you, to make sure of their contents. Take tools and nails and battens with you for securing the riven cases. Be yourself in the lazarette whilst this is doing."

"Right, sir. Where will you have the cases stowed aboard us?"

"Oh, in the lazarette. I was prevented by my fall," he exclaimed, "from examining the rest of the cargo. Do you that when the money is transhipped. I will act on your report if the weather allows. But should there come a change when we have got the money, then damn your cocoa and tin—we'll be off."

"Shall I remain in the ship during the trips, or take charge of the boat?"

"Take charge of the boat; but see all your men in first."

I faintly smiled, for here was a direction that was a little particular, methought.

"Help me on deck now, Fielding, and then go to work."

I thought to myself, "It is no time, this, to speak of Yan Bol. The matter must stand."

He leaned upon me, and, with pain and difficulty, gained the deck. All the men but one had come out of the boat, and the ship's company, saving that man and Jimmy and the fellows at the wheel and mast-head, were assembled in the gangway. They hung together in a little crowd. Impatience burnt like fire in them—impatience and expectation and anxiety, now complicated by the injury their captain had met with. When we made our appearance, they stared and shuffled, one and all, as though they were muti-neers scarce masking a madness of bloody intention, and about to make a rush aft to its execution. Is not the insanity that drink will run into the veins and brains a sweet little cherub compared with the demon that enters the soul of man out of the coin of gold or silver?

"Captain," cried Yan Bol, "I shpeaks for all handts. You vhas not hurt much, all handts hope?"

"Not much, my lads—not much, I thank you,"

g

answered Greaves, whom I had helped to seat in the chair Jimmy had placed for him, and who, whilst he remained motionless, seemed free from pain.

"Captain," again cried Yan Bol, in tones like to the noise of breakers heard in the hollows of cliffs, "again I shpeaks for all handts. Vhas der dollars safe ? "

" Yes," answered Greaves.

The men roared out a cheer—a roaring cheer it was. It seemed to be repeated in the island a mile off, as though there was a crew ashore there.

I now began to sing out the instructions which Greaves had given me. Pieces of planking for nailing over the cases were flung into the boat; lines for slings, tackles, tools, lanterns, and the like, were handed down. The crew took their seats, and we shoved off, followed by a cheer from the fellows who remained behind. There went with me six men— two Dutch, the others my countrymen. The drift of the brig, though very inconsiderable, owing to the lightness of the breeze and the apparent absolute tidelessness of the sea, had veered the island a trifle southerly, and the brig lay on a line with the edge of the cliff where the cave was. The cave was, therefore, hidden from me. I stared with great curiosity at the island as we neared it, making for the head of the westerly reef to round into the lake-like expanse within. A more hideous heap of rock shows not its head above the water. The cliffs of it, where they run to any noticeable altitude, come down to the sea in twisted masses. You would have thought the process of this island's formation had been arrested at some instant when the red-hot mass of it was writhing and pouring into the ocean over the edges of its own heaped-up stuff. No iceberg ever submitted a more fanciful sky-line; but its toad-like hue, its several hideous complexions, make it a loathly sight. The spirit shrinks from this bit of creation as from some disgusting creature.

The cave was situated in the highest front of this island. The height of this front was above two hundred feet; how much above that elevation, I know not. It was smooth and sheer, pumice-hued like the beach that swept from it into the north-east; so smooth and sheer was it that you would have said it had been split in twain from a like mass that had fallen and vanished. Assuredly some enormous convulsion had gone to the manufacture of that prodigious fissure or cave.

We pulled through the opening of the reefs, and I headed straight for the cave. So strong was my excitement that it felt like a sort of illness. I breathed with labour; the sweat lay like oil in the palms of my hands, though my hands were cold. It was not now the thoughts of the money. My excitement was no dollar-madness then. I was oppressed, to a degree I

g 2

find incommunicable, by the marvellous picture, as I
was now beholding it for the first time, of the big ship,
clothed in the dusk of the mighty tomb into which
she had backed and where she had brought up. I had
had no leisure for the sight during my first excursion :
had but glanced at it, my head being then full of
the shipwrecked people we were bringing off, and of
fancies of what might be lurking ashore. But now,
our approach being leisurely, the expanse of water
to be measured considerable, I could gaze, wonder,
realise, until emotion grew overwhelming and became
a sensation of sickness in me.

Were you to split a big stone open and find a live
toad in it you would marvel. Hundreds would assemble
to view the wonder, and a poor man might get money
by exhibiting it ; but how many much stranger things
than a live toad imprisoned in a stone would I, as a
sailor, exact the relation and sight of, ere admitting
that half the sum of that marvel of a great ship at
rest in a huge cave was approached ?

At first sight the fabric looked like a piece of
nature's handiwork, as it lay in the gloom of the
interior it had miraculously penetrated. It looked, I
say, as though the volcanic spasm, which had shorn
the lofty cliff into its bald front and wrought the prodigious fissure, had contrived the hundred fragments
and ruins of rocks, the splinters, the serpentine lengths,
the massive bulks, the pillar-shaped fragments into

the aspect of a ship, building the wonder in a sudden roar of earthquake, and leaving it a faultless similitude.

"Oars!" cried I.

We floated forwards with the arrested blades poised over the water. It was burning hot; the sun stood nearly overhead, and the surface of this strange natural harbour shone like new tin, tingling in fibres and needles of white fire back again into the light that it reflected. We were within a musket-shot of the entrance of the cave.

"On which side did you board, men?"

"To starboard, sir."

"Give way gently; and, bow, there, stand by with your boat-hook."

CHAPTER XVIII.

WE TRANSHIP THE DOLLARS.

ALTHOUGH the hour was approaching high noon, and the day very glorious, no light was in the cave beyond the length of the ship's bowsprit. A wall of darkness came to the bows of the ship; it might have been something material, something you could lean against or stick with a knife; the daylight touched it and made a twilight of it at the mouth, then died out. The long and short of it is—it is my way, anyhow, of explaining the strange thing—the filthy-coloured scoriæ, the gloomy masses of cinder, pumice, lava— call it what you will—were unreflective; light smote the stuff and perished, or was not returned, so that a thin veil of dusk clothed with deepest obscurity any hollow it lay in.

The water brimmed blue to the mouth of the cave, and then, at a few boats' lengths, slept black and thick as ink, wholly motionless this day; though I might suppose that when a large swell ran outside the breakwaters, the smaller swell of the harbour put a pulse into the black tide of the cave, though without weight enough to stir the stern-stranded ship. Yet you saw much of her when you were still on the threshold of the cavern. Her huge bows, sprawling with head-boards, loomed out of the darkness, advancing the yellow bowsprit till the cap of it was almost flush with the sides of the opening. Had the jibbooms stood, they would have forked far into daylight, and, perhaps, long ago have challenged the attention of a passing ship, and brought her people to explore the Spaniard and enrich themselves. Her lower masts were yellow, and they showed ghastly in the gloom. She had immense round tops, black and heavy, and shrouds of an almost hawser-like thickness, with a wide spread of channels and massive chain-plates. Most of the yards were across, and squared as though the machinery of the braces had worked to the music of the boatswain's pipe. Her sides were tall; she carried some swivels on her poop rail, and a few pieces caulked with tompions crouched through a half-dozen of ports, like motionless beasts of a strange shape about to spring.

To look up! To behold that lofty fabric and complication of mast and spar and rigging soaring to the dark roof, against which the topgallant masts had been ground away to the topmast heads!

Be seated in a small boat alongside a ship of six hundred or seven hundred tons, with such a height of

side as this Spaniard had, lifting her platform of deck
a full eighteen feet above the water for the eye
to follow the ascent of the lower masts from ; I say,
from the low level of a small boat, look up to the
altitude of the starry trucks of such a ship as this
Perfecta Casada; if you be no sailor, your eye will
swim as you trace the mast-heads to their airy points.
To an immeasurable height will those spars seem to
soar above you, yea, though they rise no higher than
the cross-trees. But here was a vast cave in which a
great ship—and a ship of seven hundred tons was a
great ship in my time—could lie ; and in this cave a
lofty ship *was* lying, partly afloat, partly stranded ;
the darkness in which she slumbered magnified her
proportions ; she loomed upon the sight as tall again
as she was; and half the wonder of this wonderful
show lay in the height of the black ceiling against
which her topmast heads were pressed, jamming her
into the position she had taken up, as though a ship-
wright and his men had dealt with her.

The atmosphere struck cold as snow after the
outer heat. A hush fell upon us as we floated in,
with the bowman erect ready to hook on, and the
silence was horrible, and the more horrible for the sound
thrice heard in the hush that fell upon us, of a greasy
gurgle of water, like a low, villainous, chuckling laugh.

But all this is description, and it takes me long to
submit to you what I beheld in a few breathless

moments of wonder, and awe, and admiration. We were here to load dollars, not to muse and marvel.

"Sort o' ole penguin smell knocking round, ain't there ?" said one of the crew.

"Only a Dago could have managed this job," said another. "Why don't Dagoes stay ashore ? Blast me if even a Dutchman would have made such a muck of it."

"Hold your jaw !" I roared, in a rage ; and my cry went in an echo through the cave, rebounding as a billiard ball from its cushion.

What is more diabolically and instantaneously fatal to sentiment than the vulgar talk of a vulgar Englishman ? A Spaniard, an Italian, a Portuguese, a Greek—blasphemes in your presence, and his coarseness adds to the romantic colours of the idealism you are musing on ; but let an Englishman come alongside of you, and drop an *h*, and emotion is shivered as by a thunderbolt.

The remarks of the sailors woke me up. We were alongside the ship, and the fellow in the bow had hooked on to one of the huge main-chain plates. I crawled into the channel, and over the rail, and dropped upon the deck. It was like entering a vault, and there was an odd, damp, earthy flavour in the air. I wonder, thought I, if there are two dead men in the forecastle, locked in each other's arms ? But why locked in each other's arms ? Ah, why ? Fancy

will give body to wild conceits at such a time and on
such an occasion as this.

I stood a moment at the rail; the water flowed
black as ink into the blackness over the stern.   In the
mysterious twilight that shrouded the ship, her decks
and masts looked unearthly; it was hard to conceive
that human hands had fashioned her, that the echoes
of the mortal caulker had resounded through her.   I
thought of the ship in Lycidas—

" Built in th' eclipse and rigg'd with curses dark."

Sternwards the craft died out in gloom.   The
round-house, or some such contrivance of deck struc-
ture, hung in a swollen shadow with the yellow shaft
of the mizzen-mast shooting straight up out of it.   I
seemed to catch a faint gleam of glass, a dim and
ghostly outline of doorway, of skylight, of crane-like
davits.   The deck of a ship viewed at midnight, by
the light of froth breaking round about, would
shadowily and glimmeringly show as this Spaniard
did from the gangway to the taffrail.   But forward
there was light; the radiance of the day hung, like
a sheet of blue silver, in front of the opening of the
cave, and against that brilliance—compact and undif-
fused, like the light upon the object-glass of a telescope—the bows of the ship stood out in indigo,
the tracery of the rigging exquisitely marked till it
vanished in the gloom overhead.

I bade one man remain in the boat, and the rest
to come on board and bring the lanterns, tackles,
slings, and materials for securing the damaged chests
of dollars. I then lighted one of the lanterns
and walked aft, looking with the utmost curiosity
around me, as though this ship, forsooth, instead of
being a vessel of my own time, was coeval with this
cave, and but a little younger than Noah.

The dollars were, I knew, stowed away down in the
lazarette. This queer name is given to a part of a
ship's after-hold. It is a compartment or division,
and commonly used for the stowage of stores and pro-
visions. The hatch that conducted to this place
was in the cabin. I entered the cabin—a sort of
deck-house—and paused, holding my lantern high,
and gazing about me. I observed a row of cushioned
seats or lockers, three or four round scuttles on either
hand, with dim oil paintings let into or framed to the
panels between; lamps which, when lighted, might
shine like the starry cressets of the poet; and two
square tables, one at each end. The hatch was open.
I descended and passed through a 'tween-decks, black
as ink. The lantern-light gleamed along a corridor,
and revealed a short row of berths to starboard and
larboard. And now, passing through the hatch in
this deck, I stood in the lazarette.

The floor was shallow; there were numerous
stanchions, and the white cases, which contained the

dollars, were stowed between those uprights. I approached a range of cases, and found the top one split open. I squeezed my hand through, and felt the dollars, packed in large rolls. They were as rough to the touch of the finger, with their milled edges, as any big surface of file, and cold as frost. There looked to be a great number of cases. I do not suppose that Greaves had attempted to count them. He abided by the declaration of the manifest: and since it was certain the cases had not been meddled with, no doubt the number and value were as the manifest set forth.

I halted inactively here for perhaps a minute, whilst, with lantern upheld, I ran my eye over the cases. The silence was horrible—no dimmest sob of water penetrated, no distant squeak of rat afforded relief to the ear. But here were the dollars! They were now to be secured, got into the boat, and conveyed to the brig. I called to the men, and they came below with the battens and hammer and nails. We had four lanterns burning, and there was plenty of light. In a few minutes this dead vault of hold was ringing to the blows of the hammers. I overhauled the cases, and saw that every split lid was carefully repaired before ever I dreamt of suffering a box of the metal to be lifted. The men spoke not one word, unless it were an " Ay, ay, sir," in response to a call from me. They chewed and spat with excitement, hammered and toiled with eagerness, and often did they roll their eyes over the cases, but they held their tongues. When the last of the boxes was repaired, slings were procured, a tackle rigged, and I, standing in the lazarette, tallied a quantity of the cases on deck, some of them large, and holding, as I should have reckoned by the weight, not less than three thousand to five thousand dollars apiece. I then followed the men, the gangway was cleared, and the chests lowered by tackles into the boat, where they were received and trimmed by three of the crew.

We pulled out of the harbour, deep, but not perilously deep, with silver, and when we rounded the reef I spied the brig at a distance of about a quarter of a mile away from the spot where we had left her. They had wore her and got her head round on the other tack, and clapped her aback afresh. There was a fellow stationed on the fore-royal yard; I see him in my mind's eye, as mere a pigmy as ever Gulliver handled, as he sat jockeying the yard in the slings, one hand on the tie, his legs dangling, and the loose white trousers trembling, and a hand to his brow as he sent his gaze into the remote ocean distance. The sun made a blaze of the white canvas, and their reflection trembled in sheets of quicksilver, deep in the clear cerulean beneath the shadow of the vessel's side.

The *Black Watch* looked but a little ship after the lumping fabric in the cave. Yes, she looked but a little

ship for the hundreds of leagues of ocean she had
measured, since the hour when I was lifted over her
rail nearly dead of Channel water. But small as
she was, she sat in beauty upon the sea. The long
passage had not roughened her; her sides showed like
the hide of some freshly curried mare of Arabia. She
rolled lightly, sparkles leapt from her, the colours
about her deepened, paled and deepened again, and
fingers of shadow swept through the blaze of her
canvas.

As we approached, I saw Greaves sitting in the
chair in which I had left him; he sat under a short
awning. There was a tray upon the skylight, and
bottles and glasses, and I guessed he was eating
his dinner. I looked for the lady, but saw nothing
of her. Galloon watched our approach, seated like
a monkey upon the rail, with half a fathom of red
tongue out. Bol and the others and the two Spaniards
were congregated in the gangway. The big Dutchman waited until the boat drew close; he then roared,
in a voice that could have been heard on the other side
of the island, " Hurrah, my ladts! Tree sheers for
Capt'n Greaves." And when the men had cheered,
he roared out again, " Und tree sheers more for der
dollars ! "

By the time this unwarrantable uproar—but it
was scarce worth correcting, seeing the occasion of it
—had ceased, we were alongside, and I sprang on deck.

"How have you got on, Mr. Fielding?" called Greaves from his chair, without attempting to rise.

"Very well, sir."

"How many cases?"

I gave him the number.

"Get them aboard at once," he exclaimed, "and leave them on the quarter-deck till all are shipped. See those cases aboard, and then step aft."

The men speedily hoisted the cases out of the boat. Yan Bol was conspicuously forward and energetic in the hand he gave. I stood near, and heard him say, "I vhas pleasedt mit der Spaniards for leaving dis money. Dere vhas house, vife, beer, bipes, mit songs und dances, in dese cases. Cott, vhat a veight! I likes to find more ships in a hole. Vhat drinks, vhat larks in von case only."

The sailors rumbled with laughter at the fellow, and some of the Englishmen eyed me askant, to guess my mind. I was willing, however, that Bol should run on. Greaves was near, and able to hear and judge for himself. When the last case was out of the boat, I walked aft.

Greaves said, "Send your boat's crew to dinner, and let others take their place for the next boat."

"With your leave, sir, I'll keep the men I have just returned with. They know the ropes and have nothing to learn."

"Be it so. Send the crew to dinner, but let them

bear a hand; and you can make a meal off this tray here."

There was food in plenty, and wine. Having told the boat's crew to go to their dinner, I sat down with Greaves, and ate and drank. The weather continued extraordinarily beautiful, but the wind was failing, long glassy lines of calm were already snaking along the surface of the sea, and it was fiercely hot. The horizon swam in a film; you could have seen ten miles in the morning, and not five miles now from the deck. No sights had been taken; no sights were needed when there was an island, whose situation had been accurately observed, close alongside.

" We shall have the dollars aboard by four ? " said Greaves.

" Easily, sir."

"Do you believe in the dollars now, Fielding ?" said he, with a smile.

I answered, " Yes," colouring, and asked him how he felt.

" Easier," said he; " there is no pain when I sit. A severe bruise—no more."

" Yan Bol is a bit forward and outspoken for a foremast hand, don't you think, captain ? "

" He is a Dutchman, and all Dutchmen are cheeky. The word *cheek* originates with the Dutch. Look at their sterns and look at their faces, if you want the etymology of the word *cheek*."

"I hope he'll remain cheeky only. For my part, I don't feel sure of the man."

"Too late—too late," said Greaves irritably and impatiently.

"I do not like that he should ask me the value of the treasure that is to come aboard, and I do not like that he should say that as the size of a flea is to the size of the dog that scratches it, is the proportion of the forecastle share to the whole of the money."

"If he gives me trouble," said Greaves, "I will shoot him. I will show you the rising moon through a slug-hole in the devil's skull. But do not accept Yan Bol too literally. Dutchmen will say without significance that which, in the mouth of an Englishman, might sound brutally malevolent and sinister."

"That may be, sir; I don't know the Dutch."

"I have made up my mind not to meddle with the cargo. Do not trouble to examine it. The money will be risk enough. Shrewd as old Tulp believes himself to be, and really is, the anxiety of running a quantity of tin won't be worth the purchase. If the cocoa is sweet, bring some of it off for the ship's use; and if you can meet with the four casks of tortoise-shell, we'll find room for the stuff. Four casks are easy of transhipment, but the rest we'll let be."

This was good sense. It must have taken us some

h

time to break out and tranship the tin and the wool
and the hides in hair. The smuggling of such stuff,
on our arrival home, would have taxed even the
many-sided, hard-salted cunning of a Dealman; and,
smuggling apart, without papers, how were these commodities to have been passed?

I allowed the boat's crew a quarter of an hour for
their dinner, then summoned them; and, not to repeat
the story of our first visit, by something after three
o'clock that afternoon, the weather still holding mar-
vellously radiant and all the wind gone, I had tallied
the last of the cases of dollars over the side of the
Black Watch, along with some crates of cocoa; but
the four casks of tortoise-shell I had been unable to
meet with. Whether they had been omitted, or stowed
in some secret place, I know not. Then, for an hour,
I was busy in superintending the stowage of the cases
of dollars in the brig's lazarette. Whilst I was thus
occupied, Yan Bol, with a few seamen, was sent by
the captain in the long-boat to procure fresh water
and fill up with terrapin and all else catchable that
was good for the saucepan. The Dutch boatswain
made two journeys before I was done, and was gone
ashore again for more water and turtle when I arrived
on deck after a wash and a clean-up. I reported the
dollars stowed to the captain.

"Ninety-eight thousand pounds," said he. "It is
worth the venture, I think."

"I can scarcely credit the reality now it has happened and all's well," said I.

"There are many men," said he, "who would be willing to be pressed, run-down, half-drowned, and picked up for six thousand pounds."

"Ay, indeed," said I; "and when I take up that money, Galloon, how much of it is to be your share, dear doggie?"

"The Spanish lady sleeps well."

"After four days of that island!" said I.

"What is to be done with her? I certainly cannot land her in a Spanish port. It will end, I believe, in our carrying her to England. I intend to court no unnecessary risks, and I should be courting a very unnecessary risk by looking close enough into a port to land her. No; she will sail with us to England. I hope she is amiable. I scarcely noticed that she was good-looking. I am no ladies' man—I do not care for women; and the deuce of it is, neither you nor I speak Spanish."

"She is a woman of degree," said I; "has fine manners, fine rings, and beautiful hands."

"You may have found a wife as well as a fortune in these seas, Fielding."

"Marry a Spanish woman for money?" said I. "Who'd lick honey off a thorn?"

"And why would not you marry a Spanish woman, money or no money?" said he. "Do not you know

h 2

that the best and oldest blood in the world runs in Spanish veins? You seem to sneer at the mention of old blood."

"Not at all."

"Give me old blood in a woman. With old blood you associate all the elegances, all the graces and aromas in the bearing and conduct of human nature. Vulgarity makes a toad of beauty itself. Think of Venus saying ''Ave done,' and bragging of her jewellery."

"What is a lady?"

"I expected that question. Cannot you define what any chambermaid or boots can distinguish; what any shopman, waiter, poor sailorman like you or me, can instantly *recognise?* Marry, come up! What is more teasing than the question, 'What is a gentleman?' Cocky Mr. Macaroni, with his hat over his eye and his hair dressed in imitation of his betters, says, 'Vat's a gentleman?' and the beast knows the thing every time he sees it."

"How is the pain in your side?"

"Well, it makes me wince when I move as I did then. How strange," said he, sinking his voice and looking at the island, "that I, who have been dreaming of galleons all my life, should, of the scores whose keels have cut these waters, be the one chosen to light upon yonder ship of dollars!"

"Shall you fire her before sailing?"

"No; we will leave her for the next man who may come along—for some poor devil to whom a few serons of cocoa and a thousand quintals of tin may be what the Cockney calls an 'object.'"

The sun was now low, and the west was on fire. The sea came like blood from the rim of the western line to midway the ocean plain, where the fierce light drained into thin blue that went darkening into melting violet eastwards. The brig had drifted very nearly due south of the island, opening the reefs, and baring the harbour to our sight, and disclosing the verdure that clothed a portion of the northern rocks. The long-boat lay alongside the beach, and the figures of her people came and went. I thought to myself, "A pity if Yan Bol and his sweet and manly fellows don't take a fancy to the derelict, agree among themselves to attempt to warp her afloat, and consent to remain on the island if Greaves will give them the boat; food enough they will find in the ship and on the beach."

Though the island stood steeped in the red light of sunset, it reflected nothing of the western splendour. Grimy, melancholy, livid—an ocean cinder-heap did it look in that fair evening radiance, a spadeful out of Neptune's dust-bin. I picked up the telescope to view the ship in the cave before the shadows closed the wondrous object out, and with the tracery of the spars and rigging dim in the lens I conceived myself

on board. I imagined the hour of midnight, I heard in
fancy the distant groan of surf, I heard the sob of the
black water within the cave, a faint creak from the
heart of the sepulchred vessel ; and I figured fear
growing in me even unto the beholding of appari-
tions, until a shiver ran through me as chill as
though it had come out of the cold hold of the ship
herself.

I put down the glass, meaning to laugh away my
fancies to Greaves, and beheld the Lady Aurora de la
Cueva in the act of rising through the companion-
way.

Though Greaves and I had only just now been
talking about her, I stared as though I had not known
she was aboard. It was indeed strange, after all the
months of Greaves and Yan Bol and the Dutch and
English beauties forward, to find a woman in the brig ;
to see a fine, handsome, sparkling-eyed girl stepping
out of the cabin as though she had been there from
the hour of the Downs, but secret. She bowed, I
lifted my cap, Greaves struggled to his feet with his
face full of pain. I begged him to sit, and ran below
for a chair, which I placed near his for the Lady
Aurora. She had found out that he was in pain, that
he had met with an accident, and was addressing him
as I put her chair down, her large, Spanish, glowing
eyes very wistfully fastened upon his face. He understood her, for, as I have told you, Greaves read Spanish

indifferently well, and faintly understood it when spoken; but he wanted words, and could not utter the few he possessed. He smiled and touched his side, and then pointed to the island.

It was not for me to linger near them. I went to the rail, and watched the boat and the movements of the fellows upon the beach; but I also found several opportunities in this while for observing the Lady Aurora. She had slept, and was refreshed. The fine, delicate, transparent olive of her complexion—I may say it was a very pale olive, well within the compass of the admiration of those whose love is for the white and yellow part of the sex—was touched slightly with bloom as from recent slumber. Her eyes were large, and splendid with light, remarkable for their long lashes, and of a shade that made you think of the sea at night, black and luminous, their depths filled with wandering fires as she struggled with the oppression of silence, or gazed at you as though she would speak. Her nose was slightly Jewish, rather small than big for her face, the nostrils the daintiest piece of graving I ever saw in that way. Her teeth were very good, strong and white, a little large. The quality of her clothes might have been very grand: one would judge of *that* perhaps by the rings, for this sort of thing goes on all fours as a rule; but the fit or fashion was monstrously vile to my taste. You guessed that underlying all that spread and sprawl of skirt and bodice

there sat, or stood, or reposed, the figure of a Hebe.
Hints of secret perfections there were in plenty; but
all grace of shape was overwhelmed by the cut of her
gown; it stood upon her like a candle extinguisher,
and in shape was not even fit for a nun.

"I am unable to understand the lady, Fielding,"
exclaimed Greaves. "Is Antonio forward?"

I spied the Spaniard leaning over the bows, looking
towards the island. He had gone away in the boat
on the first journey to show the men where the water
was. On her return with her freight of fresh water
he had crept over the side and sneaked forward, to
loaf and lounge and smoke in Jack Spaniard fashion.
How did I know this? Because I knew that Antonio
had been sent in the boat to point out the spring, and
his lounging in the bows with a pipe betwixt his lips
now, whilst the boat was ashore and the men busy,
told me the little yarn of loafing from start to finish.

I called, and he put his pipe in his pocket and
came aft.

"Interpret what this lady says," exclaimed Greaves.

She poured forth some sentences of Spanish. I
could trace no fatigue, no reactionary debility, such
as might attend the strain and passion of deliverance
from peril tremendous above all words to her as a
woman.

"The señorita," translated Antonio in effect—but,
as I have before said, I will not attempt a written

description of his articulation or phrases; I write that he may be intelligible—"wishes to know how long you intend to remain in this situation, and to what part of the world you are proceeding when you sail?"

"To England!" cried the lady, when Antonio had made answer out of the mouth of Greaves. "Santa Maria purissima! how shall I find my mother? If she has been rescued, she will have been conveyed to some port on the South American coast, whence she will return to Acapulco, and there await news of me. To England! Ave Maria! the world will then divide me from my mother. Blessed Virgin! I did think this ship was proceeding to a South American port. To England! I shall never see my mother again."

She exclaimed awhile in this sort of language, but untheatrically. Nay, there was a dignity in her astonishment and concern; very little tossing of hands and uprolling of eyes. The main article in the outward expression of her grief and alarm lay in the piteous look she fastened on me, as though she would rather appeal to me than to the captain; as though, indeed, she considered that since I was the first to take her by the hand on the island, and to bring her off from a situation of horror, she was entitled to look to me for all further kindnesses.

"The señorita's mother," said Greaves, "was, of course, rescued, and is, no doubt, safe and well?" Antonio turned his back upon the lady, that she might

not see him squint, and he shrugged his shoulders.
"But we have no right to suppose," continued Greaves,
looking sternly at the Spaniard, "that the ship which
rescued the señora conveyed her to a port whence
she could easily reach Acapulco. On the contrary,
in all probability the ship was bound round the Horn,
in which case the lady may be now on her way to
Europe."

Antonio translated; the Lady Aurora gazed at
him somewhat passionately, and beat the air with
a gesture of irritation, clearly unable to collect the
captain's meaning from the fellow's interpretation of it.
Antonio talked much, and gesticulated with singular
energy. The lady then appeared to comprehend.

"She says that her mother is rich," said Antonio,
"and is well known as the widow of Don Alonzo de
Cueva, the merchant of Lima. She will pay liberally
to be conveyed to Acapulco, where she has a brother
who is a priest. She will return to Acapulco because
she is sure to believe that the señora, her mother,
will seek her there."

"Tell the lady," said Greaves, "that I am truly
sorry not to be able to put her ashore at any port
where she would be within easy reach of Acapulco.
When I have filled my water-casks, I am proceeding
to England as straight as the rudder can steer the
ship, touching nowhere, and giving everything that
passes plenty of room. Yet this tell her, likewise,

that on our way to England we may chance to fall in with a vessel bound to a port on this side the South American coast. Should we fall in with such a vessel I will transfer the lady to her."

He spoke slowly, with the deliberateness of a man who is in pain whilst he discourses. Antonio made shift to render the captain's words intelligible to the lady. She asked, through the Spanish seaman, what Captain Greaves would charge to put her ashore at Lima or Valparaiso.

" It is not to be done," said Greaves; " beg her not to repeat that request."

She seemed to gather the matter of his speech by his manner. Her eyes came to mine, earnest, pleading, with a deeper shadow in their dark depths, as though tears were not far off. It was a look that made me curse my ignorance of the Spanish tongue. Much could I have said to comfort and hearten her; but though I had been able to talk as fluently as she, it was not for me to intrude *then*. I was mate, and Greaves was captain; and I stood at the rail, seeming to watch the island as it blackened to the fading crimson light, and to be keeping a look-out for the return of the long-boat.

"Was not the lady's mother proceeding to Madrid?" said Greaves.

" Yes, capitan," answered Antonio.

" If the vessel which may have picked her up is

going that way, why should she desire to return to
Acapulco ?"

" You have heard, my capitan, that the señorita
believes her mother will return to Acapulco and wait
for her there."

" How is the mother to know that the daughter is
alive ? "

Again Antonio squinted fiercely, and shrugged.

"Is there reason to suppose that the widow
imagines her daughter is saved ? Is there reason
to believe that the widow herself is saved ? Supposing her to have been picked up by a ship bound
south, why should not she proceed in the direction
that, if pursued, must ultimately land her at Cadiz, or
put her in the way of very easily reaching Madrid,
for which city, as I understand, she and her daughter
embarked at Acapulco ?   Interpret all this, will you ? "

Antonio began to translate.

" Fielding ! " exclaimed Greaves.

" Sir.'

" Call Jimmy aft."

The boy arrived.

" I am going below, Fielding," said Greaves.   " My
ribs ache consumedly.   I may get some ease by lying
flat.   Is the long-boat coming off ? "

The tall bulwarks prevented him from seeing the
lower ranges of the island.   I looked a moment; then,
to make sure, levelled the glass, and said—

" They are at this instant shoving off, sir."

" Get in the water, and then hoist your boat in," said he. " You can fill on the brig and stand north for an offing of about three miles; then heave-to afresh, and carefully observe the bearings of the island, lest it should roll down black or thick. If heavy weather happens in the night, we will proceed; for we have fresh water enough aboard to carry us along. Otherwise, we will complete our watering in the morning; for I want to make a steady run of it to the Channel, without need of a halt on any account whatever."

Whilst Greaves was giving me his instructions, Antonio was interpreting to the Lady Aurora, who frequently broke into short exclamations of " *Qué !* " " *Es esto !* " " *Será posible ?* " and while she thus exclaimed, she would look with an expression of dismay and reproach at the captain.

" If I rest my bones through the night," said Greaves, " I shall be easier or well again in the morning. Look in upon me with a report from time to time, Fielding, and tell Bol to visit me during his watch."

He rose from his chair with a face of pain, put his arm upon Jimmy's shoulder, and went below. I stepped to the gangway, calling to the fellows who were hanging about in the head to lay aft and stand by to discharge the boat and get her aboard. She

came alongside deep, and it was dark before we had
hooked the tackles into her. When she was stowed,
the topsail was swung and the brig headed about
north. There was a light wind out of the south-west.
It set the water tinkling alongside, with the noise as
of the bells of a sleigh heard afar. The young moon
lay in a red curl in the west, as though, up there, she
was still coloured by the flush of the sunset that had
blackened out to our sight. There was not a cloud.
The stars were plentiful and bright, and the dusky
ocean, flat and firm, showed as wide as the sky.

All this while the lady had remained on deck. It
was about eight o'clock, and very dark. My watch
had come round, and the brig would be in my charge
till midnight; but, watch or no watch, I should have
kept a look-out until I had secured the three-mile
offing. The island was on the starboard quarter,
scarcely distinguishable now—a dim smudge, like
smoke.

Happening to look through the skylight, I saw
the cloth laid for supper. Indeed, supper was ready.
Salt beef and ham were on the table, together with
biscuits, pickles, and a pot or two of preserves, a small
decanter of rum for my use, and a bottle of Greaves's
red wine for the lady. She had tasted nothing, as
I presumed, since her arrival on board in the morning.
She stood at the rail, looking out to sea, a pathetic
figure of loneliness, indeed, when you thought of what

she had suffered, what she was freshly delivered from; when you thought, again, of her solitude of dumbness, as you might well term her tongue's incapacity aboard this brig of English and Dutch. Most heartily did I yearn to speak soothingly and hopefully, to bid her be of good cheer when she thought of her mother, to beg her persuade herself that her mother was rescued and sailing to Europe, even as she, the señorita, was thither bound.

"Weel, weel, there's Ane abune a'!" says the gipsy in the Scotch novel, and that was the substance of what I wanted to tell the Lady Aurora.

And what did I say? Why, I just coughed to let her know that I was at her elbow. I had no other language than a cough.

She quietly looked round, and began " *Yo no lo—*' then broke off, arrested by remembering that I knew not one syllable of her tongue.

I motioned to the skylight, and pointed down and made signs for her to go below and sup. She signed to me to accompany her. I shook my head, pointing to the sails and to the sea, and cursing my ignorance that obliged me to make a baboon of myself with my limbs and head.

She bowed, and went to the companion-hatch, and on looking down a few minutes later I saw her seated at the table. She had removed her hat; her brow showed white in the lamplight under the magnificent masses of her dead-black hair. The jewels upon her fingers sparkled as, with a leisureliness that had something of stateliness in it, she helped herself to the food before her. Once again I admired the beauty of her hands, and then I turned my back upon the novel and beautiful picture of this fine Spanish woman to look to the brig.

CHAPTER XIX.

OFF THE ISLAND.

THE brig slipped cleverly through the sea. It was
like gently tearing through silk with a razor to listen
to the noise that floated aft from her cutwater. When
I guessed the island to be about three miles distant, I
hove the vessel to. Yan Bol's pipe shrilled with an
edge that seemed to fetch an echo from the furthest
reaches of the dark sea. When the sails were to the
mast, the brig lay motionless under her topsails and
standing jib.

I was about to go below to make a report to the
captain, when the lumping shadow of Bol's bulky
shape came along the deck.

"Beg pardon, Mr. Fielding," said he, with a loutish
lift of his hand in the direction of his forehead, "how
might der captain be, sir?"

"I am about to inquire."

"Dere vhas notting wrong, all handts hope?"

"No: a severe bruise. Nothing more serious, I
trust."

i

" Vhas der brick to be hove-to all night ? "

" Yaw."

" To gomblete der watering in der morning, I zooppose ? "

" Yaw."

" Vell, Mr. Fielding, der men hov oxed me to say dot if der captain vill give leave, and she vhas not too sick to be troubled by der noise, dey vould like to celebrate der recovery of der dollars by two or dree leedle songs before der vatch vhas called."

This was another way of asking for a glass of grog for all hands. There could be no objection. The men had been much exposed throughout the heat of the day, and what could more righteously warrant a harmless festal outburst than the recovery and transhipment of a hundred and forty cases of Spanish dollars ?

I entered the cabin. The Lady Aurora was still at table, but had long since ceased to eat. She lay back in her chair, her head drooped, her hands folded in the posture of one waiting. When I entered, she lifted her head and smiled, her eyes brightened, her lips moved in the first framing of a sentence; no word escaped her; she pointed to a seat, and half rose from her own chair, as though in doubt where I was used to sit. I shook my head, nodded towards the door of the captain's berth, then at the clock under the skylight, holding up my fingers that she might guess I

would join her in ten minutes ; and so I passed on, hot
in the face, and wondering whether it would be possible
for me to communicate with her without making a
fool of myself—for a fool I felt every time I gesticulated, which I now think must have been owing to
my hatred of the French.

Greaves lay in his bunk motionless, on his back,
but he was free from pain. Galloon sat on a chest
near his head. I reported the affairs of the brig, the
distance and bearings of the island, and the like. He
asked how the weather looked.

" It is a heavenly night," said I.

" It is hot in this hole," said he. " Plague seize
the awkwardness that tripped me and has floored me
thus ! One knows not what to do for a bruise of this
sort. But patience—that's the physic for every sort
of bruise, whether of the bones or of the soul. Jim
tells me the lady has supped."

" She has, sir."

" I am sorry for the poor thing ; but where is the
woman that does not always want something more
than she has ? This time yesterday she would have
given her hair—angels alive ! what would she *not* have
given ?—to be as she now is, safe aboard such a vessel
as this ; and now that she is safe aboard—rescued
from raw terrapin and the risks of the society of two
Spanish sailors (and I must like their looks better
before I give them a handsomer name than *that*)—

she craves to be with her mother—very natural, of course—who is, probably, at the bottom of the ocean; and she wants to be put ashore at Lima."

I delivered the request of the men, as expressed by Yan Bol.

"Oh, yes. Let grog be served out to all hands; and the men may sing, certainly. Disturb me? Not down here. And I like my people to be merry. Fortune has fiddled to-day; let the beggars dance."

Jimmy was in the cabin. I bade him carry a can of rum to the men, and went on deck, receiving, without knowing how to answer, a look of inquiry from the Lady Aurora as I passed her.

"The men may make merry," said I to Bol. There is grog gone forward. Tell them that the captain is free from pain; and will you keep a look-out in the waist—or in the head if you like, 'tis all one—whilst I get a bite in the cabin?"

"Yaw, dot vill I. By der vay, Mr. Fielding, vhas dere von hoondred und dirty, or vhas dere von hoondred und twenty, cases prought on boardt? Vertz swears to von hoondred und dirty; Friendt, von hoondred und twenty. I myself gounts von hoondred und dirty-two. Dere vhas a leedle vager in dis—shoost von day of a man's grog, dot vhas all."

"I made one hundred and forty cases," said I. "But are they all dollars?"

And, bursting into a laugh, I left him to chew upon that thought, and returned to the cabin.

I bowed to the lady, and took the chair I usually occupied at the table. She rose, came to my side with a bottle of claret, poured some into a glass, and made as if she would wait upon me. I was not a little confounded. Her handsome presence, her fine person embarrassed me. My career had but poorly qualified me for an easy address in conversing with ladies. Much of my life had been spent upon the ocean, in the society of some of the roughest of my own calling. For months at a stretch I had never set eyes on a woman, and when I was ashore, whether in foreign parts or in my own country, the girls I fell in with were not of a sort to teach me to know exactly what to do when I chanced upon the company of a Señorita Aurora.

I did the best I could with the imperfect and monkey-like speech of the hands and shoulders to induce her to desist from waiting upon me, and return to her chair; and in this I was helped by the arrival of Jimmy, to whom I gave several unnecessary orders, merely to emphasise to the lady the desire. I gesticulated that she should sit, and cease to do me more honour than I had impudence to support.

Presently she pointed to the bottle of claret—there stood but one bottle on the table—and looked at me in silence, but with an expression of such eloquence as Jimmy himself could not have missed the meaning of.

" Wine," said I.

" Vine," she repeated : and then to herself, " *Vino* —vine; *vino*—vine."

She next pointed to the piece of salt beef.

" Meat," said I.

" Meat—*carne*; meat—*carne*," she repeated.

She pointed to several objects. I gave her the English names, and she pronounced them deliberately, in a rich voice, invariably tacking the Spanish equivalent to the word, as though she wished me to observe it. I sat for about a quarter of an hour over my supper, and then, looking at the clock significantly, and then up through the skylight, that she might gather my intention, I rose, giving her a little bow. She rose also, and, pointing upwards, tapped her bosom, most clearly saying in that way—" May I accompany you ? "

" Si, señorita," said I, expending, as I believe, in those words the whole of my stock of her tongue.

A fine smile lighted up her face, and she addressed me ; and what I reckon she said was that it would not take me long to learn Spanish. She picked up her hat, and then, looking at the table, pointed, and, showing her white teeth, said, " Bread—*pan*; meat—*carne*; vine—*vino*;" and so on through the words I had

interpreted, making not one blunder either of pronunciation or indication of the object, saving that she
called wine *vine*, and ham *yam*.

I conducted her on deck; I believe Yan Bol had
been surveying us from the skylight; I perceived his
big figure lurching forward when I emerged, and his
way of going made me suppose that he had been
looking through the skylight with his ear bent. "An
old ape hath an old eye," thought I, as I watched him
disappear in the darkness.

The crew were assembled on the forecastle, and
singing songs there. They had rigged up two or
three lanterns, and sat in the light of them, drinking
rum-and-water out of mugs, and smoking pipes. A
strange voice was singing at that moment; I listened,
and guessed it to be one of the two Spaniards. The
girl paused and listened too. She then ejaculated,
"Ay! Ayme!" and went to the rail, and gazed out
to sea.

There blew a soft wind, cool with dew, out of the
south-west. I looked for the island, but the shadow
of it was blent like smoke with the darkness. The
ripples ran in faint, small ivory curls, and the water
was full of roaming glows of phosphorus. The Spanish
sailor ceased to sing. A fiddle struck up, screwing
and squeaking into a tune which immediately set my
toes tapping; a hoarse cough succeeded, and then
rang out the roaring voice of Travers—

" Eight bells had struck, and the starboard watch was
    called,
And the larboard watch they went to their hammocks
    down below ;
Before seven bells the case it was quite altered,
And broad upon our lee-beam we sight a lofty foe.
        Up hammocks and down chests,
        O, the boatswain he piped next,
And the drummer he was called, at quarters for to beat.
        We stowed our hammocks well
        Before we struck the bell,
And we bore down upon her with a full and flowing
    sheet !
(*Chorus*)   And we bore down upon her with a full and
    flowing she-e-t ! "

There were more verses. The chorus was always the
same ; it burst with hurricane power from the lips of
the English seamen, who sang with passion, as though
in defiance of the Dutch and Spanish listeners ; and,
indeed, the matter of the song was headlong and irre-
sistible. The lady, standing at the bulwark turned her
head to listen ; but when the noise had ended, she sank
her face afresh, put her elbow on the rail, leaned her
chin upon her hand, and so gazed straight out into
the darkness.

Much had she to think of, and her weight of
memory would be the heavier, and the colour of it
the sadder, for her inability to communicate a syllable
of what worked in her brain, when she thought of the

wreck in which her mother may have perished, or of
the livid cinder of an island on which she had been
imprisoned for four days, of her present condition, and
of her future. I wondered, as I looked at her, whether,
if she had my language, or I hers, she would be impassioned and dramatic in the recital of her adventures,
or whether she would talk quietly, describe without
vehemence of speech or motion, prove herself, in
short, the dignified, apparently cold woman I found
her in her compelled silence. This I wondered
whilst I watched her with an irritable yearning after
words that I might speak. What had been the two
sailors' behaviour to her on the island? Where and
how had she slept of nights there? What had been
her sufferings in the open boat? Who was she? Was
she visiting Madrid, to presently return to South
America? She troubled my curiosity. She was as a
book written in an unintelligible tongue, but curiously
and beautifully embellished with plates which enable
you to guess at the choiceness and profusion of the
feast you are unable to sit at.

Now Yan Bol sang a song. His voice rent the
night, and I observed the lady erect her figure as
though she hearkened with astonishment. I walked
aft to take a look at the compass, and to see that the
binnacle lamp was burning well.

"Who is this at the wheel?"

"Jorge, señor."

" You don't speak English, do you ? "

The man understood me, and shook his head
" Pretty cool fists," thought I, " to send this poor devil
aft whilst *you* enjoy yourselves with your songs and
pipes and grog! Here is a shipwrecked man; what
care you ? He is a poor rag of a man, and very fit to
be put upon; so it has been, ' Aft with ye and grip
them spokes, whilst a better man than e'er a mumping
Spaniard in all Americay comes for'ard and enjoys
himself.' " But it was not a matter to be mended
whilst the fellows were in the full of their jollification.

" *Como se llama esto?* " exclaimed a voice at my
elbow, and a small hand, gleaming with rings, was
projected into the sheen of the binnacle lamp.

I started, conceiving that the lady was still at the
bulwark rail, deep in thought or listening to the
singing.

" I do not understand," said I.

" Ow you call, señor ? " exclaimed Jorge.

She pointed to the compass, wanting its name in
English. I pronounced the word, and she echoed it
very clearly; then, lightly laying her hand upon my
arm, she took a few steps forward, and, pointing to the
sea, asked again in Spanish what that was called. In
this way I gave her some dozen words; and when
I believed she was about to ask for more terms
she, with her hand laid lightly on my arm, led me
back to the wheel, and, pointing to the compass,

pronounced its name in English, then indicated the
sea, uttering the word, and so she went through the
list she had got, blundering but once, at the word
" star," which she pronounced *zar*.

By this time the singing had come to an end:
the starbowlines, as the starboard watch were then
termed, were dropping below; the lady went to the
skylight and looked at the time ; then, coming up to
me, she put her hand out and said—

" *Buenas noches, caballero.*"

I answered, " Good-night, señorita."

She shook her head ; by the cabin lamplight flowing up through the open frames I saw her smiling.
She repeated, " Good-night, caballero," in Spanish.
Seeing her wish, I said good-night in the same
language, imitating her accent.

" *Es admirable !*" she exclaimed, and then went
toward the companion-way, meaning to go below.

But I had resolved that this handsome, amiable,
lovely Spanish lady should be made as comfortable on
board us as the resources of the brig permitted, and I
detained her by a polite gesture whilst I called to one
of the men forward to send Antonio aft. The fellow
was turned in, and he kept us waiting ten minutes
during which the lady and-I stood dumb as a pair of
ghosts, she no doubt wondering why I held her on
deck, though she did not exhibit the least uneasiness
in her bearing so far as I was able to make out in the

starlit darkness. When Antonio appeared, I requested him to ask the lady if she wished for anything the brig could supply her with. Antonio translated sulkily and sleepily.

"No, señor," said he, "the lady wants for nothing. She is wearied, and entreats permission to retire to rest."

I was convinced that the villain had manufactured this answer to enable him to return speedily to his own bed. But I was helpless.

When the lady went below, I told Antonio to send one of the men out of my watch to relieve Jorge at the wheel, and I then descended into the cabin to make a report to Greaves, and to hear how he did. Jimmy was clearing up for the night. I inquired after the captain, and the youth told me he was asleep.

"Has he complained of pain?"

"No, master."

"Where's Galloon?"

"Along with the captain, master."

"Has the dog been fed to-day?"

"Oh, yes. He had a copper-fastened buster at noon—a heart o' oak blow-out."

"What did you give him?" said I, not doubting the lad's affection for the dog, but fearing that the poor brute might have been overlooked in the hurry and excitement of the day.

" As much beef-steak as he could swallow,
master."

" There are no beef-steaks on board this ship,"
said I. " If the captain and Galloon were here, we
should have a concert. But I believe you when you
tell me that you have fed the dog."

" More'n he wanted, master."

I bade him put a spare mattress into my bunk—
we carried a stock of spare bedding, a slop lot of
Amsterdam stuff—and I then returned on deck. Two
hours of watch lay before me, and my heart went in a
gallop and my brain in a waltz through the earlier
part of that time. I found leisure for thought now :
the hush of the ocean night was upon the brig ; no
sound reached me from the forecastle. The stars
shone brightly in the dark sky, and many meteors of
crystal-white fires ran and broke over our mastheads,
bursting like rockets immeasurably distant, and
leaving glowing trails which palpitated for some
minutes.

The hope of the voyage was realised. Under foot
lay half a million of dollars, and six thousand pounds
of it were to be mine ! Is it wonderful that my spirits
should have sung, that heart and brain should have
danced ? But with this noble fulfilment of the half-
hearted hope of many weeks was mixed the romance
of the presence of a handsome Spanish woman in the
ship. One thought of her as coming on board with

the dollars—as the princess of the island, pining for
civilisation and shipping herself and the treasure of
her little dominion for the life and delights of a great
and populous city of the Old World. She it was, I
think, that set my brain a-waltzing, if it were the
dollars which made my heart gallop and my spirit
shout within me.

I tell you it was an odd, intoxicating mixture of
the picturesque, the heroic, the romantic for a plain
young sailor-man like me to put his lips to and drain
down. To be sure, the influence of the Spanish lady
upon me was no more than the influence of bright
eyes, of white teeth, of a fine person, of a head of
magnificent hair. And what sort of influence would
that be, pray? Why, heart alive O! what but a
mingling of light with thought, an aroma to haunt all
fancy of other things, giving a sparkle to the common-
place, putting foam and sweetness into cups of flatness.
Do you who are reading this know how deep, know by
the experience of months of weevils, corned horse, and
the curses of constipated sailors, how deep is the deep
monotony of life on shipboard? If the depth of this
monotony be known to you, then will you understand
why it should be that the presence—yea, the presence
merely—of a handsome woman, her glances, the flash
of her white teeth, the eloquent hinting by movement
and posture at a hidden shape of beauty, should
mingle a few threads of gold with the coarse, grey,

brine-drenched worsted of the sailor's daily life—of such a daily life as mine; should touch with lustre his -mechanic habits and trains of thought, as the wake of his ship in the night of the tropic ocean is beautified with the fiery seeds and radiant foam-bells of the sea-glow.

And now I have intelligently and poetically explained why it was that I walked out some time of the remainder of my watch on deck with my blood in a dance and my spirits singing clearly. But as I paced I grew grave under the shadow of a fancy—not yet to call it fear. Suppose the crew should rise and seize the brig? This was a *notion* that was fixedly present to Greaves during the outward passage, because he had *known*, when I doubted, that the half-million of dollars were in the ship in the cave, and upon that conviction he could base acute realisation of what *might* happen when the money was transhipped. I, on the other hand, had never seriously considered the possibility of piracy. The money must be in the brig before I could solemnly compass all the responsibility its possession implied. But the money was now on board, and six thousand pounds of it were mine, and my spirits fell as I paced the quarter-deck, looking around the wide gloom and saying to myself—" Suppose this treasure of half a million of dollars should presently start the men into a determination to seize the brig! There were but two of us—Greaves and I

—at our end of the ship. Could we count upon Jimmy? At the other end was now an addition of two Spaniards—cut-throats at heart, for all one knew— with knives as thirsty for blood as an English sailor's throat for rum."

Why should I have thought thus? Nothing whatever had happened to put fancies of this sort into my head. Was it not the being able to understand that thirty thousand of the thousands in the lazarette were to be mine that set me reflecting with a sudden dark anxiety when the question arose, Suppose the crew should rise and take the brig?

> " The needy traveller, serene and gay,
>   Walks the wild heath, and sings his toil away.
>   Does envy seize thee? Crush the upbraiding joy,
>   Increase his riches, and his peace destroy:
>   New fears in dire vicissitude invade,
>   The rustling brake alarms, and quivering shade;
>   Nor light nor darkness brings his pain relief,
>   One shows the plunder, and one hides the thief."

There was comfort, however, if not safety in this consideration: not a man forward, from Bol down to Jimmy, had any knowledge of navigation. What, then, would they be able to do with the brig if they seized her? They might spread a chart of the world and say: " Here we are *now*, and there is America, and there are the East Indies, and down there is New Holland, and up there is China; and if we steadily

head in one direction, no matter at what point of the
compass the bowsprit looks, we are bound to run
something down, whether it be a continent or one of
the poles."

Well, that is how sailors might talk in a book
designed for the young. Before the seamen forward
rose and seized this brig, that was now a very valuable
bottom as cargoes then went, they would ask of one
another : " What are we going to do with the ship when
we have her ? Where are we going to carry her, and,
having hit on a spot, how are we going to navigate
her there ? " This I chose to think, and, indeed, 1
had no doubt of it, and I drew comfort from the
conclusion ; but all the same my spirits, having
sunk, remained low throughout the rest of my
watch.

I was uneasy. I caught myself arresting my steps,
when my walk carried me towards the gangway,
whenever I heard the sound of a man's voice. O
God, to think of what a hell of passions this tiny
speck of brig was capable of holding ! To think of
the large and bloody tragedy this minim of the
building-yards could find a theatre for ! Never had I
so utterly felt human insignificance at sea as I did
this night, when I looked over the rail and searched
the smoky void of the horizon for the smudge of the
island, till, for the relief of my sight, I watched a
star.

j

"I'll tell you what it is, William Fielding," said I to myself; "your blood is over-heated, your spirits are over-excited. By this picking up to-day of a fortune—a noble fortune to you, my boy—of six thousand pounds, and by the sudden and novel companionship of a dark and splendid lady, the pulses of your body have been set a-hammering too fast. You must sleep, or excitement will make you sick."

Eight bells were struck. Bol came along, and I went below to see if the captain was awake. He addressed me on my entering his cabin. I reported the little there was to tell. He said that the pain in his side was easier; that he could move without the anguish of the afternoon.

"I shall lie by all night," said he, "and hope to be up and about again in the morning."

He then inquired about the situation of the island, the appearance of the weather, the sail under which the brig lay, whether any vessel had hove in sight, and added—

"If you should awaken in your watch, go on deck and take a look round; though I trust Bol."

I went on deck to give the Dutchman the bearings of the island and our distance from it. He was sullen with sleep. Likely as not, the can which Jimmy had filled contained more liquor than should have gone forward at once.

"Keep a bright look-out," said I. "There may come a shift of wind that will put the island under our lee, with nobody to guess that it's at hand until we're upon it."

"Ow, I'll keep a bright look-out," he answered; "but vould to Cott dere vhas no more look-outs for me! I vhas dam'dt sick of looking out. I hov been looking out, by tunder, for ofer twenty year, and hov seen noting till dis day; and den she vhas to be carried round der Hoorn to Amsterdam before she vhas all right."

I went to my berth. Excitement had subsided since my few words with Greaves. I pitched into my bunk, and was sound asleep in a minute. I was awakened by the weight of a heavy hand and by the sound of a deep voice.

"Mr. Fielding, I do not like der look of der veather. I believe dere vhas a gale of vind on her vay here."

"What is the hour, Bol?"

"She vhas a quarter past dree."

I went on deck, and observed that the sky in the north was as black as pitch. Overhead the stars were dim and few, but they burnt freely and brightly in the south. I caught a moaning tone in the wind, that had considerably freshened since I left the deck; and the brig, hove-to under whole topsails, was lying over somewhat steeply, with the seas to windward

j 2

slapping at her rounded side, hissing off in pale yeasty sheets, and flickering snappishly into the gloom to leeward.

"Call all hands and close-reef both topsails," said I.

I ran below to report to Greaves. A bracket-lamp burnt feebly in his cabin. He was wide awake, and his dark eyes, with the glance of the small yellow flame upon them, looked twice their usual size.

"It is coming on to blow, sir."

"Well, snug down and put yourself to leeward of the island, anyhow."

"Shall I heave her to, then, for watering?"

"Judge for yourself. The brig is in your hands. If it comes hard, let her go. Keep a sharp look-out for the island. Have you its bearings?"

"Bol should have them," said I. "I have been turned in since midnight."

I regained the deck. The crew were yawling at the reef-tackles and singing out at the main-braces to trim the yards for reefing. There was much noise. The wind was steadily freshening, and through the groans and pipings of it aloft ran the sharp, salt hiss of small seas bursting suddenly and with temper under the level lash of the wind. I shouted to Bol, who came out of the blackness in the waist.

"Where do you make the island?"

" She'll bear sou'-east," he answered.

I stepped to the compass.

" There's been a shift of wind since midnight. It was nor'-nor'-west, and now it's come north—since when ? "

" Ow, she freshened out of der north in a leedle squall. Dot vhas vhen I called you."

I swept the wide, dark reach of the southern line of sea with the glass ; but had the island been as big as England, it would have been sunk in the peculiar smoky thickness of the dusk that yet, strangely enough, formed a clear atmosphere for the stars to shine through. I say I swept the ocean with the glass, but to no purpose. An old sailor once laughed at me for using an ordinary day telescope at night. I told him that what would magnify a coloured object would magnify a shadow ; and he afterwards owned that he talked out of prejudice ; had looked through a telescope since in the darkness, and discovered that I was right.

The men reefed the topsails smartly, and not being able to see the island, and not choosing to trust Bol's conjectures as to its situation, I headed the brig due east, setting the reefed foresail and trysail along with some fore and aft canvas to give her heels. It blackened rapidly overhead ; every star perished. In a few minutes there was not a light visible up in God's heights ; all the fire was below, and the sea was beginning to run in flames like oil burning. This shining in the sea was a blindness to the sight, for it brought the sky down black as a midnight fog to the very sip and spit of the surge. We held on, crushing through it, for the wind, having swiftly swept up into a fresh breeze, had on a sudden roared into half a gale, and the brig was smoking forwards as she plunged, with a heel to leeward when the sea took her, that brought the white and fiery smother within hand-reach of the gangway rail.

I stood at the binnacle ; Bol was at my side ; two hands were stationed on the look-out; the crew remained on deck. They had got to hear that Bol had lost the bearings of the island, and though the watch might be called, no man was going below on such a night of sudden tempest as this, with a hurricane away behind the windward blackness, for all we knew, and this side the horizon as deadly a heap of fangs as ever bit a ship in twain.

" I vhas glad if he lightned," said Bol. " It vhas strange if der island did not show on der starboard quarter there."

" It was strange," said I, mimicking him in my temper, " that you should fall asleep in your watch on deck with land close aboard ye."

" By Cott, den——"

Rain at that instant struck the brig in a whole sheet of water. It came along with a roar and shriek of wind and wet. The cataractal drench was swept in steam off our decks by the black squall it blew along in; the fierce slap of it fired the sea, and we washed through an ocean of light, pale and green.

" By Cott, den——" bawled Bol.

" Breakers ahead!" roared a voice from the forecastle.

" Breakers on the lee-bow!" cried another voice.

It was like being blinded and shocked by lightning to hear *those* cries. They were paralysing. For an instant I looked and listened idly.

Then—" Hard a starboard every spoke! Hard a starboard every spoke!" I shouted, and flung myself upon the wheel to help the men there, roaring meanwhile to Bol to call hands to the main braces and to get the fore tack and sheet raised. He rushed forward thundering. Never had Dutchman the like of such a voice as Bol.

The brig was in the wind; she was pitching furiously head to sea, the canvas thrashing in the blackness, the gale splitting in lunatic shrieks upon every rope and spar, the strange, hoarse shouts of the seamen rising and falling in shuddering notes upon the clamour that surged above as the water rolled below.

I had fled from the wheel to the side to look for the land, and was straining my vision against the wet

obscurity in vain search of the white water of breakers,
or of the overhanging midnight shadow that should
denote the island close aboard, when—the brig struck!
a violent shock ran through the length of her; every
timber thrilled as though a mine had been sprung
under her keel. "O God, that it should have *come*
to it!"· I thought.

"Round with that fore-yard, men," I roared;
"don't let her hang! *don't* let her hang!" Again
the brig struck. A sort of raging chorus full of
curses and the passion of terror broke from the seamen as they dragged. The rain cleared as suddenly
as it had begun, the brig's head was paying off, and
my heart swelled in thanks as she listed over to larboard, trembling to a blow of sea that rose in a
mountain of milk upon her bow.

"Where are you, Fielding?" shouted the voice of
Greaves.

"Here, sir."

He was standing in the hatch, gripping the companion for support, but his voice had the old ring.
"What have you done with the brig?"

"White water was just now reported. I don't see
it. I don't see the land—yet we struck."

"No," he answered coolly, "it was we who were
struck. There is no land. Look there—and there—
and there! Those are your shoals!"

At the moment of his speaking one of the sub-

limest, most beautiful sights which the ocean, prodigal
as she is in marvels of terror and splendour, can offer
to the sight of man, was visible round about us.   In
at least a dozen different parts of the blackness that
stooped to the luminous peaks of the seas I beheld
flaming fountains, glittering lines rising and feather-
ing to the gale, coming and going, blowing pale
and yet splendid—every jet so luminous that the
scoring of the darkness by it was as defined as the
track of a rocket.   They soared and fell in a breathing
way, some near, some afar, ever varying their dis-
tances, and one snored like an escape of steam within
a biscuit toss of our weather beam, and the fiery
shower flashed on the wind betwixt our masts with
a hiss like a volley of shot tearing the surface of
water.

"A school of whales," shouted Greaves.   "One
of them plumped into us.   Now get your topsail
aback, Fielding—get your topsail aback, and stop
her till the beasts go clear, or they'll be butting
us into staves.   Jump for the well and get a
cast."

The men, hearing their captain's voice, were
quieted.   They came to the braces, and, without
disorder or any note of cursing terror in their voices,
brought the brig to a halt.   I dropped the rod and
found the vessel staunch; sounded the well four or
five times, and always found her staunch.   The

wondrous luminous appearances vanished, and the blacker hours of the night before the dawn closed upon us in an impenetrable dye, but with less weight in the wind and with less fire in the sea.

"Furl the foresail and let the brig lie as she is till dawn," said Greaves, and walked slowly from one side of the deck to the other, looking forth, pausing long to look; then, with slow motions, he went below, and stretched himself at full length upon a locker, with a hand upon his side.

My watch came round at four; but, in any case, I should have watched the brig through the darkness. Some while before dawn the wind was spent, the stars glowing, the sea fast slackening its heave, with the muck that had troubled and drenched us settling away in a shadow south and west.

At last broke the day. Melancholy is daybreak at sea. There is nothing sadder in nature; nothing that so sinks the spirits of the watcher who suffers himself to be visited by the full spirit of the sight. On shore there is the chirrup and harmonies of birds, the rosy streaking of the sky over the hill-tops; the vane of the church-spire burns, the cock crows heartily, the farmyard is in motion, the smell of the country rises in an incense as the sun springs into the sky. But at sea the cold iron-gray of the breaking morn is reflected in the boundless waste. There is nothing to catch the light of the springing sun save the clouds. The vast solitude brims into the unbroken distance, and cold is the ashen sky, and cold the picture of the ship, as it steals out of the darkness of the night. The melancholy, however, is but in the dawn's beginning. When the sun rises, there is a splendour of colours at sea which you will not find ashore. The ocean is a mirror that reverberates the light of day. Times are when the deep flings its own prismatic glories upon the sky. This have I marked at sunrise, when the flash of the luminary has sunk into the heart of the sea, when all is blueness and dazzle below, and, above, a sky of high compacted cloud, delicate as flowers and figures of frost and snow upon a window-pane, charged with the colours of the great eye of ocean looking up at it.

" There's the island," said I to myself.

I snatched up the glass, and resolved the tiny piece of shading upon the horizon into the proportions of the ugly rock of cinders. It was twelve or fourteen miles distant down on the lee quarter.

" The deuce !" thought I. " What has been our drift ? Where has the brig been running to ? And yet Greaves told me he could trust Bol !"

I looked through the skylight, and immediately the captain, who lay upon the locker, opened his eyes and fastened them upon me.

" The island is in sight, sir."

" How far distant ? "

I made answer. He asked a few questions, then bade me shift the brig's helm for the rock to complete our watering. Twenty minutes later we were standing once more for the island, with all plain sail heaped upon the brig, and a quiet air of wind blowing dead on end over the taffrail.

CHAPTER XX.

WE were off the island again by nine o'clock. Greaves was wise to fill his casks; the water was sweet, the road home long, and our peculiar care was not to be forced to look in anywhere for supplies of any sort. Yet it was as depressing as a disappointment to return to the island. Is there an uglier heap of rock in the wide world? The black lava of the scowling Galapagos yields nothing more horrid. And the spirit of its dark and horrible solitude visited you the more sharply because of the crawling, stealthy life you beheld low down by the wash of the beach, remote from the inland loneliness: the creeping shape of the elephant tortoise, of the black lizard, of crabs as huge as targets, and no further motion save what's in the air, where the ocean fowl are glancing. That island was a fit tomb for the ship which it caverned. You thought of it as a grave, of the ship as a corpse; and the ugly heap of flat split cliff and black lava climbing into spires, and front of cinderous rock corrugated

by the arrest of their glowing cataracts, fell cold upon
the sight, and colder yet upon the heart.

We sent a hand aloft, as before, to keep a look-out.
The island lay square in the north, and whilst we
hung hove-to off the reefs, at any hour something
large and armed might come sailing up from the
horizon at the back, and heave the breast of a royal
over the western or eastern point ere we could guess
that there was anything within leagues and leagues of
us. Yan Bol took charge of the long-boat, and went
ashore. It was a fine morning, but the sky looked
dim, like a blue eye after tears; the sun had his sting
of yesterday, but not his flash. A long swell swung
through the sea, but the heave was out of the north,
and we lay south, the land between; it was smooth
here, or we could have done little in the way of
watering. The corners of the land illustrated the
weight of the swell; the white water burst in clouds
there, and the noise of it came along with the voice of
a gathering storm.

Greaves was so much better of the pain in his side
that he sat at breakfast, and took a chair upon the
deck afterwards. He called me to his cabin whilst
we were heading for the island, and asked me to look
at his ribs. There was a little discolouration, such as
might attend a bruise—no more. I pressed the bones,
but he did not wince. I dug somewhat deep in the
soft part just under the liver, but he uttered no sound.

The pain was very nearly gone, he told me; yet he looked pale, and his eyes wanted their former light and old activity of glance.

I was busy in bringing the brig to a stand whilst Greaves was at breakfast, and on passing the skylight and looking down, I saw the Lady Aurora seated at table with him. When he came on deck after breakfast, she followed; Jimmy placed chairs, and she was about to sit, but catching sight of me she approached, bowing low, with a fine arch smile, and her hand extended. I supposed she meant merely to shake me by the hand, but on grasping my fingers she retained them, and I felt a foolish blush upon my face, as she drew me to the binnacle-stand, at which she pointed, saying, "Compass." She then led me to the side, and, projecting her glittering hand over the rail, said "Sea." Then, looking aloft, she laughed and shook her head, and cried—

"No zar, señor."

"Star," said I.

"*Si—star—gracias*," she exclaimed.

"Had you not better mind your eye?" exclaimed Greaves, as we approached him. "Somebody's told her the value of your share in the chinks below. She's no clipper, but she's got a devilish fine bow and run, and you'd find her bends sweetly good, I'll warrant you, were you to careen her and clear her sides. By Isten, Fielding, she'll be forging ahead, and taking you in tow if you don't mind your helm."

I made no reply. I did not greatly relish Greaves's humour. The girl's ignorance of our tongue was an appeal to our respect. But then I was twenty-four—an age of sensibility. Greaves was an older man, and though I love his memory, I must say the sea had a little blunted some of the finer points of feeling in him.

Madam Aurora took the chair which Jimmy had placed, and she and Greaves sat together, but in silence. Some business of the brig occupied my attention. Presently Greaves told me to go below and breakfast.

" I will look after the ship," said he.

I went below, and made a good breakfast. There was a dish of terrapin; the Dutch sailor Wirtz, the burly, carroty man with the deep roaring voice—but all our Dutchmen had deep voices—had somewhere learnt the art of cooking terrapin. He had stayed in the brig to dress this delicious meat, and Frank Hals, the cook, had gone ashore in his place in the long-boat. I fared sumptuously, washing the delicate morsels down with some of the *Casada's* cocoa, which had been prepared for the pot by Thomas Teach, who professed to have learnt what he knew under this head in two voyages he had made to the Dutch Spice Islands.

Galloon had followed me into the cabin, and bore me company. He sat upon his chair, and gazed at me affectionately when I talked to him. Often had I talked out my mind to Galloon. Often in quiet, lonely watches, during the outward passage, had I held his ears, whilst his fore-paws rested upon my knees, and given loose to the imaginations which the prospect of the promise of realising thirty thousand dollars raised up in me. And then, again, I loved this dog as the saviour of my life. Never could I look into his affectionate, liquid, intelligent eye, but that I would think to myself, and often say aloud to him, dog as he was, a poor four-footed beast, soulless, as it is commonly supposed, of affections to be best won by kicks and curses—that he had, by saving my life, become in a sense the creator of a man, the renewer of a being deemed by his own species immortal in spirit, so that whatever I did a dog would be answerable for; the existence of all passions in me, my pleasures and hopes and griefs, nay, my marriage, should ever I marry, and the children I begot, would be all chargeable upon a poor dog, God wot!—a strange thing to reflect on by one who has been made to believe, all his life, that he is only a little lower than the angels; and yet true as the blessed sunlight itself; for if it had not been for Galloon, long ago I should have been—what? the roe of a herring, perhaps: the liver of a cod—instead of a man, capable

k

of looking back, through a long avenue of years, and of moralising thus.

When I came on deck, I found Antonio standing in front of Greaves, cap in hand, translating for him and the lady. On my appearing, Miss Aurora exclaimed quickly and eagerly to the Spaniard, who, turning to me, said, squinting as he spoke—

" The señorita has met you before."

" Where ? " said I.

" At Lima, señor."

" Never was at Lima in my life."

He translated ; she made a little dignified gesture of impatience.

" The lady says that she has met you at the house of ——" and here Antonio named a Spanish merchant of Lima.

" No," said I, looking at her and shaking my head.

" Yes," she cried in English, and spoke rapidly to Antonio.

" She is not mistaken, caballero.   Two thumbs are alike, but two faces never."

" You never were at Lima ? " said Greaves.

" Never," I exclaimed, laughing.

" Let her have her way," said Greaves.   " Contrive to have visited Lima, and to have been a bosom friend of Don ——" and he named the Spanish merchant. " What does it signify ?   May it not mean that she is

in love with you, and that her professing to have met
you is a Spanish maiden's device to cover an advance,
as a soldier would say ? "

Antonio continued to squint. I viewed him
narrowly, and was satisfied that he had not understood the captain's words.

" Beg the lady to continue her narrative," said
Greaves.

She addressed Antonio in a few sentences at a
time. Occasionally her language was above his under-
standing; he would look at her stupidly, until she
gave him another nod. How rich was her Spanish,
how honey-sweet her utterance ! It was like listening
to singing. The memories which thronged her recital
delicately coloured with blood her pale olive cheek ;
her eyes moistened or sparkled as she spoke, or
watched while Antonio interpreted. Most of the time
her gaze was fastened upon me. It seemed as though
she put me before Greaves, as though the incident of
my having had charge of the boat which brought her
off the island, had established me in her gratitude as
her deliverer.

Her story, however, was little more than a re-
petition of what has already been related. Her mother
had been absent twenty years from Old Spain. On
the death of her husband, she sold the estate and all
her interest in the business, and went to Acapulco
with her daughter, on a visit to her brother, who was

k 2

a priest at that place; thence she and Aurora took ship for Cadiz.

The lady broke off at this to implore us, through Antonio, to tell her, as sailors, whether we believed her mother's life had been preserved. Greaves answered that he considered it very probable that her mother was alive. Who was to tell that the ship had foundered? Who was to say that she had not out-weathered the gale, been jury-rigged and worked by the survivors into port, the Señorita Aurora's mother being on board?

The girl's eyes glistened when this was translated. She smiled at Greaves, and thanked him in Spanish. An expression of pleading then entered her face, and her look took a peculiar colour of beauty from the wistfulness and plaintiveness of it. Why would not the captain set her ashore at Lima, that she might rejoin her mother, who, on landing—it mattered not at what port on the coast—was sure to make her way to Acapulco?

But Greaves shook his head, smiling into her eyes, which were impassioned with entreaty.

"I must go straight home," said he. "Do not you know that there is a treasure in our hold, which obliges me to make haste to reach England? I will take care that you safely arrive at Madrid, even should it come to myself escorting you, señorita."

She bowed, looking sadly.

" Or here," said he, extending his hand towards me, " is a cavalier who will be honoured by conducting you to Madrid."

She slightly glanced at me, then fastened her eyes upon the deck and mused for a few moments; then addressed Antonio, who, turning to me, said—but in English, you will please understand, which I do not attempt to reproduce, that you may read without hindrance—

" The lady recollects that when she met you at Lima you spoke Spanish."

" I was never at Lima," I answered, colouring and then laughing.

" Depend upon it," said Greaves, " that the fellow she met was good-looking, or recollection wouldn't be so keen."

" What was the occupation of the gentleman ? " said I to the lady, through Antonio.

" He was an English naval officer, had been imprisoned, but had been at liberty some weeks when the señorita met him."

" What was his name ? "

" She does not remember; but you are the gentleman."

" Be it so," said I, laughing.

" On slenderer evidence have men been hanged," said Greaves.

Now came a short pause. Antonio shuffled his

naked feet, sometimes looking straight, sometimes
squinting, impatient to get forward and lounge. The
long-boat had made her second trip, and lay alongside
the beach. The figures of the men crawling from the
grove of trees, trundling the casks among them, showed
like beetles in the distance. It was about eleven
o'clock. The sunlight was misty; the swell rolled
with a dull flash in the brows of it; the wind hummed
like clustering bees aloft, and swept the cheek with
the breath and kiss of fever. The slewing of the brig,
along with the sliding of the sun, pitched the glare
upon the deck, clear of the trysail, in whose shadow
we had been conversing. I called to a man to spread
the short awning. Antonio was going; the Lady
Aurora detained him.

"The señorita wishes to know," said the Spanish
seaman, "how long the voyage to England occupies."

"We mean to thrash our way home," answered
Greaves. "We shall not take long. Let us call it
three months."

"Blessed Virgin! Three months!" echoed the
girl in Spanish.

A fine look of tragic horror enlarged her eyes.
She distorted her mouth into a singular expression.
The tension paled her lips and exposed her teeth.

Greaves seemed to admire her. For *my* part, I
thought her now the most beautiful and wonderful
creature I had ever heard of—a lady who might either

be angel or devil, you could not tell which; or she might be both. Her face defied you, for it could put on twenty looks in the course of a short conversation, thanks to her heavy eyebrows, which were full of play and character, and thanks to the long lashes of her eyelids, whose drop or lift, whose languishing falls, and arch or scornful or playful erections, changed the meaning of her glances for her as she chose, rendering them, at her will, transparently eloquent, or as inscrutable as a gipsy's gaze. She put her hand upon her dress, and Antonio interpreted.

" The lady's gown will not last three months, and then, señor ? "

" Chaw ! " cried Greaves, and, pointing with something of passion to the island, he exclaimed—" Ask the lady to put the clock back till the day before yesterday is reached, and *then !* "

On this being explained, a flash of temper lighted up her eyes.

" I shall be in rags," said she, " before you reach your country."

" We have needles and thread on board," said Greaves coolly.

" You are men, and cannot conceive what it is to be a woman embarking on a long voyage, possessed of no more clothes than what she has on."

" How can we comfort her ? " said I.

" Can the señorita sew ? " said Greaves.

Certainly she could sew.

"Then," said Greaves, "if the señorita can sew, let her mind be at rest. I am the owner of a roll of fine duck, which is entirely at her service. There are yards enough to yield her as many dresses as she needs. Will she require stuff for trimming? Let her select a flag of two or three colours. Bunting makes excellent trimming. It is light and brine-proof."

Antonio bungled much, and squinted fiercely in the delivery of this; yet he contrived to make the lady faintly understand the meaning of Greaves's speech. She tapped on her knee with her fingers, and seemed to keep time with the beat of her foot to an air that she inaudibly hummed; her black eyes were downwards bent, but at swift intervals the fringes lifted, and a glance of light sparkled at me or Greaves. I noticed a pouting play of mouth. In fact, her air was that of a girl who has been spoiled by indulgence since her childhood. One figured her as the goddess of the fandango, the burden of the midnight guitar, and the heroine of a score of sweethearts.

"Duck is very well for dresses, sir," said I. "She is thinking of under-linen."

"We are not to know anything about under-linen," said Greaves. "She must make what she wants. She doesn't seem grateful enough, to please me. To bother me about dress now, after four days of that cinder, and the deliverance recent enough to keep most people hysterically sobbing and thanking God in fervent ejaculations ! "

Antonio addressed her. I guessed he wanted to know if he could go. She spoke to him, and the man, awkwardly smiling, said—

" The señorita asks if you are Catholics ? "

" Yes and no, for my part," answered Greaves, looking at her gravely. " I am heading that way. I believe I shall hoist the Papal flag yet, but it's not flying at present."

" Is the capitan a Catholic ? " repeated the lady.

" Ay, but not a Papist," said Greaves.

" Are you a Catholic, señor ? "

" I love God and hate the devil," said I. " That is my religion. It is broad, and there is room for many names upon its back."

" Is it customary, do you know, Fielding, for ladies who have just been rescued from the horrors of a volcanic island, from perils hideously increased by the association of such a yellow and, by no means, fangless worm as that "—dropping his head in a cool nod at Antonio—" to inquire into the religious faiths of their preservers ? "

The Lady Aurora spoke.

" The señorita wishes to know when you changed your religion ? "

" Ah, when, indeed ? " said I, laughing.

" You were a very good Catholic at Lima, señor ? "

" Yes, when I was at Lima, I was a very good Catholic," said I.

" Then you are the caballero the señorita supposes ? "

" Damn ye, you squinting devil, you know better ! " thundered Greaves. " Jump forward. We've had enough of this."

The man fled towards the forecastle, noiseless with naked feet. The lady looked frightened.

" Lima, señorita—*no !* " said I, smiting my bosom with force.

She gazed at me earnestly, with an expression of misgiving, then addressed me in Spanish. Greaves gathered her meaning.

" I believe she says you are not her man, if you are not a Catholic," said he ; and then pointing at me, and looking at her, he cried out, " No Catholic —no Lima—not your man, in any sense of the word. Fielding, what's that Dutch devil Bol up to ? "

I went to the side to look for the long-boat. She was at that moment coming through the two points of reef. Her oars rose and fell in the distance in hairs of gold, and she seemed to tow a hair of gold in her wake as she came out of the calm breast of the harbour into the soundless heave of the ocean. I reported her approach, and lay upon the rail, watching her and musing upon what had passed between the Spanish maid and us.

It was odd to think of a fine young woman, sitting on the deck of a vessel that had but a few hours before taken her off the desolate island which was still in view, coolly inquiring into the religious beliefs of her preservers, and looking as though, if time had been given her, she would presently overhaul our consciences. To be sure, she hoped that if she found us Catholics, she would get more of her way with us, obtain pity, sympathy enough to procure her direct conveyance to a near port. She left her chair, came close to my side, and stood looking at the boat; in a moment, pointing to it, she asked in Spanish for its name. I gave her the name, turning to look at Greaves, who was laughing softly, but with an averted face. She put more questions, pointing to the objects, and then, lightly laying her fingers upon my arm, she signed that I should take her forward, glancing at Greaves as she did so, following the look on with a full stare at me, and a shake of the head eloquent as her speech. It was for all the world as though she had said in plain English, "I don't like that man; let us leave this part of the ship."

I made her understand as best I could, by pointing to the approaching boat, and then to the yard-arm whip for slinging the casks aboard, that my duty obliged me to stop where I was. She bowed, but with a little flush, as though vexed by my refusal; indeed, in her whole instant manner, there was the irritation of your ladyship, of your exacting, well-served, much-admired, fine young madam, who is very little used to being disappointed.

I moved forward towards the gangway by two or three steps, that she might guess my work prohibited talk; and, in fact, conversation would have been impossible in a few minutes, for the long-boat was fast nearing the brig, and the job of seeing the water aboard was mine : and that was not all, either. Greaves was captain : he was on deck, watching and listening. The influence of the presence of a captain is always strong upon the seaman, whether it be of the quarter-deck or of the forecastle. Habit worked like an instinct, and disquieted me. Had Greaves been below, I daresay I should have been very glad to keep the señorita at my side, if only for the enjoyment of meeting her full gaze; for the longer I looked at her eyes, the more did I wonder at their depth and life, at their transcendent powers of repulsion and solicitation, and eloquence of rapid expression ; and the longer I listened to her voice, the more was I charmed by the sweetness and richness of it; and the longer I beheld her face, the more manifold grew its revelations. But its revelations of what ? My pen has no art to answer that question. You gaze upon the face of the deep, and beauties steal out of it to

your perception, and you know not how to define
them, you know not how to indicate them.   They
come blending in an effect that enlarges as you look,
and the sum of the steady revelation is a deepening
delight and a constant growth of wonder.   I hear you
say, "Had a woman of Spain ever the beauty you
claim or invent for this lady?" My answer is as
simple as a look—I say "Yes."   The Señorita
Aurora de la Cueva was a woman of Spain, and she
had the beauty, and more than the beauty, I feebly
attempt to describe. I care not if all the females of
Old Spain are as hideous as hobgoblins and witches;
they may all be bearded like the pard, thatched at
the brow with horse-hair, their complexions of chocolate, their figures bolsters; the Lady Aurora was beautiful; her charms I have scarce language enough to hint
at, much less portray.   This she was; and whether
you believe me or not, signifies nothing.

"And I did not much admire the woman when I
first saw her!" thought I.   In fact, had I rowed her
aboard another ship and never seen her again, I should
never have thought of her again.   "Is it to end in my
making a fool of myself?   Does a man make a fool of
himself when he falls in love?" A plague upon these
cheap cynic phrases which creep into the national
speech, and form the mirth of boys and the wisdom of
the sucklings of literature.   "But I am not in love yet,
anyhow," thought I.

" Oars ! " roared Bol, in the stern-sheets of the boat. " Standt by mit der boathook. Vy der toyfil doan somebody gif us der end of a rope ? "

A rope was flung. My Lady Aurora walked forward, calling and beckoning to Antonio. She arrived abreast of the galley, and stood there, and talked to the Spaniard, pointing about her and clearly asking for the names of things in English.

" Fielding," cried Greaves.

" Sir," I answered, facing about.

" She will be making love to you in your own tongue before another week is out," he called.

" Such a voice as hers would keep anything not deaf listening as long as she liked."

" She has a very sweet voice," he exclaimed, " and she is a very fine woman. But should she pick up our tongue, you'll find the devil that's inside of her come drifting out horns first with the earliest of her speech. Talk of your fears of the crew ! She's the sort of party to carry a ship single-handed, though the vessel mounted the guns and was manned by the complement of the *Royal Sovereign*. She is learning English for some piratic motive—it may be the dollars, it may be the brig—for she don't want to go, and I daresay she don't mean to go, round the Horn without her mother. Bol, is this the last load ? "

" Der last loadt, sir."

" Bear a hand then to whip the water aboard, and let us get away."

It was a quarter before one by the time we had chocked and secured the long-boat, and were ready to start on a passage that was to carry us over many thousands of miles of salt water. The breeze had freshened; soft small clouds, like shadings in pencil, were sailing up off the edge of the sea into the misty blue overhead; the lustre of the sun was still pale and brassy, and a look of wind was in the yellow of the disc-shaped spread of radiance, out of which he looked like an eye of fire in a target of gold.

" Make sail, Fielding," called Greaves from his chair, on which he had been sitting ever since he came on deck, though in all those hours he had not once complained of pain. " Make sail, and heap it on her. Bring her head due south, and let her go."

The braces of the yards of the main were manned, the wheel turned, the canvas filled as the fiery breath, that was now brushing the sea, and that seemed to come the hotter for the very dimness of the sunshine, gushed over the quarter. We squared away to it; and now the island slided by, opening features of its swart, melancholy, loathly rocks, which had been in-visible before. The milk-white burst of surge made the base of the cliff in the wash of it black. I noticed a hovering of pale radiance upon the patch of verdure where the grove or wood stood. It was no more than a patch to our distant eye; it was like the dance of the South African silver-tree. The verdure had the gleam of an emerald, and you thought of a gem on the sallow breast of Death.

I was full of the business of making sail, yet could find an eye for the island as it veered away on the quarter. Greaves gazed at it intently; so did the Lady Aurora as she stood at the rail, with her profile cut clear and keen as a marble bust against the sky over the horizon. The mouth of the cave yawned upon us, then narrowed, then thinned into a slice, then vanished round a shoulder of cliff.

"Pull, you toytils! Shoomp und run!" bawled Bol, in his hurricane note, to the two Spaniards who were loafing near the galley, lazily looking on at the work that was going forward. "Dis vhas not der islandt—dis vhas no shipwreck. Shoomp, or I make you fly mit a sharge of goonpowder in der slack of yer breeks."

The royals were sheeted home; trysail, flying-jib, staysails set; for it was a quartering wind, and there was scarce a cloth that we could throw abroad but could do serviceable work. They called this sort of sailing in our time *going along all fluking,* the weather-clew of the mainsail up and the lee-clew dully lifting its weight of blocks and hawser-like sheets and thick frame of foot and bolt-rope.

"Set all stu'n'-sails!" cried Greaves; and soon out

to windward soared to their several yard-arms and to
their boom-ends those wide, overhanging spaces of
sail, clothing the brig in surf-white cloths from the
royal mast-heads to the very heave of the brine, when
she rolled her swinging-boom to windward.

"Pipe to dinner!" called Greaves.

The sweet, clear strains of Yan Bol's whistle found
a hundred echoes in the hollows on high. Aurora
gazed upwards, as though looking for the birds. The
men had worked hard, and were pale with heat and
sweat. They had worked with a will in making sail.
Even the Dutchmen had sprung along and aloft with
a blue-jacket's activity; for we were homeward bound!
—a cry in every marine heart magical in its inspiration
of swift and eager labour. With dripping brows the
men stood looking at the receding island, whilst Yan
Bol whistled them to dinner; and when the burly
Dutch boatswain let fall the pipe upon his breast to
the length of its laniard, all hands, moved by feelings
which made every throat one for the moment, roared
out a long, wild cheer of farewell to the island,
flourishing caps and arms to it, as though its heights
were crowded with friends who could see and hear
them.

"Look at Galloon!" cried Greaves.

The dog was on the taffrail, and every bark he
sent at the island was like a loud hurrah, with the
significance the noise took from the wagging of the

l

creature's tail and the set of the whole figure of
him.

"He knows we are homeward bound," said
Greaves.

"And that the dollars are aboard," said I.

Miss Aurora went to the dog, caressed and talked
to him. The lad Jimmy's head showed at the galley
door. Greaves hailed him to know when dinner
would be ready.

"Another twenty minutes, master."

"Heave the log, Fielding, and let's get the pace at
the start."

All expression of pain was now passed out of his
face; likewise had his natural, fresh colour returned
to him. The triumph of this time had kindled his
eyes anew, and there was pride and content in the
looks which he cast around his brig and over the rail
at the island. And I think if ever there was a man
who had a right to feel satisfied with himself and
his work, Greaves, at this time, was he; for, truly,
something more than talent had gone to the discovery of the dollars in the caverned ship. Mere
accident it was that had disclosed the vessel, but it
needed the genius of a great adventurer to light upon
the dollars, to note all the particulars of the Spanish
manifest, to hold the secret behind his teeth till he
got home, to inspire such an old hunks as Bartholo-
mew Tulp with confidence enough to shed his blood,

or, in other words, to disburse his money, in the furtherance of this enterprise of recovery.

I called a couple of men aft, and hove the log. What is the log ? It is a reel round which are wound many fathoms of line; at the end of the line is attached a piece of wood, sometimes a canvas bag, designed to grip the water when it is hove overboard. The line is spaced into knots, and the running of it is timed by a glass of sand. This log is one of the oldest contrivances we have at sea. With it the early navigators groped their way about the world. It found them New Holland and the Indies, and both Americas. It was their longitude and often their latitude. It was their chronometer and sextant. We use it still, and cannot better it. A simple and noble old contrivance is the log. May the mariner never lose faith in it! Crutched by the log on one side, and the lead on the other, he may hobble round the globe in safety, defiant of shoals, regardless of fogs.

I hove the log, and made the speed seven knots.

"A good start!" exclaimed Greaves, rising and coming slowly to the rail, and looking over. He walked without inconvenience or pain, and stood with a thoughtful face, gazing at the satin-white sheets of foam sliding past. Madam Aurora left Galloon and came to my side, but Galloon followed her—never

l 2

went there to sea a friendlier, a more affectionate dog.
The men were hauling in the dripping log-line and
reeling it up.   The lady with a smile said with a very
good accent, "How do you call it?"   I laughed as I
pronounced the word *log*.   Oh, what should it convey
to the imagination of a Spanish maiden?

She understood, however, for what purpose it had
been used, and with eloquent gestures inquired the
speed.   I held up my fingers.

"*Quien lo hubiera creido?*" cried she.

"She is not grumbling, I hope," called Greaves
from the rail, and he slowly approached us.

The lady looked for a little while very earnestly at
the captain, with a world of meaning in her beautiful
eyes—meaning so eloquent in *desire* of expression
that it was pathetic to witness the arrest of speech in
her gaze and face.   She then with grace and dignity
motioned round the sea.

"It is very wide, and the voyage before us is
a long one—I understand that," interpreted Greaves;
and never did man peruse lineaments more speaking or translate glances more radiant and expres-
sive.

She then placed the forefinger of her right hand
upon her lips to signify silence or dumbness.

"Which means," said Greaves, "that you can't
speak our tongue, and don't like the prospect ac-
cordingly."

She then took her dress in her hand, putting on a most mournful countenance.

"Yaw, yaw," cried Greaves, with a little irritation, "we have discussed that matter, madam. But there is white duck below—duck for the duck, what d'ye say, Fielding?—and there are hussifs in the fok's'le."

I believed that her dumb-show was at an end. Not at all. Clasping her hands, sparkling with the several rings she wore, and raising them in a posture of supplication to the level of her mouth, she upturned her face to the sky, and with an inimitable expression of entreaty, of piteous prayer rather, insomuch that her eyes seemed to swim and her lips to work, she stood whilst you could have counted ten.

"Sainted and purest of all the Marias, put pity into the heart of this British captain, and cause him to set me ashore, for the sea is wide and the voyage is long; and I am possessed by a dumb devil and cast among heretics; and I have but one gown; and, O Maria and ye saints! candles shall ye have in plenty, mortification will I undergo, prayers by the fathom will I recite, choice gifts will I make to Holy Mother Church, if ye will but soften the heart of the durned, slab-sided skipper who stands opposite me, interpreting my mind. There ye have it, Fielding. That's what her gestures said, that's what her eyes looked. But I tell you what—this sort of thing will grow tiresome presently. You must bear a hand and teach her to speak English."

"Dinner's on the table, master," said Jimmy, putting his head through the companion-way.

"Call Yan Bol aft to stand a look-out whilst we dine, Fielding," said Greaves, "and give your arm to the lady and bring her below; she don't like me."

CHAPTER XXI.

A FIGHT.

WE had swept the island out of sight before we left
the dinner-table. When I came on deck, the horizon
had closed somewhat upon us. The ocean was a weak
blue, and ran with a frosty sparkle into a sort of film
or thickness that went all round the sea. The breeze
had freshened, and it whipped the waters into little
billows with yearning and snapping heads of foam,
and it was pouring its increasing volume into the lofty
height and wide expanse of canvas under which the
brig was thrusting along in a staggering, rushing way,
the glass-smooth curve of brine at the bow breaking
abreast of the gangway with a twelve-knot flash of
the foam into the throbbing race of the long wake.

We kept her so throughout the afternoon until six
o'clock, when the evening began to darken eastwards:
we then took in the lower and topgallant studding-
sails, but left her to drag the fore topmast studding-
sail if she could not carry it, for this was wind to make
the most of: we could not, to our impatience, come

up with the Horn too soon; many parallels were there for our keel to cut before we should find ourselves abreast of that headland; degrees of latitude lying like hurdles for the brig to take along that mighty and majestic course of ocean.

That same night of the day of our departure from the island, Greaves came out of the cabin and walked the deck with me. He had been amusing himself for an hour below with the company of the Señorita Aurora. From time to time I had watched them through the skylight. He smoked a cigar; a glass of grog stood at his elbow, some wine and ship's biscuit before the lady. He held a pencil, and from time to time wrote, looking up at her; and she would bend over the paper, read, give him a dignified nod, take the pencil, and herself write.

But it seemed to me that she forced herself to endure this tuition. She held herself as much away from him as the obligation of writing and extending her hand and receiving the paper permitted. This went on till about nine o'clock. The lady then withdrew, and Greaves came on deck, as I have said.

" This is fine sailing," said he.

" Ay, indeed. I would part with some of those dollars below for a month of it."

" I have been teaching the girl English, and have picked up some Spanish words from her. She is an apt scholar; her mind is as swift as the light in her

eyes. It is clever of her to wish to learn English.
We can't be always sending for that fellow Antonio.
She seemed astonished when I talked of three months;
but she knows, she *must* know, that the run might
occupy a vessel more than three months. What
change would the skipper of the craft she sailed out
of Acapulco in be willing to give out of *four* months,
ay, and perhaps five, in a passage to Cadiz ? "

"She, perhaps, thought of herself as being without
clothes when you talked of three months, and so cried
out."

"Well, it is clever of her to wish to learn English.
Here she is, and here she's likely to remain until we
send her ashore in the Downs."

"But why ?"

"Why ? "

"Is there no chance of something coming along,"
said I, "in which we can send her to a port this side
America ? "

"She knows there is a big treasure on board."

"That's sure."

"She knows that it is Spanish money, and how got
by us."

"True."

"Well, now, send her out of this brig with our
secret in her head, and we stand to be chased by the
chap we put her aboard of."

"Not if she be an English ship."

"I'd trust no Englishman in this part of the world. Figure a craft as heavily armed again as our little brig; figure *that*, and then count our crew forward there. I'll have no risks. I'll speak nothing. We have got what we came to fetch, and this is to be my last voyage. I am a rich man now. There are thirty-six thousand pounds belonging to me below. No, Fielding, the lady will have to go along with us. You shall teach her English; she shall teach me Spanish. She shall pour out tea, act the hostess, sing: the very spirit of melody swells her fine throat every time she opens her lips. She shall make dresses for herself and under-linen."

"And the two Spaniards?"

"They must go along with us too. They are a worthless, skulking pair of fellows, I fear; but we must keep 'em."

"They get no dollars?" said I.

"Not so much as shall buy them soap. We have saved their lives; that's good pay for such service as they'll render. What shall you do with your money?"

"Well, I have often considered, captain," I answered. "I believe I shall buy a little house, put what remains out at interest, and go a-fishing for the rest of my days. And you?"

"First of all," he answered, "I shall knock off the sea. I shall then strike deep inland, and look for a

little estate in the heart of a Midland shire. I do not
know that I shall marry. Should I marry, it will be
with a lady of my own degree in life. I will play the
gentleman only so far as I am entitled by my condition to represent one. I will be no sham. There is
no yard-arm high enough for the hanging of the men
who, having got or inherited money, set up as country
gentlemen, still splashed with the mud of the gutter
out of which their fathers crawled, shaking themselves
—illiterate, vulgar, scorned by the footmen who stand
behind their chairs, belly - crawlers, title - lickers,
toadies. Faugh! I once made a rhyme on shams
—four lines—the only rhymes I ever made in my
life—

> " Pull up your blinds, that all the world may see
> The house you live in and the man you be.
> The blinds are up, and now the sun hath shone :
> The house is empty, and the man is gone."

" By which you mean to imply——" said I.

" By which I mean to imply," he interrupted,
" that if the lines don't tell their own story, they must
be deuced bad."

He stopped to look at the compass. The night
was dark, but the dusk had cleared. The clouds
raced swiftly over the stars, and the wind blew strong,
but with no increase of weight since we had taken in
the studding-sails. The brig rushed along, leaving a

meteor's line of light astern of her. The dim squares
of her royals swayed on high with the floating stroke
of a pendulum. I admired the dark and pallid picture of the little fabric speeding lonely through this
vast field of night.

Greaves came from the binnacle and stood beside
me.

"Fielding," he exclaimed, with cordiality strong in
his voice, "it rejoices my heart when I reflect that I,
whose life you saved, should, by a very miracle of
chance, be the one man chosen, as it were, to sub-
stantially, and I may say handsomely, serve you."

"I shall walk through my days blessing your
name," said I, grasping the hand he extended. "And
how have you repaid me? You have not only preserved me from drowning: you make me easy for the
rest of my time."

"The accounts are squared to my taste," said he.
"I am very well satisfied. To-morrow I shall want
you to take stock of the cases in the lazarette. You
found them heavy?"

"All, sir."

"And all are full, no doubt. But you shall make
sure for me."

"I shall want help," said I. "Whom shall I choose
amongst the crew?"

"It matters not," he answered. "All hands know
the money is there."

"Yes; but it is an *idea* to them now. When they come to see the sparkle of the white dollars!"

"There is no good in distrusting them," said he. "I am aware that your fears run that way. When we were outward bound, your fears ran in another direction," he added drily. "Let me tell you this: whether we choose to trust the men or not, they're aboard; they man the ship; they are the people who are to navigate her home. We *must* trust them," he repeated with emphasis. "In fact," he continued after a short pause, "I would set an example of good faith by letting them understand how entirely I trust them. Therefore to-morrow take Bol and two others of the men who were left aboard me when you went to the *Casada*, and examine the cases in their presence, you testing, they moving the boxes for you."

I replied in the customary sea phrase; for this was a direct order, the wisdom of which it was no duty of mine to challenge. Shortly afterwards he went below.

It blew so fresh that night and next day, however, that the sea ran too high to enable me to get below amongst the cases. It was a spell of wild, hard weather for that part of the world, though it never blew so fierce as to oblige us to heave-to. The gale held steady on the quarter, and we stormed along, the white seas rising in clouds as high as the foretop, and blowing ahead like vast bursts of steam from the hatchway.

Greaves pressed the brig, and she rushed through the surge in madness. I never before saw a vessel spring through the seas as did the *Black Watch* at this time under a single-reefed foresail and double-reefed topsails. She'd be in a smother forward, just a seething dazzle of yeast 'twixt the forecastle rails, everything hidden that way in a snowstorm, so that you'd think the whole length of her was thundering into the boiling whiteness about her bows; but in a breath she'd leap, black and streaming, to the height of the lifting sea, with a toss of the head that filled the wind with crystals and prisms of brine, whilst a long-drawn whistling and hooting came out of the fabric of her slanting masts, and the water blew forward in white smoke from the gushing scuppers.

Then came a change; the dawn of the third morning painted a delicate lilac along the eastern sky, and when the sun rose over the wide Pacific the morning was one of cloudless splendour.

At eight o'clock Yan Bol came aft to take charge of the deck. I told him that presently we would be going into the lazarette to take stock of the cases of silver, and that the captain would keep a look-out whilst he was below. A dull light glittered in the eyes of the big Dutchman. He grinned and said, " Vill not she be a long shob, Mr. Fielding ?"

" Yes," said I.

" How long shall she take a man to gount a tousand dollars ? Und dere vhas hoondreds und tousands of dollars to gount below."

" Do you think I mean to count the dollars ? "

" Yaw."

I arched my eyebrows at him, and then gave him my back.

" Vell, I vhas sorry. I like gounting money. Dere vhas a shoy in der feel of money if so be ash he vhas gold or silver—I do not love copper—dot makes me happier, Mr. Fielding, dan any odder pleasure. Ox me vhy und I tells you ? Because vhen I gounts money she vhas mine own. No man gives me his money to gount. She vhas mine own ; but leedle I have, and vhen I gounts her it vhas after long years, so dot der pleasure vhas all der same as a pipe und a pot to a man vhen he comes out of der lockoop."

Whilst I breakfasted I enjoyed some conversation in dumb-show with the Lady Aurora—dumb-show, for the most part, I should say—for a number of English words she now possessed, and I was astonished not more by her memory than by the excellence of her pronunciation. Her knowledge of a single word uttered by me seemed to light up the whole phrase to her perception. Her gaze would continue passionately wistful and expectant whenever she listened with a desire to understand ; and whenever she seized, or thought she had seized, the sense of what was said, a flush visited her cheeks, her whole face brightened.

There was a degree of eagerness in this desire of hers to learn English that was a little perplexing. It was an earnestness—call it an enthusiasm, if you will —that went beyond my idea of her need. It was intelligible that she should wish to make herself understood. She would now know that she was to be locked up in a ship with a number of Englishmen for three or four months; what more reasonable than that she should desire to make her wants intelligible without being forced upon so disagreeable and ignorant an interpreter as Antonio, and without seeking expression in grimaces and the lunatic language of the eyebrows, shoulders, and hands? What more reasonable, I ask? But her earnestness, her zeal, her satisfaction when she understood, caused me to wonder somewhat when I thought of her in this way. She was on a desert island a few days ago, with small prospect of deliverance from as frightful a fate as could well befall a woman. For all she knew, her mother was drowned; she might be an orphan, and who was to tell what property belonging to her and her mother had sunk in the Spaniard from which she had escaped, supposing that vessel to have foundered? And yet, spite of all this, her spirits were good, her beauty growing as the lingering traces of her suffering died out. She took an interest in everything her eye rested upon, questioning me like a child, questioning Greaves—nay, walking forward, as I have told you, to ask Antonio for the English names of things ; and all the while her troubles, so far as she was able to express them, did not go beyond an anxiety as to clothes for herself and an eagerness to pick up our tongue.

These thoughts ran in my head as I ate my breakfast, whilst she talked to me by gesticulation, occasionally uttering a word or two in English, and listening with shining eyes to the sentences I let fall in my own speech. Greaves lay upon a locker. He listened, sometimes smiling, but rarely spoke. He complained this morning of an aching in his side where he had hurt himself, and said that he feared he had made a mistake in walking yesterday ; he was afraid he had overworked the bruised ribs ; but he looked well, and when he spoke there was a heartiness in his voice. It was as likely as not that he had angered the bruise by too much walking about the decks, and I advised him to lie up until the pain went.

However, the brig was to be watched whilst I went into the lazarette with Bol and the others, so I sent Jimmy on deck with a chair, and when I had breakfasted Greaves got up, put his hand upon my shoulder, and together we ascended the companion-ladder.

Yan Bol was carpenter as well as bo'sun and sailmaker. I bade him fetch the necessary tools for

m

opening the cases and securing them again. With us went Henry Call and another—I forget who that man was. We lighted a couple of lanterns, and going into the cabin lifted the lazarette hatch that was just abaft the companion-steps. The Lady Aurora came to the square hole to look at us, and inquired by signs what we were going to do. I shrugged Spanish fashion, and made a face at her, that she might gather that what we were going to do was entirely beyond the art of my shoulders and arms to communicate.

"Doan she shpeak no English, Mr. Fielding?" said Bol, as he handed down his tools to Call, who was already in the lazarette.

"No," said I.

"Vell, I, Yan Bol, teaches him herself in a month for von of her rings."

"Over with ye, Bol. Catch hold of this lantern."

He dropped through the hatch, and I followed, and Miss Aurora stood at the edge of the square of the hole, holding by the companion-steps and peering down.

There were one hundred and forty cases; we examined every one of them; it was a tedious job. I felt mighty reluctant at first to let Bol prize open the lids and gaze with the others at the dull, frosty glitter of the long rolls of dollars; but a little reflection made me sensible of the force of Greaves's argument. If the crew were not to be trusted, what was to be done?

And was it not a mere piece of cheap quarter-deck subtlety on my part to hold that the *idea* of the dollars being aft was not the same as *seeing* them?

There was no need to watch very anxiously; the dollars were packed as tightly as though the metal had been poured red-hot into the cases and hardened in solid blocks. There was never a nail on Bol's stump-ended fingers that could have scratched a coin out.

"Vhas dere goldt here as vell ash silver?" he inquired.

"No."

"Oxcuse me, Mr. Fielding, but how vhas you to know?"

"How was anybody to know what these cases contained at all? Shove ahead, will ye? and ask fewer questions. Are we to be here all day?"

It was as hot as fire in this lazarette. Our blood was speedily in a blaze and our clothes soaked. The three Jews who were summoned from the province of Babylon to be hove into a burning furnace suffered not as we did. Bol's eyes took a gummy look and turned dull as bits of jelly-fish; yet the three fellows were perfectly happy in staring at the silver and pulling the cases about. Every time a lid was lifted their heads came together in the sheen of the lantern, and rude sounds of rejoicing broke from them.

"How many sprees goes to each box?"

m 2

"There's an Atlantic Ocean of drink in this here case alone."

"Smite me, but if this gets blown the girls'll be coming down to meet the brig afore she's reported."

"She vhas a handsome coin. I likes to feel her in mine pocket. How much vhas she vurth, Mr. Fielding?"

"All that you shall be able to buy with her. Next case, and bear a hand."

"How many tousand dollars vhas dere in all?"

"Enough to stiffen you with sausage and to keep ye oozy with schnapps."

We worked our way to the bottom case, and every case was chock-a-block, as we say at sea—filled flush —and the dollars by the lantern light resembled exquisitely wrought chain armour. I saw that every case was securely nailed; the boxes were restowed. We then climbed out of the lazarette, and Bol and the others went forward whilst I put on the hatch, padlocked it, and withdrew the key.

I plunged my fire-red face in water, quickly shifted, and quitted the cabin, tired, burning hot, but very well satisfied with the morning's work. Greaves was seated in a chair, and Miss Aurora walked the deck, in the shadow of the little awning, pacing the planks abreast of him. Her carriage—to use the old-fashioned word—had she been draped as the beauties of her person demanded, would have been lofty yet flowing, dignified yet easy and floating, graceful as the motions of a dancer who swims from the dance into walking; but the barbaric cut of her gown spoiled all. Never did I behold a woman's dress so ridiculously shaped. It was a grief to an English eye, for in my country the girls' costumes were just such as would have hit and sweetened by suggestion the form of Miss Aurora. Well do I remember the English girl's style of 1815: the neckerchief with its peep of white breast, the girdle under the swelling bosom, the fair up-and-down fall of drapery thence. Never do I recall that costume, with its hat of chip or leghorn, without a fancy of the smell of buttercups and daisies, the flavour of cream, the scent of a milkmaid fresh from the udder.

I handed the key to Greaves. He put it in his pocket, and gazed at me inquiringly.

"It's all right, sir, to the bottom dollar," said I.

"Good," he exclaimed.

"It is so much right," said I, "that I am disposed to think there is more money than the manifest represents."

"There are five hundred and fifty thousand dollars in one hundred and forty cases. I wish there may be more, but I suspect the entry was correct. What did the men say?"

"Yan Bol was all a-rumble with questions. There will be much talk forward."

"There has been much talk aft," he exclaimed, smiling. "Sailors are human, and those fellows yonder are to pocket twelve hundred dollars apiece beside their wages on this job. Let them talk. Let imagination run away with them. Let the fiddle be jigging in their ears; let their Polls be seated on their knees—in fancy. Keep their hearts willing, for this bucket has to be whipped home."

The Lady Aurora looked and listened as she paced abreast of us. Her eyes, full of light, often rested on me. Greaves ran his gaze slightly over her figure, and leaning back in his chair and looking away, that she might not suspect he talked of her, said—

"Our dark and lonely friend is mighty full of curiosity. I can believe that Eve was such another. When Eve walked round the apple-tree and looked up at the fruit, with her head a little on one side, she wore just the sort of expression the dark and lonely party puts on when she motions a question."

"*Que hora es, señor?*" said the lady.

Greaves made her understand, by pronouncing the word "one" in Spanish and by gesticulating the remainder of his meaning, that it was drawing on to two o'clock.

"She may be hungry," said I.

"She shall be fed in a few minutes," said Greaves.

The girl seated herself on the skylight and watched the motion of Greaves's lips, listening, at the same time,

with a little frown of attention to the pronunciation
of the words he coolly delivered.

"I was observing," said he, with an askant glance
at her, "that the dark and lonely party is mighty full
of curiosity. She tried to pump me about the dollars
below; wanted to know what you were doing in the
hold; asked the value of the treasure."

"How did you understand her?"

"She beckoned to Antonio; but when I found she
had no more to say than *that*, I sent him forward
again, with a sea-blessing on his head. And when I
was taking sights she put out her hand for my quad-
rant. I let her hold it. She clapped it to her eye—
shutting the eye to which she put it, of course—fell
to fingering the thing, and I took it from her. I wish
she wasn't so handsome. A little moustache, a pretty
shadowing of beard, the Valladolid complexion, and a
few chocolate teeth, would make the difference I want,
to enable me to look my meaning when she teases me
with questions. But who could be angry with the
owner of those eyes?"

He gazed at her fully. She averted her face suddenly. I fancied I caught a fleeting expression of
aversion, or, at all events, of distrust. She flashed her
eyes upon me with a gaze as significant as though she
understood what Greaves had been talking about, rose
from the skylight, and motioned me to walk with
her. Greaves left his chair and stepped slowly to the

companion-way. At this moment Jimmy came along
with the cabin dinner. The lady, inclining her face
to my ear, spoke low in Spanish, pointed to the cabin
skylight, shook her head, then pressed her forefinger
to her lip; all which, in plain English, meant—" I don't
like him."   I could have answered that she owed
her life to him as master of the ship, and that his
off'hand manners were British, and meant nothing.

" Dinner," said I.

" Dinner," she repeated, smiling.

She repeated the word several times.

" Will you come ? " said I.

These words she likewise repeated ; then, giving
me a little bow, she extended her hand, that I might
conduct her below.

The evening of this same day was soft and beautiful, rich with the lights of heaven ; the ocean so calm
that some of the most brilliant of the luminaries found
reflection in the water—tremulous, wire-like lines of
silver ; yet had the breeze body enough to give the
brig way. It came fanning and breathing cool as dew
off the dark surface of the sea, and the refreshment of
it after the fiery heat of the day was as drink to the
parched throat.

I walked in the gangway, smoking a pipe. It was
shortly after eight o'clock. Yan Bol was aft with
Greaves. The Lady Aurora was in the cabin, writing
with a pencil. Some seamen were in the bows of the

brig ; their shadowy figures flitted to and fro, all very quietly. Voices proceeded from the other side of the caboose ; the speakers did not probably know that I walked near. I could not choose but listen. One was Antonio, the other Wirtz, and the third Thomas Teach.

"What I don't understand's this," said the voice of Teach. "Th'ole man" (meaning Captain Greaves) "falls in with that there ship locked up in the island, and boards her. He finds the silver—why didn't he take it, instead of leaving it with a chance of the vessel going to pieces, or some covey a-nabbing the dollars afore he could come back for them ? "

"Dot may seem all right to you," said Wirtz, "but see here, Tommy ; shuppose der captain had took der dollars into der ship he commanded vhen he falls in mit der island : vhat do his crew say ? Und vhen he arrives vhat vhas he to do mit der dollars ? Gif dem oop to der owners of his ship ? By Cott, he see dem dom'd first. If he keep der dollars for himself, how vhas he going to landt dem on der sly mitout der crew asking him for one half, maybe, and making him like as he can hang himself for der rest ? Dot's vhere she vhas. No, no," rumbled the man in his deep Dutch voice, "der capt'n know his beesiness. Dis trip for der dollars vhas vhat you English call shipshape und Pristol fashion."

" Is the dollars to be run, I wonder, when we gets home ? " said Teach.

" Do you mean shmuggled ? "

" Yaw, smuggled's the word, Yonny," said Teach.

" Vell, if dey vhas not run dey vhas seized."

" Who's agoing to seize 'em ? "

" Ox der captain."

" I'd blow the blooming brains out of any man's head as laid a finger on my share," said Teach.

" Yaw, und you gif me der pleasure of seeing you hanging oop by der neck. Den I pulls off my hat, und I say, How vhas she oop dere mit you ? Vas he pretty windy oop dere ? "

" When I gets my share," said Teach after a pause, " I'm a-going in for a buster. There'll be no half-laughs and purser's grins about the gallivanting. I've chalked out for myself. There's Galen always a-telling us what he's going to do with his money ; sometimes he's a-going to buy a share in a vessel ; then, no, dumm'd if he is, he'll buy a house and put his young woman into it : then, no, dumm'd if he'll do that, he'll clap his money in a bank, and wait till the figures grow big enough to allow of his living like a gent for the remainder of his days."

" Vhen I gets my money dis vhas my shoke," said the Dutchman. " My girl shall teach me to eat. She shall puy me a silver fork. By Cott, I drink mine beer out of silver. Every day I hov veal broth und sausages, peas und salad, stewed apple und ham, und pickled herrings mit smoked beef, und butter und sheese, und I shplits myself mit almonds und raisins."

"I like the taste of the Dutch!" cried Antonio in a voice that sounded thin and almost shrill after Wirtz's. "When I get my money, see what it shall bring me; white cod and onions from Galicia, walnuts from Biscay, oranges from Mercia, sausages from Estremadura"—here he loudly smacked his lips—"sweet citrons and iced barley-water, and water-melons. Vaya! what have you to say now to your veal broth and salt herrings? And I will have Malaga raisins, and my olives shall come from Seville, and my grapes and figs from Valencia. Vaya! I am a Spaniard, and this is how a Spaniard chooses. All that is good may be had in Madrid, and all that is good will I have when my share is paid me."

There fell a short silence as of astonishment.

"Share!" cried Wirtz in a low, deep, trembling voice. "Share didt you say? Shpeak again. I like to hear dot verdt vonce more."

"Share! What share are ye talking about? Ye ain't thinking of the dollars below, I hope?" said Teach in a tone of menace.

"I expect a share," said the Spaniard.

"Oxpect—say dot again. I likes to hear you shpeak," said Wirtz, with an accent that made me figure him doubling his fist.

"Aren't I a sailor on board this ship?" said Antonio.

" A *sailor*, d'ye call yourself?" cried Teach. "Well," he snapped, "suppose y'are, what then?"

"I have a right to a share."

"And do you tink you get a share?"

"I have a right to a share," repeated the Spaniard in a sullen note.

"Call her a shoke or I will fight mit you," said Wirtz.

"I will not fight," said the Spaniard in a dogged voice. "I have a right to a share. The capitan will pay me and Jorge. We are sailors with you, and are helping to navigate this brig to your country. The dollars are Spanish; they are money of my own country. The capitan is a gentleman, and will not wrong me and Jorge, and we will receive our share as a part of the crew."

This was followed by a Dutch oath, by a crash and a low cry.

"Hullo, there—hullo!" I called. "What are you men about there on t'other side the caboose?"

I sprang across the deck, and, by such light as the stars made, beheld Antonio in the act of getting on to his legs.

"Mind! He may have a knife!" shouted Teach.

The Spaniard, uttering a malediction, whipped a blade from a sheath that lay strapped to his hip, and

flung it upon the deck. The point of the weapon
pierced the plank, and the knife stood upright.

"I am no assassin! I do not draw knives upon
men!" cried Antonio.

"Who knocked this man down?" I demanded.

"I—Vertz."

"You are a bully and a ruffian. This is a shipwrecked man, scarce recovered from great sufferings.
He is half your size, too."

"He talked of his share, Heer Fielding, und my
bloodt poiled. We safe his life, he eats und drinks,
und der toyfil has der impudence to talk of his
share."

"Forward there! What is wrong?" cried the
voice of Greaves. "Where is Mr. Fielding?"

"Here, sir."

"What is wrong, I am asking."

"Come aft to the captain, the three of you," said I;
and I led the way.

All hands were on deck at this hour. The forecastle was roasting, and the watch below lay about
the forward part of the decks. The whole crew,
therefore, heard the noise, were drawn by it, and followed me as I went aft, Teach loitering in my wake
to tell those who brought up the rear that "the
blooming Spaniard was swearing he'd a right to a
share of the dollars, and that he was bragging as how
he meant to spend his money in Madrid on onions

and figs, when he was brought up with a round turn
by Yonny Vertz's fist."

It is strange that unto the eye of memory the
picture which the brig at this hour made should stand
the most clearly cut, the most sharply defined of all
my recollections of her. Why is this? Because, perhaps, of the accentuation that night-scene took from
the shadowy heap of the men assembled upon the
quarter-deck, from the quarrel beside the caboose,
from the significance that must come into any sort
of difficulty aboard us from the treasure in the
lazarette.

The sails soared dark and still in the weak night-
wind; a brook-like bubbling noise of water rose from
under the bows; the vessel was steeped in the dye of
the night; but there was a faint shining in the air
round about the illuminated binnacle, and a dim sheen
hovered over the cabin skylight. The sea sloped vast
and flat to the scintillant wall of the sky. The voices
of the men deepened upon the ear the silence out
upon the ocean. It was a night to set the mind
running upon that saying, and realising it: "*And
darkness was upon the face of the deep; and the
Spirit of God moved upon the face of the waters.*"

"What's wrong?" said Greaves.

The shapeless figure of Bol came trudging from
the neighbourhood of the wheel to listen.

"There's been some sort of discussion between

Wirtz and Antonio," said I, " and Wirtz knocked the Spaniard down."

" Captain," exclaimed Wirtz, " all hands likes to know if der Spaniards you safe shares in der dollars ? "

" Who began the row ? " said Greaves.

" Señor," exclaimed Antonio, " I was speaking of the food that we eat in my country—— "

" Captain," bawled Teach, " he was a-bragging of the cod and onions, the nuts and barley-water, he meant to treat hisself to out of his share, as he calls it, when he gets to his home."

" She made mine plood poil," cried Wirtz ; " und she laughs at me vhen I shpeaks of vhat ve eats in mine own country."

" Señor," exclaimed Antonio, " have not Jorge and me a right to a share ? "

" Of what ? "

" Of the money in the cases—of my country's money—that you take out of the Spanish ship."

" Bol shall slit your nose if you talk like that. You rascal ! is it not enough that we have saved your life ? And what d'ye mean by your country's money ? Of what country are you ? "

" I am of Spain, señor ; born at Salamanca."

" There is no money in your country," shouted Greaves. " Ye are paupers all, cowards all, sneaks and rogues to a man." Yan Bol laughed deep.

"Speak again of the money below being the money of your country and we'll hang ye."

"Señor," said Antonio, "am I and Jorge to receive no money for working as sailors in this ship?"

"Not so much as will purchase you a rag to wind round your greasy ankles."

A half-smothered laugh broke from Wirtz and others.

"We ask, then, that you land us," said the Spaniard, whose audacity in continuing to address Greaves was scarcely less astonishing than the captain's extraordinary exhibition of temper and wilder display of words.

"Mind that you are not landed at the bottom of the sea, with a twenty-four-pound shot to keep you there," cried Greaves. "Wirtz, did you knock that man down?"

"Yaw, captain," responded Wirtz, in a voice that made one guess at the grin upon his face.

"You are a big man, Wirtz, and Antonio is a little man. Wirtz, I wish you may not be a coward at heart. Know you not," cried Greaves, elevating his voice, "that it is written, 'make not an hungry soul sorrowful; neither provoke a man in his distress'? The soul of Antonio is hungry for dollars, and you have made him sorrowful; he is in distress, being shipwrecked and having lost all his clothes, and you have provoked him. Your grog is stopped for a week, Wirtz."

" By Cott, but dot vhas hardt upon a man," said the Dutchman.

" Now get forward, all hands," exclaimed Greaves; "but mark you this: any man who raises his hand against another on board this brig goes into irons and forfeits his share of dollars. This is to be a peaceful and a smiling ship. We are going to get home sweetly and soberly; then comes your enjoyment— the pleasures of beasts or men, as you choose. Let no man say no to this."

He walked aft; I thought he would stay to have a word with me. Instead he immediately descended into the cabin. The men moved forward, talking amongst themselves, some of them laughing.

Yan Bol came up to me and said—

" I tell you vhat, Mr. Fielding; der Captain Greaves vhas a very fine shentleman."

" Very."

" How he talks—mine Cott, how he talks! I would give half mine dollars to talk like dot shentle-man."

" He is an educated man, and speaks well."

" Yaw, vell indeedt. I like der sheek of Antonio in oxbecting a share. But he oxbects no longer, ha!"

I turned from the Dutchman and looked through the skylight, and saw Greaves sitting at table, leaning his head upon his hand. The Lady Aurora continued to write, but once or twice whilst I watched she lifted

n

her eyes to look at the captain. I was weary, and passed below to go to my cabin. Greaves had left the table, and was entering his own berth as I descended the companion-steps. The materials for a glass of grog were on a swing tray. Whilst I mixed myself a tumbler the girl rose and handed me the paper she had been writing upon. The sheets had been torn by Greaves from an old log-book, and they were filled by her with Spanish names with their English meanings. I ran my eye over the writing, which was a very neat, clean Spanish hand, and nodded and smiled, and returned the pages to her, saying "*Bueno.*" Then, emptying my glass, I gave her a bow, bade her good-night in Spanish, received her answer of " Good-night, sir," well expressed in English, and passed into my berth.

CHAPTER XXII

GREAVES SICKENS.

THIS time gives a date to a change that came over Greaves. It was the change of sickness. He grew feverish, irritable, fanciful; his appetite fell away; the light in his eyes dimmed; sometimes he would put on a staring look, as though he beheld something beyond that at which he gazed.

I had been struck by his manner, and more by his manner than by his speech, when he lectured Wirtz and flung at Antonio the Spaniard, as you have read in the last chapter. Yet of itself this would not have been a matter to rest very weightily upon my mind, seeing that all along I had considered Greaves as a little, just a little, mad at the root. But soon the incident took significance as being a first lifting of the curtain, so to speak, upon a new and somewhat crazy behaviour in my friend. I hoped at first it was the heat that unsettled his nerves, and that the Horn would give me back my old, odd, hearty, generous shipmate and messmate. Then I feared that the blow

n 2

he had dealt himself when he stumbled in the hold of the *Cusada* had been silently and painlessly working bitter mischief in the organ of the liver, or in parts adjacent thereto. If the liver was hurt, the strangeness of the man might be accounted for. I have suffered from the liver in my time, and know what it is to have felt mad; I say I have known moments—O God, avert the like of them from me and from those I love—when I could scarce restrain myself from breaking windows, kicking at the shins of all who approached me, knocking my head against the wall, yelling with the yell of one who drops in a fit; and all the while my brain was as healthy as the healthiest that ever filled a human skull, and nothing was wanted but a musketry of calomel pills to dislodge the fiend that was jockeying my liver and galloping the whole fabric of my being down the easy descent.

It will not be supposed that the change in Greaves was sudden. It uttered itself at capricious intervals, and at the beginning was more visible in the mood than in the man.

For example, it was, I think, about four days after the little incident which brings the last chapter to a close. I had charge of the deck from eight to midnight. Miss Aurora had passed half an hour with me sometimes asking questions by gestures distinguishable by the light of the moon, sometimes attempting strange sentences in English, all the words correctly pronounced, but so misplaced that with true British politeness I was for ever breaking into a laugh at her. A moment there had been when she was in earnest. She came to a stand, her face fronting the moon, so that I witnessed the working of it, her eyes with a little silver flame in each liquid depth dark as the sea over the side. She spoke in Spanish, with here and there a word of English. It seemed to me she referred to the voyage. I fancied that I coaxed out of her words the meaning that she desired to continue in the brig and was content. How did I gather this, when I tell you in the next breath that I could not understand her? Well, it was my *fancy* of her meaning that I give you; but whether I understood her or not, she motioned with an air of tragic distress, clasped her hands, looked up at the stars, and cried in English, "Sad—sad—not understand— sad." We then resumed our walk, and presently she left me.

Now it was that Greaves arrived. He smoked a long, curled pipe of Turkish workmanship, and moved noiseless in slippers. The moonlight whitened his face and silvered his hair and blackened his eyes till, elsewhere, I might have looked twice without knowing him. We were to the southward of the Lima parallel, our course south by west. The Bolivian coast trends inward. Our course gave us to larboard a wide sweep of open ocean, and this we should hold down to the latitude of 50°; after which the chance was small of our falling in with anything armed under Spanish colours.

We had made noble progress, taking the days all round, and this night we were curtseying onwards with a pretty breeze off the larboard beam—a wind that ran the waters gushing white to the bends; and overhead were all the stars, and the moon in their midst dimming a circle of them, and under the moon the play of the sea was like a torrent of boiling silver.

" This is a desolate ocean," said Greaves.

" So much the better for us," said I.

" Oh yes, so much the better for us.   But the solitude of the sea is a burden that the heart don't always beat lightly under.   Is solitude a material thing ?   It has the weight of substance when it settles upon the spirits."

I let him talk on.   He was fond of big, fine words, and the stranger he became the more heroic grew his vein.

" Any more rows forward amongst the men ? "

" I have heard of none."

" I had two men who fought through a voyage. They had sailed together before, and fought throughout.   'They will fight whilst they meet on earth,' said the boatswain of the ship to me, ' and they will fight if they catch sight of each other at the Resurrection.' " He puffed a cloud of smoke upon the wind, and looked round the sea. "I am unsettled in my faith," said he: "I am troubled by doubts. I believe I am almost Roman Catholic, but lack sufficient credulity to enable me to bring up in that faith. I will tell you what I mean to believe in," continued he, halting in his walk, compelling me to stand, and looking me full in the face; "I am going to believe in the transmigration of souls."

"Oh, you'll wish to choose your next body before deciding, won't you?" said I. "You wouldn't be a flea or a cockroach?"

"The flea, and perhaps the cockroach, have short lives," said he gravely, "and the next entry might be into something noble. But stop till I tell you why I am going to believe in the transmigration of souls. I had a dream a few nights since; I dreamt that I was a Jewess. I beheld my face in a glass, and admired it vastly. My eyes flashed and were full of fire; my lips were scarlet. I wore something white about my head. I knew that I was a Jewess. Shadowy faces of many races of people approached, looked me close in the eyes, felt my face with their hands, accosted me, and I could not speak. I was suffocated with the want of speech. But on a sudden I obtained relief. I opened my mouth and spoke, and the words I spoke were Hebrew."

"D'ye know Hebrew?" said I.

"A stupid question to ask a sailor."

" How do you know you spoke in Hebrew ? "

" Because it wasn't Greek ; because it wasn't
Welsh ; because—because—man, it was just Hebrew."

" And how does transmigration offer here ? "
said I.

· " I was my own soul informing the body of a
Jewess. My soul, of course, couldn't utter itself, as
it was fresh from the body of an Englishman, until
it had filled up, as smoke might, every cranny and
brain-cell of the shape it possessed; until it had
penetrated to the crypts and dark foundations of the
woman's heart. Then, seeking vent, my soul broke
through the lips of the Jewess. In what tongue, d'ye
ask ? In what but the tongue of her nation ? "

" This," thought I, " is the Lady Aurora's doing.
She it is who's the Jewess of my poor friend's dream.
The fiery eyes, if not the scarlet lips, are hers, and
hers the arrest and suffocation of speech."

But I guessed it would anger him to put this; yet
it grieved me to hear this nonsense in his mouth, and
the more because his looks by the moon, that shone
upon us whilst he discoursed, gave a gloomy accentuation of—what shall I call it ? not yet madness; not
yet craziness; let me rather speak of it as wildness
—to his words.

He walked with me for above an hour, talking
on this absurdity of transmigration, and reasoning

illogically, and often with irreverence, on points relating to the salvation of man. It is a bad sign when religion gets into a man's head and acidly turns into windiness and nightmare imaginations, as sweet milk hardens into curdy flatulence in the belly of the suckling.

I sought to shift the helm of his mind by talking about the dollars below; by speaking about the crew and my secret distrust of Yan Bol; by calling his attention to the look of his brig as she floated, with aslant spars, through the moonlight, flowing lengths of the sails curving in alabaster beyond the shadow in their hollows, the water, black as ink under her bowsprit, pouring aft in fire and snow. But all to no purpose. He looked, and seemed not to see; he repeated, in a mouthing, absent way, my sentences about Bol and other matters, and immediately struck back again into his talk about heaven, his soul, the Jewess he had dreamt of, and the like.

But even without seeing him, even without hearing him, I should have known that there was something wrong with the man by the behaviour of his dog. I do not say that all dogs have souls; but I am as sure that Galloon had a soul of his own, after its kind, as that my eyes are mates. As a change slowly came over Greaves, so slowly changed Galloon. I would notice the dog watching his master's face at table, and found a score of human emotions in the creature's expression. I'd see him lying at Greaves's door if the captain was within, when formerly he would be on deck cruising about among the men or skylarking aft with me. If I called him, he'd come slowly. There was no more capering up to me, no more buoyant greetings, no leapings and lickings and short eager yelps of salutation in response to the many things I'd say to him. "We make much of human love," I would think whilst caressing the dog or looking at him, "and the love of man we call a passion; but the love of the dog we call an instinct. Yet is not the instinct nobler than the passion? Purity it has that is faultless. Is human passion pure to faultlessness? There is selfishness in human passion, but the love of yonder dog for its master is without selfishness. Many qualities enter into the passion of love; but the love of yonder dog is a primary quality in him. It is as gold amongst metals. Supposing analysis possible, then analyse the brute's affection, and you find not a hair's weight, not a dust-grain's bulk, of vitiating element."

The Lady Aurora was quick to notice the change in Greaves. Her lids moved swiftly upon her eyes, and their lashes were a veil, and she had an art of glancing without seeming to glance. She did not like him, and would not appear to see him more often than courtesy obliged. Her rapid glances, therefore, on occasions when she would have found other occupation for her eyes told me that she was struck by

the man's looks, that she wondered at them, and
guessed their significance. I was no doctor. For all
I could tell, she might have some knowledge under
that head. I fancied this from her manner of looking
at Greaves.

So one day, when she and I were alone in the
cabin, Bol on the look-out above, and the captain in
his berth, I endeavoured to converse with her about
my friend; but to no purpose. Intelligibility vanished
in signs, shakes of the head, dumb pointings to the
brow and ribs. She had, indeed, picked up a little
English. She was able to pronounce the names of
various articles of food, also had several English
nautical terms at her tongue's end; but when it
came to trying to talk about Greaves's state of health,
there was nothing for it but to crook our brows,
hunch our backs, and work meaning into nonsense
with postures.

Yet I managed to discover that the lady and I
were agreed in this: that Greaves had received some
internal injury from his fall, that it was slowly sicken-
ing him, and affecting his mind.

Nevertheless, he went about as usual, punctually
took sights, attended at meals, was up and down
during the day and night. He was very rational in all
the orders he gave to the men, in all direct instructions
to me respecting shipboard discipline and routine. It
was by fits and starts that his growing wildness showed,

and always when he had me alone; and then the
matter of his discourse was dreams and religion and
death. Not that he talked as though he supposed
his end was approaching; upon his words lay no
shadow of the melancholy that is cast by the dread
event when the heart knows, dimly and mysteriously,
that it is coming. He chattered as if for argument's
sake; postulated to disprove his own assertions; but
he was seldom logical, often devout, filled to the very
twang of his nose with fervour, and at other times,
and on a sudden, as impious as young John Bunyan.

What think you of this character of a seaman, of
a plain North Country merchant seaman; *you* whose
ideas of the nautical man are gotten from Smollett's
studies, from the delightful portraits of dear Captain
Marryat? But, Jack, bless ye! *you* who have been
to sea, *you* who have sailed ten times round the world,
who have swung your hammock in a score of forecastles, and who have out-weathered Satan himself in
a dozen different aspects of ship's captains, *you*, mate,
will approve this sketch, will recognise its truth, will
tell the land-lubbers that at sea are many varieties of
men—men who swear not, who are gentle, faithful in
their duty below; men who are a little crazy, who
drink deeply, and are devils in their thoughts and
madmen in their behaviour, but trucklers and slaverers
to those who hire them; men who are hearty, pimpled,
broad of beam, verdant with the grog-blossom and

green in naught else, moist in the weather eye, and bow-legged by great seas.

One Sunday morning, when we had left the island a little more or less than three weeks behind us, Greaves said to me at the breakfast-table—

"I shall hold Divine Service this morning on deck."

I stared, but said nothing.

"I'll read a portion of the Church of England liturgy to the men," said he, "and a chapter out of the Bible. What chapter do you recommend?"

I was at a loss.

"Give them something interesting," said I, "something that will carry them along with you."

"Right," he exclaimed, with a little light of vivacity kindling in his somewhat sunken and somewhat leaden eye; "what d'ye say to a fight out of Joshua?"

"I do not think," I answered, "that a good fight out of Joshua could be bettered."

"I'll give 'em that chapter," said he, "in which the son of Nun corks the five kings up in a cave and then hangs them. Not that there's any moral that I can see in that sort of narrative. It is an Ebrew Gazette extraordinary—a pitiful, bloody business from beginning to end. But if the reading of a chapter of it causes even one of the sailors to take an interest in the Bible, I shall have done some good."

"So you will."

"Do you know the men's persuasions?"

"Not I, captain."

"The Spaniards are Roman Catholics, of course. The Dutchmen and the others will be of us if they're of anything. When you go on deck, tell Bol to see that the crew clean themselves, and let him muster and bring them aft for Divine Service at half-past ten."

"Ay, ay, sir."

Miss Aurora sat over against me at this meal as at most others; she stared at me as though something was wrong. I did not wonder: I had been unable to conceal my astonishment at Greaves's orders for Divine Service. Down to this moment he had never read a prayer to the men, never exhibited the least disposition to do so, never imported the faintest shadow of anything religious into the dull and swinish routine of the brig. It was somewhat late in the day to lay up on *that* tack, methought. But it was for me to obey, and I went on deck, leaving Greaves sitting. Miss Aurora followed, and touched my elbow as I passed through the companion-hatch.

"What is it?" said she, in English.

"Nothing, nothing," I answered, smiling and shaking my head; for it would have given me a deal too much to act, with Yan Bol and the fellow at the wheel as spectators, to gesticulate Greaves's intention to collect all hands to prayers.

" No danger ? " said she, speaking again in English.

" No, no," I responded, heartily.

She touched her forehead, clasped her hands, and turned up her eyes to heaven with one of her incomparable expressions of tragic melancholy, sighed heavily, and returned to the cabin.

" Bol," said I, stepping up to the great Dutchman where he stood near the wheel, " you will see that the men clean themselves and muster aft by half-past ten for Divine Service."

" Vhat's dot ? " said he.

" Prayers."

He looked at Teach, who was at the helm, and a smile crawled over his face, as wind creeps over a surface of sea. His smile wrinkled his massive visage to the line of his hair.

" Brayers, Mr. Fielding ! Dot vhas strange after all dese months. For vhat vhas ve to pray now dot der dollars vhas on boardt ? "

" Reason the matter with the captain if you choose. You have your instructions."

" Ay, ay, sir. Mr. Fielding, may I hov a verdt mit you ? "

He spoke respectfully, and moved from the wheel. He was a man I had been careful to give a wide berth to throughout the voyage; but also was he a man whom, for my own peace sake, I had been at some pains not to give offence to. The familiarity of the fellow was Dutch. I never could make sure that it was more than a characteristic of his countrymen with him, and that he meant insolence when he spoke insolently. I bore in mind, moreover, that secretly he, and no doubt the rest of the crew, viewed me as an interloper—as one who would, probably, share far more handsomely than they in the treasure, without having entered at Amsterdam or having formed a part of the original scheme of the expedition. This consideration, then, made me wary in my relations with Yan Bol.

He moved from the wheel out of earshot of the fellow there, and said, in a rumbling voice of subdued thunder—

" I oxbects dot der captain vhas not fery vell, Mr. Fielding ? "

" He is not very well."

" She vhas a bad shob if he vhas to took und die."

" Yaw ; but what is it you wish to say to me ? "

" I hov nothing to say, Mr. Fielding, oxcept vhat I hov said. Der men likes to know how der captain vhas. Vhen I goes forwardt und tells dem dot dey most lay aft und bray, dey vhas for vanting to know if der captain vhas all right mit his headt. Oxcuse me, Mr. Fielding, but vhas it all right mit der captain's headt ? "

" We are talking of the captain," said I.

" Ay, ay, sir ; und I shpeaks mit all respect. You

vhas first mate; I oct second. It vhas right ve shpeaks together vhen der capt'n's health vhas in trouble."

"You are able to judge of his state as well as I, Bol."

"No; you live close mit him. My end of der ship vhas yonder."

His voice seemed to deepen yet as he spoke these words, whilst he pointed with his vast square hand to the forecastle. I held my peace, sending a look to windward and at the wheel as a hint to him to go. He stood awhile viewing me and appearing to consider, all with a heavy Dutch leisureliness of manner and expression, as though his thoughts rose slow, like whales, to the surface of his intelligence, spouted and sunk before he could harpoon them; then saying, "Vell, brayers at half-past ten; dot vhas a strange idea now der money vhas on boardt," he walked forward.

This being Sunday morning, the men had nothing to do, and lounged about the galley, smoking and conversing. I watched Bol approach them. He stood abreast of a knot and delivered his orders. *That* I gathered from the stares, the starts, the hoarse laugh, the rude forecastle joke sent in a growling shout across to a mate at a distance. A little later, however, the fellows came together in a body, somewhat forward of the caboose, some of them out of my

o

sight until my steps carried me to the gangway. Yan Bol stood amongst them. It was clear to me that they were talking over this new scheme of a prayer meeting aft. I kept well away, and heard nothing but the rumbling of their voices; but it was easy to guess that the most of their talk ran on the captain's health and intellect, and I reckoned that, if they had already noticed any strangeness in him, this call to prayers would go further to prove him mad in their eyes than the insanest shipboard order he could have delivered.

Some while, however, before there was need for Bol to send the men to clean themselves, Jimmy came out of the cabin and said that the captain wished to speak to me. The morning was fine, the breeze steady, and the sea smooth. The deck was to be safely left for a short interval. I called an order to the helmsman, and went below.

Greaves was pacing the cabin floor. The Lady Aurora was in her berth, perhaps at her devotions. Galloon was upon a chair, wistfully watching his master as he measured the cabin. Greaves's face worked with excitement and agitation; his walk was equally suggestive of distress and disorder. Were there such a thing as news at sea, I might have supposed that something heart-shaking had come to him.

"Fielding," he cried, as I stood viewing him from the bottom of the companion-ladder, "I can't read prayers to the men. The devil's right. He's put it into my head that I'm too wicked, that I've been too great a sinner in the past, and am still altogether too vile to read prayers."

"Do not attempt to do so, then," said I.

"I might be struck dead for profanity," said he. "There's a feeling here"—he laid his hand upon his heart—"that warns me I shall drop if I open my lips in the recital of a prayer to the men. Look how nervous I am!" he exclaimed, with a wild, hard smile; and approaching me close he extended his hands, which trembled violently, and then, turning up the palms, he disclosed the channels or lines in them wet with perspiration. "Tell the men," said he, "that I am too ill to read prayers. Next Sunday, perhaps——"

He threw himself upon a locker, and hid his face upon the table. I watched him for a few minutes, then, going on deck, beckoned to Bol and told him there would be no prayers that morning. The Dutchman threw a suspicious look at the skylight and walked forward.

After this incident anxiety increased upon me until it became indescribably great. I had supposed that the hurt Greaves had done himself, through the connection which exists between the liver and the brain, affected his mind; but now, when he was growing worse, I reckoned he had struck his head as well as

o 2

his side. Be this as it will, his intellect was giving
way, his health every day decaying, and I say that
when I grew sensible of this, when I understood that
unless he took a turn and mended apace he must die,
anxiety made my days bitter.

My old fear of the crew revived. That fear had
been hushed somewhat by the behaviour of the men,
but it grew clamorous when I thought of Greaves as
dead and buried in the sea, of the treasure of half a
million of dollars in the lazarette, of myself as standing alone in the brig, with no man in authority to
support me, without even the moral backing of good-
will I might have got from the men had I shipped at
Amsterdam and formed one of the Tulp party.

The dead days became dreams and visions to my
memory when I thought backwards and recalled the
Royal Brunswicker, Captain Spalding, my arrival in
the Downs, the gibbet on the sand-hills, the press-gang,
the long outward passage to the island, and the hopes
and fears which came and went when Greaves talked
rationally of the dollars, then irrationally of dreams
and the like, and so on, and so on. I did pray very
eagerly in my heart that he would be spared. Indeed,
I loved the man. He had saved my life, he had en-
riched me, he had proved a generous, cordial, and
cheery shipmate and messmate. I say I loved him,
and on several occasions when I was on deck alone,
walking out the weary hours of the night watch, did I

look up at the stars and ask of God to deliver my friend
from the death whose hand was closing upon him.
These petitions would I murmur till my eyes were
wet. It was hard that he should be called away in
the prime of his time after years of the stern and
barren servitude of the sea, at the moment when a
noble prize, gained, as I would think, with high adven-
turous skill, was his.

But I never could discover, at this time at all
events, that he had the smallest idea he was in a bad
way. What was visible to me and the sailors, to the
Spanish lady, yes, and to his own dog, himself did not
see—at least, by never a word that fell from his lips
did he give me to guess he knew he was ill. Sometimes he'd complain of weakness and keep his bed;
he'd wonder what had become of his appetite, that
was all; he never went further. It was I, mainly,
who took sights and kept the ship's reckoning, who,
in fact, navigated the brig, and did the work of her
master. Miss Aurora's sympathies with him were
strong at the start—that is, when she saw how ill he
was, and how his illness was increasing upon him.
She'd make efforts to anticipate his wants at table;
with her own hands she'd boil chocolate for him in th
caboose and bring it to the cabin; she let me understand she wished to nurse him. But whether it was
because of simple dislike, or because his poor head,
muddling the fine woman whom he had rescued with

the speechless Jewess of his dream, excited in him
some inscrutable fear or aversion, I know not; he would
have nothing to say to her, looked away when she
spoke, repelled whatever she offered, often shrank
when she approached—was so crazily discourteous, in
a word, that I was obliged to take the girl aside and,
by signs and such words as were now current between
us, advise her to keep clear of him.

As to *her*, she spent much of her time in sewing
and in attempting to master the English tongue out
of some books which I borrowed from Greaves's cabin,
and with such help as I had time to give her. We
had plenty of needles and thread on board. Greaves,
before his illness grew, had given Miss Aurora a handsome roll of pure white duck, or drill—I forget now
which it was—to do what she pleased with. I had
found some remnants of bunting, of different colours,
that she might amuse herself, if she chose, with
Greaves's notion of trimming her dresses; then I had
borrowed a thimble from the forecastle. You will
suppose that it was not a *tight* fit; but she managed
with it. And so she went to work, sewing in the
cabin or in her own berth: and I see her now, with
my mind's eye, as she sits under the skylight, stitching
away like any sempstress earning a living, the jewels
upon her fingers flashing as her hand rises and falls.

One morning she came out of her berth dressed in
a gown of her own manufacture. It was built on

original lines, and it suited her. I believe she had shaped it to enable her to get about with ease, to allow her to step without inconvenience up the companion-ladder and through the hatch, to pass through the cabin betwixt the table and the lockers without being dragged, and sometimes held, by the folds of her skirt, and to freely move in her little bedroom. The dress she had been cast away in had hardly permitted this liberty. It was voluminous enough to have yielded her three clinging skirts; it caught the wind when she was on deck, and blew out like a topsail in a squall when the yard is on the cap. I admired her vastly in this costume of her own making. The cut answered something to my own taste in female apparel: the waist rose high, the sleeves were tight, the dip and swell of her shape were defined. I had always suspected that a nobly-proportioned woman lay awkwardly hid in the dress that had heretofore clothed her, and I guessed I had been right when I looked at her this morning and marked the curve of the breast, the width of the shoulders, the fine, swinging, lofty carriage.

The dress was snow-white; it fell in with the colour of her face. Her cheeks seemed the whiter for the whiteness of her clothes. She had trimmed her dress with triple lines of red bunting; and, for my part, I should never want to see a prettier or more effective gown on a maiden for sea use.

She stood in the door of her berth, looking archly at me. Galloon growled, scarce knowing her for the moment. Greaves was in his berth, for by this time he was ailing badly. She looked down her dress, coloured slightly, then walked up to me and said—

"How you like it? How you like it?" turning herself about a little coquettishly.

Admiration will often make a man laugh; and I laughed to see her in that dress, and laughed to hear her address me in English; and laughed yet again, but always admiringly, at her spirited, courting manner of turning her figure about, that I might get a view of her clothes.

"It is very good indeed," said I.

"*Si*, it is very good," she repeated after me.

She then sought to express herself further, and, failing, signed to let me know that she had now two dresses, and that presently she would have three. I pronounced some word of applause in Spanish, which she obliged me to repeat, that I might catch the correct pronunciation, and we then sat down to breakfast.

I have told you that she wore some very handsome rings, and on this occasion it was that I took particular notice of a remarkable ring which she carried on her left hand. She followed my gaze, and stretched out her hand to my face. I imagined she intended that I should kiss her hand, for I was a fool in the customs of nations, and honestly knew not but that a man's kissing a woman's hand thus held out to him, almost to his lips, as it were, was some Spanish fashion of significant civility which she would expect me to attend to; so I bent my head and put my mouth to her hand.

She coloured, her eyes flashed, she looked confused; then smiled, shook her head, and pointed to the ring. I was young and ingenuous, and the blood rose to my face when I understood that I had blundered; but I held my peace, and looked at the ring. A moment later she pulled it off and put it into my hand. It was a very rich ring, formed of ten precious stones of different sorts and a medallion of the crucifix. I turned it about, admiring it. She watched me earnestly, and then, with a smile and a sigh, said—

"You are not Catolique."

"No," said I.

She motioned to let me know she could tell as much by my ignorance of the use of that ring; and then, taking the thing from me, she went through a pretty and dramatic pantomime, reciting "Aves" whilst she touched the ring, and winding up with a sentence out of the "Paternoster." She put on the ring after she had made an end of her pretty pantomime, and, looking again at me earnestly, repeated, with the same dramatic sigh—

"You are not Catolique."

" No," said I.

" You will be Catolique ? " she exclaimed, in very fairly pronounced English, still wearing a wistful and impassioned expression.

I slowly shook my head. She sighed again, and looked very downcast ; but I was wanted on deck, and could sit at table no longer ; so I left her.

CHAPTER XXIII

THE WHALER.

ALL this while the crew went on quietly with the work of the ship, giving me no trouble, nor occasioning me further anxiety than such as arose from my fear of how it might prove with us should the captain die. This will I say of Bol: a better boatswain never trod the decks of a vessel. I carried by nature a critical eye, and whilst Greaves lay ill my vigilance was redoubled; but not once had I cause to find fault with Yan Bol's part in the duties of the brig.

We wanted, indeed, the freshening of the paint-pot, but in all other respects we were as smart a little ship, as we blew towards the Horn, as though we had quitted the Thames but a week before. Our brass guns sparkled, our decks were yacht-like with holystoning, our rigging might have been newly set up by riggers of the king. Every detail of the furniture aloft was carefully seen to, from the eyes of the royal rigging to the laniards of the channel dead-eyes.

The men feared Bol; his vast bulk of beef, and the

granite lumps which swelled in muscle to the movement of his arms, made him the match for any two of
them. The delivery of his lungs was the cannon's
roar. I have seen a stout fellow stagger as though to
a blow, sway in the recoil of a man who is hit hard, on
Yan Bol thrusting his huge mouth into the fellow's
face and exploding in passion an order betwixt his
eyes. But though the crew feared him, they also liked
him; he acted as second mate, indeed, but throughout with reluctance; was their shipmate and forecastle
associate first of all, the man who ate out of their kids
and drank out of their scuttle butt, who slung his
hammock in their bedroom, showed them what to do
and often how to do it, occasionally went aloft with
them, yarned and smoked with them. So much for
Yan Bol.

Greaves had a just and considerable admiration for him, the fullest confidence in him as a
sailor, and counted him the best boatswain he had
ever heard of; and I agreed with him—going, however, rather farther, for I had distrusted the man from
the beginning, and my distrust of him was now deeper
than ever it had been, and I would have given half
my share of the money in the lazarette had we been
blown away from the island when he was ashore and
forced to proceed without him.

The two Spaniards were bad sailors, lazy and reck-
less. Bol could do nothing with them. They skulked

when there was business to be done aloft, were not to
be trusted at the wheel, and it came at last to our
putting them to help the cook and do the dirty work
of the ship when they were not at sail-making—for, to
be sure, they were smart hands with their palms and
needles. There were no more fights, no more assertions by Antonio and his mate Jorge of their claims to
a share. In talking to me one day about them Bol
said it was the wish of the crew to turn them out of
the brig at the first chance.

" The captain won't hear of it," said I.

The Dutchman asked why.

" Because," said I, " the Spaniards know that there
is treasure on board. They also know it is Spanish
treasure, and how got by us. Suppose you tranship
them : they arrive at a port, and state what they know.
The news that we have salved the treasure reaches the
ears of the owner of it, who thereupon makes application for restitution. Our business is to keep clear of
difficulties."

" Yaw, dot do I see. But hark you, Mr. Fielding,
ve keep der Spaniards und ve arrive home, und der
Spaniards go ashore, und den? I ox, und den? Vill
dey not shpeak all der same as dey vould shpoke in
von of der own ports down here?"

" I have considered that; so, too, has Captain
Greaves. There is a remedy, but it does not lie in
transferring them in these seas."

He shrugged his shoulders, and the subject dropped.

But the long and short of Greaves's policy in this particular matter was: get the money home in safety first, bring off the treasure clear of the fifty sea risks and perils of the age—the gale, the shoal, the leak, the pirate, the enemy's ships of the State. It will be time enough to trouble yourself with what the Spaniards and others of the crew may whisper ashore when the money has been landed, divided, exchanged into gold of the realm, with plenty of leisure for a disappearance that might run into time should the news of the salving of the treasure of the *Casada* ever reach the ears of the owners of the silver.

We carried good strong winds to the southward. The days grew shorter; there was an edge in the weather, let the breeze blow whence it would; the swell of the sea was long and dark. We bent strong canvas for rounding the Horn, and in other ways prepared for a conflict which in those days had a significance that has departed from that wrestle. The seamen put on warm clothes; there was never a need now for the small awning aft; the sun shone white, as though the dazzle of his disc was the reflection of his beam on snow. I say his light was white, and often cold, when we had yet to swim many hundreds of miles to fetch the parallel of the Horn.

In all the weeks we occupied in measuring our way from the island ere rounding the headland for the

Atlantic we fell in with but one ship. It was our good
luck, and there was nothing surprising in it either.
In this present year of my writing my story it may be
your chance to sail over a thousand leagues of Pacific
water and meet with nothing. It was a lonelier ocean
in my time than it is now. Northward, on the equatorial parallel, there was, indeed, some life; but southward the great liquid highway that now every year
foams to the shearing stems of half a thousand stately
ships, was, in the year of the *Black Watch*, scarce less
barren as a breast of sea than when it was swept for
the galleon by the perspective glasses of Dampier and
Woodes Rogers.

We fell in with a little ship and spoke her, and the
speaking her proved one of the most memorable of all
the incidents in this strange expedition, as you shall
presently learn if you choose to proceed.

Greaves was on this day very weak; he had risen
to breakfast, sat like the spectre of death at table, his
sunken, leaden, black eyes wandering from me to Miss
Aurora with the seeking gaze of one who strives to
collect his wits; then, rising with a little convulsion
of his figure, he leaned with his hand upon the table and
said, in a small voice, looking downwards and slightly
smiling—

" I must return to my bunk. It isn't the machinery
that's wrong; the spring has slackened, and wants
setting up afresh."

I took him by the arm, helped him to his cabin, and stood looking on, waiting to be of service, whilst Jimmy pulled off his coat and shoes. I believed he would speak seriously of his illness, for I guessed that if he felt as bad as he looked he would count himself a dying man. But he had not one word to say about his sensations or condition. When he was in bed, I stood beside him; he lay with his eyes wide open, viewing me steadfastly in silence. Presently he said—

"Why do you stand there? It is all right with me. Get back to your breakfast and finish it, Fielding. Whose look-out is it?"

"Mine, sir."

"Why do you stand there?"

"I wish to see if I can be of use to you," said I, making a step towards the door.

"I am truly obliged. Jimmy does all I need. I want you to think of nothing but the brig. I shall be quite well—I feel it, I am sure of it—before we have climbed far up the Atlantic. By Isten, Fielding, but it warms me to the very heart of my soul to reflect that you are in charge—you and not Van Laar. Van Laar it might have been, with Michael Greaves helpless in his cabin, and the Horn coming aboard. Lord, Lord, wonderful are Thy ways!" said he, turning up his eyes. "Now get ye to your breakfast. The machinery is all right, I tell you; the spring's fallen slack, the old clock loses, but the tick's steady, Fielding—the tick's steady, my lad, and a few days will make the time right with me; so get you to your breakfast."

I re-entered the cabin and seated myself.

"The captain is bad," said the Lady Aurora.

I answered with a sorrowful nod. She clasped her hands, looked at me across the table anxiously, and said—

"He die."

"*Que hacer ?*" ("What is to be done ?") I answered, for by this time I had picked up a number of phrases from her.

She slightly shrugged her shoulders and shook her head, and, pointing upwards, exclaimed in Spanish—

"It is as God wills."

Then, again fixing her fine eyes, full of fire and feeling, upon me, she, by nods and gestures, contrived to make me understand this question—

"Suppose the captain dies, how is the brig to get to England ?"

I smiled and pointed to myself, and made her gather that, whilst I was on board, the brig was pretty sure, in some fashion or other, to head on a true course for England.

We continued to exchange our meaning in this fashion whilst I finished breakfast. Conversation

p

between us was scarcely now the hard labour it formerly was. She had a number of words in my tongue and I some in hers; then, by being much together—or, as I would rather put it, having by this time held many conversations in our fashion of discoursing—we had got to distinguish shades of signification which had been wasted before in one another's gaze and gestures. Her looks were eloquence itself. Even now was I able to collect her mind when she talked to me with her face only; when she would talk to me, I say, for five minutes at a time, merely with the expressions of her face, never opening her lips. Her eyes were charged with the language of light and passions. She could look grief, dismay, concern, horror, pity—all other emotions, indeed—with an incomparable skill, force, and beauty of mute delivery.

I went on deck, and stepped to the side, as was my custom, to peer ahead. Bol, who stood near the skylight, called out—

"A sail!"

He pointed over the starboard bow, and, looking that way, I spied the delicate white gleam of a ship's canvas. It was what we should call a fine, hard day, the atmosphere strong and tonical, cold, but without harshness or rawness. The breeze was fresh off the larboard beam, and swept with a rushing noise betwixt our masts—the breath of the young giant whose dam was the snow-darkened Antarctic hurricane. The

surge was a long, steady sweep of sea, tall and wide,
of the deepest blue I had ever beheld. The brig, with
her yards braced well forward, the bowlines triced out,
and every cloth that would draw pulling white as
milk in the white sunshine from stay and yard and
gaff and boom, was sweeping through the water with
the speed of smoke down the wind. Magnificently
buoyant was the vessel's motion. The yeast of her
wake seethed to her counter as she curtseyed. Large
birds were flying over the track of snow astern.

"What is that craft going to prove, Bol?" said I,
taking up the glass.

"Dot vhas not long to findt out," he answered.

In those times our telescopes were not as yours
are now. I levelled the long and heavy tube, but it
resolved me no more of the ship ahead than this—
that a ship she was.

"Shall ve shift our hellum und edge avay?" said
Bol.

"I will let you know," said I, walking aft.

I waited a bit, looked at the sail again, and found
we were picking her up as though she were at anchor.
By this time also, most of her fabric having lifted
above the sea-line, I was able to tell that she was
square-rigged, like ourselves, but that, unlike the
Black Watch, she had short topgallant - masts;
whence, as you will suppose, I set her down at once
as a trader. This and our overhauling her so rapidly

p 2

—which means, suppose her an enemy, then she had no more chance of getting alongside of us than a land-crab a scudding rabbit—determined me to hold on as we were.

You see, I was in charge of the brig, and could do as I chose. Yet was it right that I should report the sail to Greaves, and I called to Yan Bol, who stood in the waist, and bade him keep a look-out for a few minutes whilst I went below. Jimmy came out of the captain's berth as I entered the cabin. The lad held open the door, and I passed in.

"I have come to report a sail right ahead, sir."

He turned his eyes upon me with such a look as you may behold in the gaze of an old man straining after memory.

"A sail?" he exclaimed.

"Yes, sir."

"Ay, ay."

He smiled strangely, fetched a long, trembling breath, and said—

"Suppose she should prove a galleon? We are rich enough, Fielding. Leave her alone—leave her alone."

"She is no galleon. She is a small trader, I reckon, and will be abreast of us and astern whilst we're talking about her."

"We have as much as we need," said he. "Don't imperil what you've got, man. D'ye know, Fielding, I

fear my sight's beginning to fail me. Jimmy gave me
the Bible just now. The type's big, and it came and
went in a dissolving way like a wriggle of worms in
water. I would to God there was a priest aboard. I
want to ask some questions."

He closed his eyes, and with them closed repeated,
" I want to ask some questions."

I waited, supposing he would look at me. He
kept his eyes shut; so, bidding Jimmy, who stood in
the door, to have a care of his master, and to keep
within reach of his hail, I returned to the deck, very
heavy in my spirits; for the departure of this man
did then seem to me a question of hours instead of
days, nay weeks, as I had lately thought, so ill did he
look, so darkly and miserably did his manner and
speech accentuate the menace of his face.

It was not very long before I made out the vessel
ahead to be a whaler. I knew *that* by her heavy davits,
crowd of boats, and square, sawed-off look when she
cocked her stern at us. I showed Dutch colours,
scarce doubting as yet but that the stranger would
prove a Yankee, for in those days, as now, many
American vessels fished in those waters, pursuing their
gigantic game into seas where the British flag was
rarely flown—that is, over anything in search of
grease. But the Dutch flag had not been blowing three
minutes from our gaff-end when up floated the red flag
of England to the mizzenmast head of the stranger.

She was a little ship: to describe her exactly, she
was ship-rigged on the fore and main, whilst on her
schooner-mizzenmast she carried a cross-jack and
topsail-yard. She lifted, ragged with weeds, to the
heads of the seas, and washed along, heavily rolling
and pitching, and blowing white water off her bows,
whale-like. I shifted the helm to close her, for the
sake of the sight of a strange face, for the sound of a
strange human voice. She was abreast of us some
time before noon, and there lay before us, foaming and
plunging, as quaint a picture as the ocean at that time
had to offer, liberally furnished as her breast was with
romantic structures. She was as broad as she was
long, of a greasy rusty black, and when the sea
knocked her over she threw up her round of bottom
till you watched for the keel; and the long grass
streamed away from her as she rolled like hair from
the head of a plunging mermaid. Many faces sur-
veyed us from over her rail. Her sails fitted her ill,
and were dark with use. After every roll and plunge
the water poured like a mountain torrent out of her
head-boards and channels; but I had read her name
as we approached—her name and the name of the
town she hailed from. She was the *Virginia Creeper*,
of Whitby.

Whitby! I had never visited that town; but I
knew it in fancy, through the famous Cook's association with the place, almost as well as I knew in reality

the little towns of Deal and Sandwich. It was just one of those magical English words to sweep the mind and the imaginations of the mind clean out of the countless leagues of the Pacific into the narrow miles of one's own home waters, there to behold again with a dreamer's gaze the milk-white coasts of the south, the chocolate coasts of the north, the red sail of the smack plunging to the North Sea, the brown sail of the barge creeping close inshore, the projection of black and tarry timber pier, with its cluster of bright-hued wherries, the length of sparkling white sand, the shingly incline, the careened boat, the figure of its owner at work upon it with a tar-brush.

We foamed along together, broadside to broadside, within musket-shot, and I hailed the whaler and was answered.

The man who responded stood in the mizzen rigging. He wore a round glazed hat, a shawl about his throat, a monkey-coat to his knees. He sang out to know what ship I was, and I answered that we were the *Black Watch*, of London, chartered by a merchant of Amsterdam, and that the captain and mate and most of the crew were Englishmen. We were bound to London, I roared to him, omitting to answer his question where we were from. Then, in answer, he shouted that he was the *Virginia Creeper*, of and from Whitby, ten months out, had met with shocking bad luck, and was bound out of these seas for

the South Atlantic. All the whales had gone east.
Sorry we were in such a hurry. He would have been
glad to come aboard for a yarn, and for what news
from home we had to give him. Were we still fight-
ing the Yankees? A Yankee privateer had spoke him
in the South Atlantic, and the captain of the vessel
sent a mate aboard him with a box of cigars, and this
message—that the whaler was a ship he never meddled
with, no matter under what colour he found her; that
he honoured a calling that had given his own nation
her finest race of seamen; and when he sailed away
he dipped to the *Virginia Creeper* as to a friend. All
this I was able to hear. The man, who spoke as a
Quaker, delivered his words with a strong, slightly
nasal voice, and his words came clear as the sound of
a bell through the washing hiss of the water and the
roar aloft.

I found time to shout back that our captain was
dangerously ill, and to ask the master of the whaler,
as I supposed the man to be, if he knew aught of
physic—of the treatment of injuries. He shook his
head vehemently, crying "No!" thrice, as though he
would instantly kill any hope the sight of him had
excited in *that* way; and, indeed, what should a sailor
know of physic and the treatment of such a sickness
as was fast killing Greaves? I asked the question
to ease my conscience and to satisfy the crew, who
were listening. I figured him coming aboard and

stifling a groan when he saw Greaves, vexing the poor, languishing man with useless questions, put to mark his sympathy, and then coming out of the berth to tell me it was a bad case.

We sped onwards. The voice would no longer carry, and the whaler veered astern almost into our wake, with a wild slap of her foresail, as she plunged a heavy curtsey of farewell at us.

My notes of what befell me in this memorable year of Waterloo gives much to my memory, but not everything; and I am unable to recollect the exact situation of the brig when we fell in with the *Virginia Creeper* westwards of the Horn. I am sure, however, that we were something to the southward of the island of John Fernandez, somewhere about the latitude of Valdivia. This I suppose from remembrance of the climate. But be it as it may, it was now, on this date of our speaking the Whitby whaler, that I confidently supposed my poor friend Greaves would not live to see the end of the week. I have told you so; but guess my surprise when, on coming on deck at four o'clock that same afternoon, I found him seated on a chair, wrapped in a warm cloak. Yan Bol walked to and fro near him. They had been talking. I had heard the Dutchman's deep voice as I stepped through the hatch. But if Greaves had looked a dying man in his berth, he showed, to be sure, ghastly sick by the light of the day. I had

seen much of him below, yet I started when my eyes
went to his face now, as though, down to this moment,
I had not observed the dreadful change that had
happened in him.   Galloon lay at his feet.   The
poor man smiled faintly on seeing me, and said in a
weak voice—

"Did not I tell you I should be better presently?
The machinery's sound; and when that's so, Nature
is your one artist to make it the right time of day
with ye."

I conversed a little with him.   Yan Bol stood by.
I told him about the whaler.   He motioned with a
trembling white hand, and said he had heard all
about it from Yan Bol.   Presently he wandered somewhat in his speech, and rose falteringly, sending a
sort of blind, groping look round the decks; but he
was too feeble to hold his body erect, and the swing
of the brig, as she reeled to a sea, flung him roughly
back upon his chair.

"Let me take you below," said I.

He looked at me as though he did not know me,
and talked to himself.   I motioned to Bol with my
head, and we each took an arm, and tenderly—and I
say that there was a tenderness in Yan Bol's handling
of the poor fellow that gave me such an opinion of
his heart as helped me for a little while like a fresh
spirit in that time of my distress, anxiety, and fear
—very tenderly, I say, we partly carried, partly

supported, the captain into the cabin, whence he
went, leaning on Jimmy, to his berth, looking behind him somewhat wildly at us who stood watching him, and talking without any sense that I could
collect.

"Mr. Fielding," said Yan Bol as we regained the
deck, "der captain vhas a deadt man."

"I wondered to find him out of his berth."

"He vhas von minute talking like ash you or me,
und der next he vhas grazy mit fancies. I likes to
know how dot vhas mit der brain. Von minute he
oxes me questions about der vhaler, as you might; der
next he looks at me und say, 'Vhas your name Yan
Bol?' 'It vhas,' I answered. 'Vhat vhas der natural
figure of der Toyfell?' he oxes. 'Dot vhas a question
for der minister,' says I. 'Last night,' he says, 'dere
vhas a full moon, und I saw a reflection like she
might be a bat's upon der brightness of der moon.
Dot reflection sailed slowly across. I ox you,' says
he, 'vhas dot der reflection of der Toyfell—dot, you
must know, is Brince of der vinds?' I keeps mine
own counsel, und valks a leedle, und pretends dot der
brig vants looking after; und vhen I comes back he
oxes me anoder question dot vhas no longer grazy,
but like ash you might ox. Now, how vhas dot,
Mr. Fielding?"

"I am as ignorant as you," said I; "but his end
is at hand. He will not long talk, sensibly or crazily.

God help him, and bless us all! It is a heavy blow to
befall this little brig—'tis a heavier blow to befall the
poor gentleman who has shown us how to fill our
pockets with dollars, whose own share would make
him a happy and prosperous man for life."

"Dot vhas so," said Bol ; and our conversation
ended.

Seeing that Greaves's mind was loosened, I no
longer expected him to realise the near approach of
death. I ceased, therefore, to be surprised that he
did not speak to me about his condition. Sometimes
I would ask myself whether it was not my duty, as
his friend, to touch upon the subject of his state at
some favourable moment when his faculties were
strong enough for coherent discourse. He was dying.
He must soon die. He could not live to round the
Horn. How would he wish the money he had earned
by this venture to be disposed of ? Thirty thousand
pounds was a large fortune. I knew that he was
fatherless and motherless, but no more of him did I
know than that. I had never heard him speak of his
relations; indeed, throughout he had been silent on
the subject of his parentage and beginnings, though
he had never wanted in candour when he talked of
his first going to sea, his struggles and failures and
sufferings in the vocation.

But as often as I thought it proper to speak to
him, so often did I shrink from what was, perhaps, an

obligation. No; I could not find it in me to tell him that he was a dying man.

The weather grew colder, and we met with some hard gales out of the south-east, which knocked us away fifty leagues to the westward out of our course. It was Cape Horn weather, though we were not up with that headland yet. The dark-green seas rolled fierce and high; the sky hung low and sallow, and fled in scud. We stormed our way along under reefed canvas, showing all that we durst, and making good average way, seeing that the gale was off the bow and the seas like cliffs for the little brig to burst through.

Anxiety lay very heavy upon me all this time. I had confidence in Yan Bol's seamanship, but I had more faith in myself; and I was up and down in my watch below to look after the brig, till, when the twenty-four hours had come round, I would find I had not passed two of them in sleep.

The cold found the Lady Aurora without warm apparel. The dress she had been shipwrecked in was of some gay, glossy stuff, plentiful in skirt, and as warm as a cobweb. What was to be done? It was not to be borne that she should sit shivering in the cabin for the want of apparel that would enable her to look abroad whenever she had a mind to pass through the hatch; so, after turning the matter over in my mind, one morning, soon after our meeting

with the whaler, I ordered Jimmy and another to
bring the slop-chest into the cabin. It was a great
box, and one of two. Both were of Tulp's providing.
The old chap guessed he saw his way to making
money out of the sailors by putting cheap clothes
aboard for sale, and it was likely enough he would
find his little venture in this way answerable to his
expectations when we got home, for already one of
the chests was emptied of two-thirds of its contents,
the sailors (I being one of them) having purchased
at an advance of about eighty per cent. upon what
would be rated ashore as a very high selling price.

Well, one of the slop-chests was brought up and
put in the cabin. I had tried to make Miss Aurora
understand what I meant—to no purpose. Now,
lifting the lid of the chest, she standing by me and
looking down upon the queer collection of sailors'
clothing, I pulled out a monkey-coat, big enough for
the sheathing of even Yan Bol's bolster-like figure,
and, holding it up, went to work to make myself
intelligible. I put the coat on her. I then touched
it here and there to signify that, by shaping a waist
and cutting in at the dip of the back, by shortening the
sleeves and fixing the velvet collar to suit her throat,
she might make a very good figure of a jacket for
herself out of the coat. I then took a cap from the
chest, and I placed it upon her head, advising, as best
I could by signs and words, that she should stitch

flaps to it to shelter her ears, with strings to keep the
thing on her head in wind. I went further still, being
resolved that the lady should go warmly clad round
the Horn, and, calling to Jimmy, bade him bring me
up a bale of spare blankets. I heartily longed for a
Spanish dictionary, that I might give her the word
petticoat out of it. However, she caught my drift
after a little, on my selecting one of the finest of the
blankets and putting it about her and holding it to
her waist. She nodded and laughed.

I witnessed no embarrassment, and, in honest
truth, there was no cause for embarrassment. Yet I
do not suppose that an English girl—at least, that
many English girls —would have made this little
business of suggesting apparel, and hinting at clothing
which a man is not supposed to know anything at all
about until he is married, so pleasant and easy as did
this Spanish maiden.

Well, her ladyship was now supplied with materials
for warm clothing, and that same afternoon she went
to work on the coat. Hard work it was. She wanted
shears for such cloth as that, and managed with difficulty with a sailor's knife fresh from the grindstone ;
yet by next afternoon, having worked all that day
and all next morning, she had given something of the
shape of her own figure to the coat. She put it on
for me to look at. It wrapped her bravely ; and
when, with white teeth showing, she placed the cap

on her head, her beauty—and beauty, dark speaking, impressive, I must call it—took a quality of brightness, a piquancy that comes to beauty from male attire; in her case wanting when ordinarily dressed, of such gravity and dignity was her bearing, of such a natural, womanly loftiness were the whole figure and looks of her.

END OF VOL. II.

Printed by CASSELL & COMPANY, LIMITED, La Belle Sauvage, London, E.C.

Illustrated, Fine-Art, and other Volumes.

Abbeys and Churches of England and Wales, The: Descriptive, Historical, Pictorial. Series II. 21s.

A Blot of Ink. Translated from the French by Q and PAUL FRANCKE. 5s.

Adventure, The World of. Fully Illustrated. In Three Vols. 9s. each.

Africa and its Explorers, The Story of. By DR. ROBERT BROWN, F.L.S. Illustrated. Vol. I., 7s. 6d.

Agrarian Tenures. By the Rt. Hon. G. SHAW-LEFEVRE, M.P. 10s. 6d.

Anthea. By CÉCILE CASSAVETTI (a Russian). A Sensational Story, based on authentic facts of the time of the Greek War of Independence. 10s. 6d.

Arabian Nights Entertainments, Cassell's Pictorial. 10s. 6d.

Architectural Drawing. By R. PHENÉ SPIERS. Illustrated. 10s. 6d.

Art, The Magazine of. Yearly Vol. With 12 Photogravures, Etchings, &c., and about 400 Illustrations. 16s.

Artistic Anatomy. By Prof. M. DUVAL. *Cheap Edition.* 3s. 6d.

Atlas, The Universal. A New and Complete General Atlas of the World, with 117 Pages of Maps, handsomely produced in Colours, and a Complete Index to about 125,000 Names. Cloth, 30s. net ; or half-morocco, 35s. net.

Bashkirtseff, Marie, The Journal of. *Cheap Edition.* 7s. 6d.

Bashkirtseff, Marie, The Letters of. 7s. 6d.

Beetles, Butterflies, Moths, and Other Insects. By A. W. KAPPEL, F.L.S., F.E.S., and W. EGMONT KIRBY. With 12 Coloured Plates. 3s. 6d.

Biographical Dictionary, Cassell's New. 7s. 6d.

Birds' Nests, Eggs, and Egg-Collecting. By R. KEARTON. Illustrated with 16 Coloured Plates. 5s.

Blue Pavilions, The. By Q, Author of "Dead Man's Rock," &c. 6s.

Bob Lovell's Career. A Story of American Railway Life. By EDWARD S. ELLIS. 5s.

Breechloader, The, and How to Use It. By W. W. GREENER. 2s.

British Ballads. With 275 Original Illustrations. In Two Vols. 15s.

British Battles on Land and Sea. By JAMES GRANT. With about 600 Illustrations. Three Vols., 4to, £1 7s.; *Library Edition,* £1 10s.

British Battles, Recent. Illustrated. 4to, 9s.; *Library Edition,* 10s.

Butterflies and Moths, European. With 61 Coloured Plates. 35s.

Canaries and Cage-Birds, The Illustrated Book of. With 56 Fac-simile Coloured Plates, 35s. Half-morocco, £2 5s.

Carnation Manual, The. Edited and Issued by the National Carnation and Picotee Society (Southern Section). 3s. 6d.

Cassell's Family Magazine. Yearly Vol. Illustrated. 9s.

Cathedrals, Abbeys, and Churches of England and Wales. Descriptive, Historical, Pictorial. *Popular Edition.* Two Vols. 25s.

Celebrities of the Century. *Cheap Edition.* 10s. 6d.

Cities of the World. Four Vols. Illustrated. 7s. 6d. each.

Civil Service, Guide to Employment in the. 3s. 6d.

Climate and Health Resorts. By Dr BURNEY YEO. 7s. 6d.

Clinical Manuals for Practitioners and Students of Medicine. A List of Volumes forwarded post free on application to the Publishers.

Colonist's Medical Handbook, The. By E. A. BARTON, M.R.C.S. 2s. 6d.

Colour. By Prof. A. H. CHURCH. With Coloured Plates. 3s. 6d.

Columbus, The Career of. By CHARLES ELTON, Q.C. 10s. 6d.

Commercial Botany of the Nineteenth Century. 3s. 6d.

Cookery, A Year's. By PHYLLIS BROWNE. 3s. 6d.

Cookery, Cassell's Shilling. 384 pages, limp cloth, 1s.

Cookery, Vegetarian. By A. G. PAYNE. 1s. 6d.

Cooking by Gas, The Art of. By MARIE J. SUGG. Illustrated. 3s. 6d.

Cottage Gardening, Poultry, Bees, Allotments, Food, House, Window and Town Gardens. Edited by W. ROBINSON, F.L.S., Author of "The English Flower Garden." Fully Illustrated. First Half-yearly Volume. Cloth, 2s. 6d.

Countries of the World, The. By ROBERT BROWN, M.A., Ph.D., &c. Complete in Six Vols., with about 750 Illustrations. 4to, 7s. 6d. each.

Cyclopædia, Cassell's Concise. Brought down to the latest date. With about 600 Illustrations. *Cheap Edition.* 7s. 6d.

Cyclopædia, Cassell's Miniature. Containing 30,000 subjects. Cloth, 2s. 6d. ; half-roxburgh, 4s.

Daughter of the South, A ; and Shorter Stories. By Mrs. BURTON HARRISON. 4s.

Dickens, Character Sketches from. FIRST, SECOND, and THIRD SERIES. With Six Original Drawings in each by F. BARNARD. 21s. each.

Dick Whittington, A Modern. By JAMES PAYN. In One Vol., 6s.

Dog, Illustrated Book of the. By VERO SHAW, B.A. With 28 Coloured Plates. Cloth bevelled, 35s. ; half-morocco, 45s.

Domestic Dictionary, The. Illustrated. Cloth, 7s. 6d.

Doré Bible, The. With 200 Full-page Illustrations by DORÉ. 15s.

Doré Gallery, The. With 250 Illustrations by DORÉ. 4to, 42s.

Doré's Dante's Inferno. Illustrated by GUSTAVE DORÉ. With Introduction by A. J. BUTLER. Cloth gilt or buckram, 7s. 6d.

Doré's Milton's Paradise Lost. Illustrated by DORÉ. 4to, 21s.

Dr. Dumány's Wife. A Novel. By MAURUS JÓKAI. 6s.

Dulce Domum. Rhymes and Songs for Children. Edited by JOHN FARMER, Author of "Gaudeamus," &c. Old Notation and Words. 5s. N.B.—The words of the Songs in "Dulce Domum" (with the Airs both in Tonic Sol-fa and Old Notation) can be had in Two Parts, 6d. each.

Earth, Our, and its Story. By Dr. ROBERT BROWN, F.L.S. With Coloured Plates and numerous Wood Engravings. Three Vols. 9s. each.

Edinburgh, Old and New. With 600 Illustrations. Three Vols. 9s. each.

Egypt : Descriptive, Historical, and Picturesque. By Prof. G. EBERS. With 800 Original Engravings. *Popular Edition.* In Two Vols. 42s.

Electricity in the Service of Man. Illustrated. 9s.

Electricity, Practical. By Prof. W. E. AYRTON. 7s. 6d.

Encyclopædic Dictionary, The. In Fourteen Divisional Vols., 10s. 6d. each ; or Seven Vols., half-morocco, 21s. each ; half-russia, 25s.

England, Cassell's Illustrated History of. With 2,000 Illustrations. Ten Vols., 4to, 9s. each. *Revised Edition.* Vols. I. to VI 9s. each.

English Dictionary, Cassell's. Giving definitions of more than 100,000 Words and Phrases. Cloth, 7s. 6d. *Cheap Edition.* 3s. 6d.

English History, The Dictionary of. *Cheap Edition.* 10s. 6d.

English Literature, Dictionary of. By W. DAVENPORT ADAMS. *Cheap Edition,* 7s. 6d. ; Roxburgh, 10s. 6d.

English Literature, Library of. By Prof. HENRY MORLEY. Complete in Five Vols., 7s. 6d. each.

English Literature, Morley's First Sketch of. *Revised Edition.* 7s. 6d.
English Literature, The Story of. By ANNA BUCKLAND. 3s. 6d.
English Writers. By Prof. HENRY MORLEY. Vols. I. to IX. 5s. each.
Æsop's Fables. Illustrated by ERNEST GRISET. Cloth, 3s. 6d.
Etiquette of Good Society. 1s. ; cloth, 1s. 6d.
Europe, Cassell's Pocket Guide to. Edition for 1893. Leather, 6s.
Fairway Island. By HORACE HUTCHINSON. With 4 Full-page Plates. 5s.
Faith Doctor, The. A Novel. By Dr. EDWARD EGGLESTON. 6s.
Family Physician, The. By Eminent PHYSICIANS and SURGEONS.
    New and Revised Edition. Cloth, 21s. ; Roxburgh, 25s.
Father Stafford. A Novel. By ANTHONY HOPE. 6s.
Field Naturalist's Handbook, The. By the Revs. J. G. WOOD and
    THEODORE WOOD. *Cheap Edition.* 2s. 6d.
Figuier's Popular Scientific Works. With Several Hundred Illustra-
    tions in each. Newly Revised and Corrected. 3s. 6d. each.
    THE HUMAN RACE. | MAMMALIA. | OCEAN WORLD.
        THE INSECT WORLD.   REPTILES AND BIRDS.
    WORLD BEFORE THE DELUGE. THE VEGETABLE WORLD.
Flora's Feast. A Masque of Flowers. Penned and Pictured by WALTER
    CRANE. With 40 Pages in Colours. 5s.
Football, The Rugby Union Game. Edited by REV. F. MARSHALL.
    Illustrated. 7s. 6d.
Fraser, John Drummond. By PHILALETHES. A Story of Jesuit
    Intrigue in the Church of England. 5s.
Garden Flowers, Familiar. By SHIRLEY HIBBERD. With Coloured
    Plates by F. E. HULME, F.L.S. Complete in Five Series. 12s. 6d. each.
Gardening, Cassell's Popular. Illustrated. Four Vols. 5s. each.
George Saxon, The Reputation of. By MORLEY ROBERTS. 5s.
Gilbert, Elizabeth, and her Work for the Blind. By FRANCES
    MARTIN. 2s. 6d.
Gleanings from Popular Authors. Two Vols. With Original Illus-
    trations. 4to, 9s. each. Two Vols. in One, 15s.
Gulliver's Travels. With 88 Engravings by MORTEN. *Cheap Edition.*
    Cloth, 3s. 6d. ; cloth gilt, 5s.
Gun and its Development, The. By W. W. GREENER. With 500
    Illustrations. 10s. 6d.
Health at School. By CLEMENT DUKES, M.D., B.S. 7s. 6d.
Heavens, The Story of the. By Sir ROBERT STAWELL BALL, LL.D.,
    F.R.S., F.R.A.S. With Coloured Plates. *Popular Edition.* 12s. 6d.
Heroes of Britain in Peace and War. With 300 Original Illus-
    trations. *Cheap Edition.* Two Vols., 3s. 6d. each ; or Two Vols. in
    One, cloth gilt, 7s. 6d.
Hiram Golf's Religion ; or, the "Shoemaker by the Grace of
    God." 2s.
History, A Foot-note to. Eight Years of Trouble in Samoa. By
    ROBERT LOUIS STEVENSON. 6s.
Historic Houses of the United Kingdom. Profusely Illustrated. 10s. 6d.
Hors de Combat ; or, Three Weeks in a Hospital. Founded on
    Facts. By GERTRUDE & ETHEL ARMITAGE SOUTHAM. Illustrated. 5s.
Horse, The Book of the. By SAMUEL SIDNEY. With 28 Fac-simile
    Coloured Plates. *Enlarged Edition.* Demy 4to, 35s. ; half-morocco, 45s.
Houghton, Lord : The Life, Letters, and Friendships of Richard
    Monckton Milnes, First Lord Houghton. By T. WEMYSS
    REID. In Two Vols., with Two Portraits. 32s.
Household, Cassell's Book of the. Complete in Four Vols. 5s. each.
    Four Vols. in Two, half-morocco, 25s.
Hygiene and Public Health. By B. ARTHUR WHITELEGGE, M.D. 7s. 6d.

India, Cassell's History of. By JAMES GRANT. With about 400 Illustrations. Two Vols., 9s. each. One Vol., 15s.

In-door Amusements, Card Games, and Fireside Fun, Cassell's Book of. *Cheap Edition.* 2s.

Into the Unknown: A Romance of South Africa. By LAWRENCE FLETCHER. 4s.

"I Saw Three Ships," and other Winter's Tales. By Q, Author of "Dead Man's Rock," &c. 6s.

Island Nights' Entertainments. By R. L. STEVENSON. Illustrated, 6s.

Italy from the Fall of Napoleon I. in 1815 to 1890. By J. W. PROBYN. *New and Cheaper Edition.* 3s. 6d.

Joy and Health. By MARTELLIUS. 3s. 6d. *Édition de Luxe,* 7s. 6d.

Kennel Guide, The Practical. By Dr. GORDON STABLES. 1s.

Khiva, A Ride to. By Col. FRED. BURNABY. 1s. 6d.

"La Bella," and Others. Being Certain Stories Recollected by Egerton Castle, Author of "Consequences." 6s.

Ladies' Physician, The. By a London Physician. 6s.

Lady's Dressing-room, The. Translated from the French of BARONESS STAFFE by LADY COLIN CAMPBELL. 3s. 6d.

Leona. By Mrs. MOLESWORTH. 6s.

Letts's Diaries and other Time-saving Publications published exclusively by CASSELL & COMPANY. (*A list free on application.*)

Little Minister, The. By J. M. BARRIE. One Vol. 6s.

Locomotive Engine, The Biography of a. By HENRY FRITH. 5s.

Loftus, Lord Augustus, The Diplomatic Reminiscences of, 1837-1862. With Portrait. Two Vols., 32s.

London, Greater. By EDWARD WALFORD. Two Vols. With about 400 Illustrations. 9s. each.

London, Old and New. Six Vols., each containing about 200 Illustrations and Maps. Cloth, 9s. each.

London Street Arabs. By Mrs. H. M. STANLEY. Illustrated, 5s.

Mathew, Father, His Life and Times. By F. J. MATHEW. 2s. 6d.

Medicine Lady, The. By L. T. MEADE. In One Vol., 6s.

Medicine, Manuals for Students of. (*A List forwarded post free.*)

Modern Europe, A History of. By C. A. FYFFE, M.A. Complete in Three Vols., with full-page Illustrations, 7s. 6d. each.

Mount Desolation. An Australian Romance. By W. CARLTON DAWE. 5s.

Music, Illustrated History of. By EMIL NAUMANN. Edited by the Rev. Sir F. A. GORE OUSELEY, Bart. Illustrated. Two Vols. 31s. 6d.

Musical and Dramatic Copyright, The Law of. By EDWARD CUTLER, THOMAS EUSTACE SMITH, and FREDERIC E. WEATHERLY, Barristers-at-Law. 3s. 6d.

Napier, Life and Letters of the Rt. Hon. Sir Joseph, Bart., LL.D., &c. By A. C. EWALD, F.S.A. *New and Revised Edition.* 7s. 6d.

National Library, Cassell's. In Volumes. Paper covers, 3d.; cloth, 6d. (*A Complete List of the Volumes post free on application.*)

Natural History, Cassell's Concise. By E. PERCEVAL WRIGHT, M.A., M.D., F.L.S. With several Hundred Illustrations. 7s. 6d.

Natural History, Cassell's New. Edited by Prof. P. MARTIN DUNCAN, M.B., F.R.S., F.G.S. Complete in Six Vols. With about 2,000 Illustrations. Cloth, 9s. each.

Nature's Wonder Workers. By KATE R. LOVELL. Illustrated. 3s. 6d.

Nursing for the Home and for the Hospital, A Handbook of. By CATHERINE J. WOOD. *Cheap Edition.* 1s. 6d. ; cloth, 2s.

Nursing of Sick Children, A Handbook for the. By CATHERINE J. WOOD. 2s. 6d.

O'Driscoll's Weird, and other Stories. By A. WERNER. 5s.

Odyssey, The Modern ; or, Ulysses up to Date. Cloth gilt, 10s. 6d.

Ohio, The New. A Story of East and West. By EDWARD EVERETT HALE. 6s.

Oil Painting, A Manual of. By the Hon. JOHN COLLIER. 2s. 6d.

Orchid Hunter, Travels and Adventures of an. By ALBERT MILLICAN. Fully Illustrated. 12s. 6d.

Our Own Country. Six Vols. With 1,200 Illustrations. 7s. 6d. each.

Out of the Jaws of Death. By FRANK BARRETT. In One Vol.. 6s.

Painting, The English School of. *Cheap Edition.* 3s. 6d.

Painting, Practical Guides to. With Coloured Plates :—

MARINE PAINTING. 5s.	TREE PAINTING. 5s.
ANIMAL PAINTING. 5s.	WATER-COLOUR PAINTING. 5s.
CHINA PAINTING. 5s.	NEUTRAL TINT. 5s.
FIGURE PAINTING. 7s. 6d.	SEPIA, in Two Vols., 3s. each ; or in One Vol., 5s.
ELEMENTARY FLOWER PAINT-ING. 3s.	FLOWERS, AND HOW TO PAINT THEM. 5s.

Peoples of the World, The. In Six Vols. By Dr. ROBERT BROWN. Illustrated. 7s. 6d. each.

Perfect Gentleman, The. By the Rev. A. SMYTHE-PALMER, D.D. 3s. 6d.

Phillips, Watts, Artist and Playwright. By Miss E. WATTS PHILLIPS. With 32 Plates. 10s. 6d.

Photography for Amateurs. By T. C. HEPWORTH. *Enlarged and Revised Edition.* Illustrated. 1s.; or cloth, 1s. 6d.

Phrase and Fable, Dictionary of. By the Rev. Dr. BREWER. *Cheap Edition, Enlarged,* cloth, 3s. 6d. ; or with leather back, 4s. 6d.

Physiology for Students, Elementary. By A. T. SCHOFIELD, M.D., M.R.C.S., &c. Illustrated. 7s. 6d.

Picturesque America. Complete in Four Vols., with 48 Exquisite Steel Plates and about 800 Original Wood Engravings. £2 2s. each.

Picturesque Canada. With 600 Original Illustrations. Two Vols. £6 6s. the Set.

Picturesque Europe. Complete in Five Vols. Each containing 13 Exquisite Steel Plates, from Original Drawings, and nearly 200 Original Illustrations. Cloth, £21; half-morocco, £31 10s. ; morocco gilt, £52 10s. POPULAR EDITION. In Five Vols., 18s. each.

Picturesque Mediterranean, The. With Magnificent Original Illustrations by the leading Artists of the Day. Complete in Two Vols. £2 2s. each.

Pigeon Keeper, The Practical. By LEWIS WRIGHT. Illustrated. 3s. 6d.

Pigeons, The Book of. By ROBERT FULTON. Edited and Arranged by L. WRIGHT. With 50 Coloured Plates, 31s. 6d. ; half-morocco, £2 2s.

Pity and of Death, The Book of. By PIERRE LOTI. Translated by T. P. O'CONNOR, M.P. 5s.

Playthings and Parodies. Short Stories by BARRY PAIN. 5s.

Poems, Aubrey de Vere's. A Selection. Edited by J. DENNIS. 3s. 6d.

Poetry, The Nature and Elements of. By E. C. STEDMAN. 6s.

Poets, Cassell's Miniature Library of the. Price 1s. each Vol.

Portrait Gallery, The Cabinet. First, Second, and Third Series, each containing 36 Cabinet Photographs of Eminent Men and Women. With Biographical Sketches. 15s. each.

Poultry Keeper, The Practical. By L. WRIGHT. Illustrated. 3s. 6d.

Poultry, The Book of. By LEWIS WRIGHT. *Popular Edition.* 10s. 6d.

Poultry, The Illustrated Book of. By LEWIS WRIGHT. With Fifty Coloured Plates. *New and Revised Edition.* Cloth, 31s. 6d.

Queen Summer ; or, The Tourney of the Lily and the Rose. With Forty Pages of Designs in Colours by WALTER CRANE. 6s.

Queen Victoria, The Life and Times of. By ROBERT WILSON. Complete in Two Vols. With numerous Illustrations. 9s. each.

Rabbit-Keeper, The Practical. By CUNICULUS. Illustrated. 3s. 6d.

Raffles Haw, The Doings of. By A. CONAN DOYLE. 5s.

Railway Guides, Official Illustrated. With Illustrations, Maps, &c. Price 1s. each; or in cloth, 2s. each.

GREAT EASTERN RAILWAY.	GREAT WESTERN RAILWAY.
GREAT NORTHERN RAILWAY.	LONDON AND SOUTH-WESTERN
LONDON, BRIGHTON AND SOUTH COAST RAILWAY.	RAILWAY.
LONDON AND NORTH-WESTERN RAILWAY.	MIDLAND RAILWAY.
	SOUTH-EASTERN RAILWAY.

Rovings of a Restless Boy, The. By KATHARINE B. FOOT. Illustrated. 5s.

Railway Library, Cassell's. Crown 8vo, boards, 2s. each.

METZEROTT, SHOEMAKER. By KATHARINE P. WOODS.	THE PHANTOM CITY. By W. WESTALL.
DAVID TODD. By DAVID MACLURE.	JACK GORDON, KNIGHT ERRANT, GOTHAM, 1883. By BARCLAY NORTH.
THE ASTONISHING HISTORY OF TROY TOWN. By Q.	THE DIAMOND BUTTON. By BARCLAY NORTH.
THE ADMIRABLE LADY BIDDY FANE. By FRANK BARRETT.	ANOTHER'S CRIME. By JULIAN HAWTHORNE.
COMMODORE JUNK. By G. MANVILLE FENN.	THE YOKE OF THE THORAH. By SIDNEY LUSKA.
ST. CUTHBERT'S TOWER. By FLORENCE WARDEN.	WHO IS JOHN NOMAN? By CHARLES HENRY BECKETT.
THE MAN WITH A THUMB. By BARCLAY NORTH.	THE TRAGEDY OF BRINKWATER. By MARTHA L. MOODEY.
BY RIGHT NOT LAW. By R. SHERARD.	AN AMERICAN PENMAN. By JULIAN HAWTHORNE.
WITHIN SOUND OF THE WEIR. By THOMAS ST. E. HAKE.	SECTION 558; or, THE FATAL LETTER. By JULIAN HAWTHORNE.
UNDER A STRANGE MASK. By FRANK BARRETT.	THE BROWN STONE BOY. By W. H. BISHOP.
THE COOMBSBERROW MYSTERY. By JAMES COLWALL.	A TRAGIC MYSTERY. By JULIAN HAWTHORNE.
DEAD MAN'S ROCK. By Q.	THE GREAT BANK ROBBERY. By JULIAN HAWTHORNE.
A QUEER RACE. By W. WESTALL.	
CAPTAIN TRAFALGAR. By WESTALL and LAURIE.	

Redgrave, Richard, C.B., R.A. Memoir. Compiled from his Diary. By F. M. REDGRAVE. 10s. 6d.

Rivers of Great Britain : Descriptive, Historical, Pictorial.
THE ROYAL RIVER: The Thames, from Source to Sea. *Popular Edition,* 16s.
RIVERS OF THE EAST COAST. With highly finished Engravings. *Popular Edition,* 16s.

Robinson Crusoe, Cassell's New Fine-Art Edition of. With upwards of 100 Original Illustrations. 7s. 6d.

Romance, The World of. Illustrated. Cloth, 9s.

Russo-Turkish War, Cassell's History of. With about 500 Illustrations. Two Vols. 9s. each.

Salisbury Parliament, A Diary of the. By H. W. LUCY. Illustrated by HARRY FURNISS. 21s.

Saturday Journal, Cassell's. Yearly Volume, cloth, 7s. 6d.

Scarabæus. The Story of an African Beetle. By the MARQUISE CLARA LANZA and JAMES CLARENCE HARVEY. Cloth, 5s.

Science for All. Edited by Dr. Robert Brown. *Revised Edition.* Illustrated. Five Vols. 9s. each.

Science, The Year Book of. Edited by Prof. Bonney, F.R.S. 7s. 6d.

Sculpture, A Primer of. By E. Roscoe Mullins. With Illustrations. 2s.6d.

Sea, The: Its Stirring Story of Adventure, Peril, and Heroism. By F. Whymper. With 400 Illustrations. Four Vols. 7s. 6d. each.

Shadow of a Song, The. A Novel. By Cecil Harley. 5s.

Shaftesbury, The Seventh Earl of, K.G., The Life and Work of. By Edwin Hodder. *Cheap Edition.* 3s. 6d.

Shakespeare, The Plays of. Edited by Professor Henry Morley. Complete in Thirteen Vols., cloth, 21s. ; half-morocco, cloth sides, 42s.

Shakespeare, Cassell's Quarto Edition. Containing about 600 Illustrations by H. C. Selous. Complete in Three Vols., cloth gilt, £3 3s.

Shakespeare, Miniature. Illustrated. In Twelve Vols., in box, 12s. ; or in Red Paste Grain (box to match), with spring catch, 21s.

Shakspere, The International. *Édition de Luxe.*
"KING HENRY VIII." Illustrated by Sir James Linton, P.R.I. *(Price on application.)*
"OTHELLO." Illustrated by Frank Dicksee, R.A. £3 10s.
"KING HENRY IV." Illustrated by Eduard Grützner. £3 10s.
"AS YOU LIKE IT." Illustrated by Émile Bayard. £3 10s.
"ROMEO AND JULIET." Illustrated by F. Dicksee, R.A. Is now out of print, and scarce.

Shakspere, The Leopold. With 400 Illustrations. *Cheap Edition.* 3s. 6d. Cloth gilt, gilt edges, 5s. ; Roxburgh, 7s. 6d.

Shakspere, The Royal. With Steel Plates and Wood Engravings. Three Vols. 15s. each.

Sketches, The Art of Making and Using. From the French of G. Fraipont. By Clara Bell. With 50 Illustrations. 2s. 6d.

Smuggling Days and Smuggling Ways; or, The Story of a Lost Art. By Commander the Hon. Henry N. Shore, R.N. With numerous Plans and Drawings by the Author. 7s. 6d.

Snare of the Fowler, The. By Mrs. Alexander. In One Vol., 6s.

Social Welfare, Subjects of. By Sir Lyon Playfair, K.C.B. 7s. 6d.

Sports and Pastimes, Cassell's Complete Book of. *Cheap Edition.* With more than 900 Illustrations. Medium 8vo, 992 pages, cloth, 3s. 6d.

Squire, The. By Mrs. Parr. In One Vol., 6s.

Standard Library, Cassell's. Cloth, 2s. each.

Shirley.	Adventures of Mr. Ledbury.	Jack Hinton.
Coningsby.		Poe's Works.
Mary Barton.	Ivanhoe.	Old Mortality.
The Antiquary.	Oliver Twist.	The Hour and the Man.
Nicholas Nickleby (Two Vols.).	Selections from Hood's Works.	Handy Andy.
Jane Eyre.	Longfellow's Prose Works.	Scarlet Letter.
Wuthering Heights.		Pickwick (Two Vols.).
Dombey and Son (Two Vols.).	Sense and Sensibility.	Last of the Mohicans.
	Lytton's Plays.	Pride and Prejudice.
The Prairie.	Tales, Poems, and Sketches. Bret Harte.	Yellowplush Papers.
Night and Morning.		Tales of the Borders.
Kenilworth.	Martin Chuzzlewit (Two Vols.).	Last Days of Palmyra.
Ingoldsby Legends.		Washington Irving's Sketch-Book.
Tower of London.	The Prince of the House of David.	The Talisman.
The Pioneers.		Rienzi.
Charles O'Malley.	Sheridan's Plays.	Old Curiosity Shop.
Barnaby Rudge.	Uncle Tom's Cabin.	Heart of Midlothian.
Cakes and Ale.	Deerslayer.	Last Days of Pompeii.
The King's Own.	Rome and the Early Christians.	American Humour.
People I have Met.		Sketches by Boz.
The Pathfinder.	The Trials of Margaret Lyndsay.	Macaulay's Lays and Essays
Evelina.		
Scott's Poems.	Harry Lorrequer.	
Last of the Barons.	Eugene Aram.	

Star-Land. By Sir R. S. Ball, LL.D., &c. Illustrated. 6s.

Storehouse of General Information, Cassell's. With Wood Engravings, Maps, and Coloured Plates. In Vols., 5s. each.

Story of Francis Cludde, The. By STANLEY J. WEYMAN. 6s.
Story Poems. For Young and Old. Edited by E. DAVENPORT. 3s. 6d.
Successful Life, The. By AN ELDER BROTHER. 3s. 6d.
Sybil Knox; or, Home Again: a Story of To-day. By EDWARD
  E. HALE, Author of "East and West," &c. 6s.
Teaching in Three Continents. By W. C. GRASBY 6s.
Tenting on the Plains; or, General Custer in Kansas and Texas.
  By ELIZABETH B. CUSTER. Illustrated. 5s.
Thackeray, Character Sketches from. Six New and Original Draw-
  ings by FREDERICK BARNARD, reproduced in Photogravure. 21s.
The "Short Story" Library.

Noughts and Crosses. By Q. 5s.	Eleven Possible Cases. By Various
Otto the Knight, &c. By OCTAVE	Authors. 6s.
THANET. 5s.	Felicia. By Miss FANNY MURFREE. 5s.
Fourteen to One, &c. By ELIZA-	The Poet's Audience, and Delilah.
BETH STUART PHELPS. 5s.	By CLARA SAVILE CLARKE. 5s.

The "Treasure Island" Series. *Cheap Illustrated Editions.* Cloth,
  3s. 6d. each.

King Solomon's Mines. By H.	The Splendid Spur. By Q.
RIDER HAGGARD.	The Master of Ballantrae. By
Kidnapped. By R. L. STEVENSON.	ROBERT LOUIS STEVENSON.
Treasure Island. By ROBERT	The Black Arrow. By ROBERT
LOUIS STEVENSON.	LOUIS STEVENSON.

Tiny Luttrell. By E. W. HORNUNG, Author of "A Bride from the Bush."
  Crown 8vo, cloth gilt, Two Vols. 21s.
Trees, Familiar. By G. S. BOULGER, F.L.S. Two Series. With 40
  full-page Coloured Plates by W. H. J. BOOT. 12s. 6d. each.
"Unicode": the Universal Telegraphic Phrase Book. *Desk or
  Pocket Edition.* 2s. 6d.
United States, Cassell's History of the. By the late EDMUND
  OLLIER. With 600 Illustrations. Three Vols. 9s. each.
Universal History, Cassell's Illustrated. Four Vols. 9s. each.
Verses Grave and Gay. By ELLEN THORNEYCROFT FOWLER. 3s. 6d.
Vision of Saints, A. By LEWIS MORRIS. *Édition de Luxe.* With 20
  Full-page Illustrations. 21s.
Waterloo Letters. Edited by MAJOR-GENERAL H. T. SIBORNE, late
  Colonel R.E. With numerous Maps and Plans of the Battlefield. 21s.
Wild Birds, Familiar. By W. SWAYSLAND. Four Series. With 40
  Coloured Plates in each. 12s. 6d. each.
Wild Flowers, Familiar. By F. E. HULME, F.L.S., F.S.A. Five
  Series. With 40 Coloured Plates in each. 12s. 6d. each.
Wood, Rev. J. G., Life of the. By the Rev. THEODORE WOOD.
  Extra crown 8vo, cloth. *Cheap Edition.* 5s.
Work. The Illustrated Journal for Mechanics. Vol. IV., for 1893, 6s. 6d.
World of Wit and Humour, The. With 400 Illustrations. 7s. 6d.
World of Wonders. Two Vols. With 400 Illustrations. 7s. 6d. each.
Wrecker, The. By ROBERT LOUIS STEVENSON and LLOYD OSBOURNE.
  Illustrated. 6s.
Yule Tide. Cassell's Christmas Annual. 1s.
Zero, the Slaver: A Romance of Equatorial Africa. By LAWRENCE
  FLETCHER. 4s.

ILLUSTRATED MAGAZINES.

The Quiver. ENLARGED SERIES. Monthly, 6d.
Cassell's Family Magazine. Monthly, 7d.
"Little Folks" Magazine. Monthly, 6d.
The Magazine of Art. Monthly, 1s.
"Chums." Illustrated Paper for Boys. Weekly, 1d.; Monthly, 6d.
Cassell's Saturday Journal. Weekly, 1d.; Monthly, 6d.
Work. Weekly, 1d.; Monthly, 6d.

CASSELL'S COMPLETE CATALOGUE, containing particulars of upwards of
  One Thousand Volumes, will be sent post free on application.

CASSELL & COMPANY, LIMITED, *Ludgate Hill, London.*

Bibles and Religious Works.

Bible, Cassell's Illustrated Family. With 900 Illustrations. Leather, gilt edges, £2 10s.

Bible Educator, The. Edited by the Very Rev. Dean PLUMPTRE, D.D., With Illustrations, Maps, &c. Four Vols., cloth, 6s. each.

Bible Student in the British Museum, The. By the Rev. J. G. KITCHIN, M.A. *New and Revised Edition.* 1s. 4d.

Biblewomen and Nurses. Yearly Volume. Illustrated. 3s.

Bunyan's Pilgrim's Progress. Illustrated throughout. Cloth, 3s. 6d. ; cloth gilt, gilt edges, 5s.

Child's Bible, The. With 200 Illustrations. *150th Thousand.* 7s. 6d.

Child's Life of Christ, The. With 200 Illustrations. 7s. 6d.

"Come, ye Children." Illustrated. By Rev. BENJAMIN WAUGH. 5s.

Conquests of the Cross. With numerous Illustrations. Complete in Three Vols. 9s. each.

Doré Bible. With 238 Illustrations by GUSTAVE DORÉ. Small folio, best morocco, gilt edges, £15. *Popular Edition.* With 200 Illustrations. 15s.

Early Days of Christianity, The. By the Ven. Archdeacon FARRAR, D.D., F.R.S. LIBRARY EDITION. Two Vols., 24s. ; morocco, £2 2s. POPULAR EDITION. Complete in One Volume, cloth, 6s. ; cloth, gilt edges, 7s. 6d. ; Persian morocco, 10s. 6d. ; tree-calf, 15s.

Family Prayer-Book, The. Edited by Rev. Canon GARBETT, M.A., and Rev. S. MARTIN. Extra crown 4to, cloth, 5s. ; morocco, 18s.

Gleanings after Harvest. Studies and Sketches by the Rev. JOHN R. VERNON, M.A. Illustrated. 6s.

"Graven in the Rock." By the Rev. Dr. SAMUEL KINNS, F.R.A.S., Author of "Moses and Geology." Illustrated. 12s. 6d.

"Heart Chords." A Series of Works by Eminent Divines. Bound in cloth, red edges, One Shilling each.

MY BIBLE. By the Right Rev. W. BOYD CARPENTER. Bishop of Ripon.	MY GROWTH IN DIVINE LIFE. By the Rev. Preb. REYNOLDS, M.A.
MY FATHER. By the Right Rev. ASHTON OXENDEN, late Bishop of Montreal.	MY SOUL. By the Rev. P. B. POWER, M.A.
MY WORK FOR GOD. By the Right Rev. Bishop COTTERILL.	MY HEREAFTER. By the Very Rev. Dean BICKERSTETH.
MY OBJECT IN LIFE. By the Ven. Archdeacon FARRAR, D.D.	MY WALK WITH GOD. By the Very Rev. Dean MONTGOMERY.
MY ASPIRATIONS. By the Rev. G. MATHESON, D.D.	MY AIDS TO THE DIVINE LIFE. By the Very Rev. Dean BOYLE.
MY EMOTIONAL LIFE. By the Rev. Preb. CHADWICK, D.D.	MY SOURCES OF STRENGTH. By the Rev. E. E. JENKINS, M.A., Secretary
MY BODY. By the Rev. Prof. W. G. BLAIKIE, D.D.	of Wesleyan Missionary Society.

Helps to Belief. A Series of Helpful Manuals on the Religious Difficulties of the Day. Edited by the Rev. TEIGNMOUTH SHORE, M.A., Canon of Worcester. Cloth, 1s. each.

CREATION. By Dr. H. Goodwin, the late Lord Bishop of Carlisle.	MIRACLES. By the Rev. Brownlow Maitland, M.A.
THE DIVINITY OF OUR LORD. By the Lord Bishop of Derry.	PRAYER. By the Rev. T. Teignmouth Shore, M.A.
THE MORALITY OF THE OLD TESTAMENT. By the Rev. Newman Smyth, D.D.	THE ATONEMENT. By William Connor Magee, D.D., Late Archbishop of York.

Holy Land and the Bible, The. By the Rev. C. GEIKIE, D.D., LL.D. (Edin.). Two Vols., 24s. *Illustrated Edition*, One Vol., 21s.

Lectures on Christianity and Socialism. By the Right Rev. ALFRED BARRY, D.D. Cloth, 3s. 6d.

Life of Christ, The. By the Ven. Archdeacon FARRAR, D.D., F.R.S. LIBRARY EDITION. Two Vols. Cloth, 24s.; morocco, 42s. CHEAP ILLUSTRATED EDITION. Cloth, 7s. 6d.; cloth, full gilt, gilt edges, 10s. 6d. POPULAR EDITION, in One Vol., 8vo, cloth, 6s.; cloth, gilt edges, 7s. 6d.; Persian morocco, gilt edges, 10s. 6d.; tree-calf, 15s.

Marriage Ring, The. By WILLIAM LANDELS, D.D. *New and Cheaper Edition.* 3s. 6d.

Morning and Evening Prayers for Workhouses and other Institutions. Selected by LOUISA TWINING. 2s.

Moses and Geology; or, The Harmony of the Bible with Science. By the Rev. SAMUEL KINNS, Ph.D., F.R.A.S. Illustrated. *New Edition* on Larger and Superior Paper. 8s. 6d.

My Comfort in Sorrow. By HUGH MACMILLAN, D.D. 1s.

New Light on the Bible and the Holy Land. By B. T. A. EVETTS, M.A. Illustrated. 21s.

New Testament Commentary for English Readers, The. Edited by the Rt. Rev. C. J. ELLICOTT, D.D., Lord Bishop of Gloucester and Bristol. In Three Volumes. 21s. each. Vol. I.—The Four Gospels. Vol. II.—The Acts, Romans, Corinthians, Galatians. Vol. III.—The remaining Books of the New Testament.

New Testament Commentary. Edited by Bishop ELLICOTT. Handy Volume Edition. St. Matthew, 3s. 6d. St. Mark, 3s. St. Luke, 3s. 6d. St. John, 3s. 6d. The Acts of the Apostles, 3s. 6d. Romans, 2s. 6d. Corinthians I. and II., 3s. Galatians, Ephesians, and Philippians, 3s. Colossians, Thessalonians, and Timothy, 3s. Titus, Philemon, Hebrews, and James, 3s. Peter, Jude, and John, 3s. The Revelation, 3s. An Introduction to the New Testament, 3s. 6d.

Old Testament Commentary for English Readers, The. Edited by the Right Rev. C. J. ELLICOTT, D.D., Lord Bishop of Gloucester and Bristol. Complete in Five Vols. 21s. each. Vol. I.—Genesis to Numbers. Vol. II.—Deuteronomy to Samuel II. Vol. III.—Kings I. to Esther. Vol. IV.—Job to Isaiah. Vol. V.—Jeremiah to Malachi.

Old Testament Commentary. Edited by Bishop ELLICOTT. Handy Volume Edition. Genesis, 3s. 6d. Exodus, 3s. Leviticus, 3s. Numbers, 2s. 6d. Deuteronomy, 2s. 6d.

Protestantism, The History of. By the Rev. J. A. WYLIE, LL.D. Containing upwards of 600 Original Illustrations. Three Vols. 9s. each.

Quiver Yearly Volume, The. With about 600 Original Illustrations. 7s. 6d.

Religion, The Dictionary of. By the Rev. W. BENHAM, B.D. *Cheap Edition.* 10s. 6d.

St. George for England; and other Sermons preached to Children. By the Rev. T. TEIGNMOUTH SHORE, M.A., Canon of Worcester. 5s.

St. Paul, The Life and Work of. By the Ven. Archdeacon FARRAR, D.D., F.R.S., Chaplain-in-Ordinary to the Queen. LIBRARY EDITION. Two Vols., cloth, 24s.; calf, 42s. ILLUSTRATED EDITION, complete in One Volume, with about 300 Illustrations, £1 1s.; morocco, £2 2s. POPULAR EDITION. One Volume, 8vo, cloth, 6s.; cloth, gilt edges, 7s. 6d.; Persian morocco, 10s. 6d.; tree-calf, 15s.

Shall We Know One Another in Heaven? By the Rt. Rev. J. C. RYLE, D.D., Bishop of Liverpool. *Cheap Edition.* Paper covers, 6d.

Signa Christi. By the Rev. JAMES AITCHISON. 5s.

"Sunday," Its Origin, History, and Present Obligation. By the Ven. Archdeacon HESSEY, D.C.L. *Fifth Edition.* 7s. 6d.

Twilight of Life, The. Words of Counsel and Comfort for the Aged. By the Rev. JOHN ELLERTON, M.A. 1s. 6d.

Educational Works and Students' Manuals.

Agricultural Text-Books, Cassell's. (The "Downton" Series.) Edited by JOHN WRIGHTSON, Professor of Agriculture. Fully Illustrated, 2s. 6d. each. Farm Crops.—By Prof. WRIGHTSON. Soils and Manures.—By J. M. H. MUNRO, D.Sc. (London), F.I.C., F.C.S. Live Stock.—By Prof. WRIGHTSON.

Alphabet, Cassell's Pictorial. 3s. 6d.

Arithmetics, The Modern School. By GEORGE RICKS, B.Sc. Lond. With Test Cards. (*List on application.*)

Atlas, Cassell's Popular. Containing 24 Coloured Maps. 2s. 6d.

Book-Keeping. By THEODORE JONES. For Schools, 2s.; cloth, 3s. For the Million, 2s.; cloth, 3s. Books for Jones's System, 2s.

Chemistry, The Public School. By J. H. ANDERSON, M.A. 2s. 6d.

Classical Texts for Schools, Cassell's. (*A List post free on application.*)

Cookery for Schools. By LIZZIE HERITAGE. 6d.

Copy-Books, Cassell's Graduated. *Eighteen Books.* 2d. each.

Copy-Books, The Modern School. *Twelve Books.* 2d. each.

Drawing Copies, Cassell's Modern School Freehand. First Grade, 1s.; Second Grade, 2s.

Drawing Copies, Cassell's "New Standard." *Complete in Fourteen Books.* 2d., 3d., and 4d. each.

Energy and Motion. By WILLIAM PAICE, M.A. Illustrated. 1s. 6d.

Euclid, Cassell's. Edited by Prof. WALLACE, M.A. 1s.

Euclid, The First Four Books of. *New Edition.* In paper, 6d.; cloth, 9d.

Experimental Geometry. By PAUL BERT. Illustrated. 1s. 6d.

French, Cassell's Lessons in. *New and Revised Edition.* Parts I. and II., each 2s. 6d.; complete, 4s. 6d. Key, 1s. 6d.

French-English and English-French Dictionary. *Entirely New and Enlarged Edition.* 1,150 pages, 8vo, cloth, 3s. 6d.

French Reader, Cassell's Public School. By G. S. CONRAD. 2s. 6d.

Gaudeamus. Songs for Colleges and Schools. Edited by JOHN FARMER. 5s. Words only, paper covers, 6d.; cloth, 9d.

German Dictionary, Cassell's New (German-English, English-German). *Cheap Edition.* Cloth, 3s. 6d.

Hand-and-Eye Training. By G. RICKS, B.Sc. 2 Vols., with 16 Coloured Plates in each Vol. Cr. 4to, 6s. each. Cards for Class Use, 5 sets, 1s. each.

Historical Cartoons, Cassell's Coloured. Size 45 in. × 35 in., 2s. each. Mounted on canvas and varnished, with rollers, 5s. each.

Historical Course for Schools, Cassell's. Illustrated throughout. I.—Stories from English History, 1s. II.—The Simple Outline of English History, 1s. 3d. III.—The Class History of England, 2s. 6d.

Latin Dictionary, Cassell's New. (Latin-English and English-Latin.) Revised by J. R. V. MARCHANT, M.A., and J. F. CHARLES, B.A. Cloth, 3s. 6d.

Latin Primer, The First. By Prof. POSTGATE. 1s.

Latin Primer, The New. By Prof. J. P. POSTGATE. Crown 8vo, 2s. 6d.

Latin Prose for Lower Forms. By M. A. BAYFIELD, M.A. 2s. 6d.

Laundry Work (How to Teach It). By Mrs. E. LORD. 6d.

Laws of Every-Day Life. By H. O. ARNOLD-FORSTER, M.P. 1s. 6d. *Special Edition* on Green Paper for Persons with Weak Eyesight. 2s.

Little Folks' History of England. Illustrated. 1s. 6d.

Making of the Home, The. By Mrs. SAMUEL A. BARNETT. 1s. 6d.

Map-Building Series, Cassell's. Outline Maps prepared by H. O. ARNOLD-FORSTER, M.P. Per Set of Twelve, 1s.

Marlborough Books:—Arithmetic Examples, 3s. French Exercises, 3s. 6d. French Grammar, 2s. 6d. German do., 3s. 6d.

Mechanics and Machine Design, Numerical Examples in Practical. By R. G. BLAINE, M.E. *New and Revised Edition.* With 69 Diagrams. Cloth, 2s. 6d.

Mechanics for Young Beginners, A First Book of. By the Rev.
J. G. EASTON, M.A. 4s. 6d.

"Model Joint" Wall Sheets, for Instruction in Manual Training. By
S. BARTER. Eight Sheets, 2s. 6d. each.

Natural History Coloured Wall Sheets, Cassell's New. 18
Subjects. Size 39 by 31 in. Mounted on rollers and varnished. 3s. each.

Object Lessons from Nature. By Prof. L. C. MIALL, F.L.S. Fully
Illustrated. *New and Enlarged Edition.* Two Vols., 1s. 6d. each.

Perspective, The Principles of. By G. TROBRIDGE. Illustrated. Paper,
1s. 6d. ; cloth, 2s. 6d.

Physiology for Schools. By A. T. SCHOFIELD, M.D., M.R.C.S., &c.
Illustrated. Cloth, 1s. 9d. ; Three Parts, paper covers, 5d. each ; or
cloth limp, 6d. each.

Poetry Readers, Cassell's New. Illustrated. 12 Books, 1d. each ; or
complete in one Vol., cloth, 1s. 6d.

Popular Educator, Cassell's NEW. With Revised Text, New Maps,
New Coloured Plates, New Type, &c. In 8 Vols., 5s. each ; or in
Four Vols., half-morocco, 50s. the set.

Readers, Cassell's "Higher Class." (*List on application.*)

Readers, Cassell's Readable. Illustrated. (*List on application.*)

Readers for Infant Schools, Coloured. Three Books. 4d. each.

Reader, The Citizen. By H. O. ARNOLD-FORSTER, M.P. Illustrated.
1s. 6d. Also a *Scottish Edition,* cloth, 1s. 6d.

Reader, The Temperance. By Rev. J. DENNIS HIRD. Cr. 8vo, 1s. 6d.

Readers, The "Modern School" Geographical. (*List on application.*)

Readers, The "Modern School." Illustrated. (*List on application.*)

Reckoning, Howard's Anglo-American Art of. By C. FRUSHER
HOWARD. Paper covers, 1s. ; cloth, 2s. *New Edition,* 5s.

Round the Empire. By G. R. PARKIN. Fully Illustrated. 1s. 6d.

Science Applied to Work. By J. A. BOWER. 1s.

Science of Everyday Life. By J. A. BOWER. Illustrated. 1s.

**Shade from Models, Common Objects, and Casts of Ornament,
How to.** By W. E. SPARKES. With 25 Plates by the Author. 3s.

Shakspere's Plays for School Use. 5 Books. Illustrated. 6d. each.

Spelling, A Complete Manual of. By J. D. MORELL, LL.D. 1s.

Technical Manuals, Cassell's. Illustrated throughout :—
Handrailing and Staircasing, 3s. 6d.—Bricklayers, Drawing for, 3s.—
Building Construction, 2s. — Cabinet-Makers, Drawing for, 3s. —
Carpenters and Joiners, Drawing for, 3s. 6d.—Gothic Stonework, 3s.—
Linear Drawing and Practical Geometry, 2s.—Linear Drawing and
Projection.—The Two Vols. in One, 3s. 6d.—Machinists and Engineers,
Drawing for, 4s. 6d.—Metal-Plate Workers, Drawing for, 3s.—Model
Drawing, 3s.—Orthographical and Isometrical Projection, 2s.—Practical
Perspective, 3s.—Stonemasons, Drawing for, 3s.—Applied Mechanics,
by Sir R. S. Ball, LL.D., 2s.—Systematic Drawing and Shading, 2s.

Technical Educator, Cassell's. *Revised Edition.* Four Vols. 5s. each.

Technology, Manuals of. Edited by Prof. AYRTON, F.R.S., and
RICHARD WORMELL, D.Sc., M.A. Illustrated throughout :—
The Dyeing of Textile Fabrics, by Prof. Hummel, 5s.—Watch and
Clock Making, by D. Glasgow, Vice-President of the British Horo-
logical Institute, 4s. 6d.—Steel and Iron, by Prof. W. H. Greenwood,
F.C.S., M.I.C.E., &c., 5s.—Spinning Woollen and Worsted, by W. S.
B. McLaren, M.P., 4s. 6d.—Design in Textile Fabrics, by T. R. Ashen-
hurst, 4s. 6d.—Practical Mechanics, by Prof. Perry, M.E., 3s. 6d.—
Cutting Tools Worked by Hand and Machine, by Prof. Smith, 3s. 6d.

Things New and Old ; or, Stories from English History. By
H. O. ARNOLD-FORSTER, M.P. Fully Illustrated, and strongly bound
in Cloth. Standards I. & II., 9d. each ; Standard III., 1s. ;
Standard IV., 1s. 3d. ; Standards V., VI., & VII., 1s. 6d. each.

This World of Ours. By H. O. ARNOLD-FORSTER, M.P. Illusd. 3s. 6d

Books for Young People.

"Little Folks" Half-Yearly Volume. Containing 432 4to pages, with about 200 Illustrations, and Pictures in Colour. Boards, 3s. 6d.; cloth, 5s.

Bo-Peep. A Book for the Little Ones. With Original Stories and Verses. Illustrated throughout. Yearly Volume. Boards, 2s. 6d. ; cloth, 3s. 6d.

Bashful Fifteen. By L. T. MEADE. Illustrated. 3s. 6d.

The Peep of Day. *Cassell's Illustrated Edition.* 2s. 6d.

Maggie Steele's Diary. By E. A. DILLWYN. 2s. 6d.

A Bundle of Tales. By MAGGIE BROWNE (Author of "Wanted—a King," &c.), SAM BROWNE, and AUNT ETHEL. 3s. 6d.

Fairy Tales in other Lands. By JULIA GODDARD. Illustrated. 3s. 6d.

Pleasant Work for Busy Fingers. By MAGGIE BROWNE. Illustrated. 5s.

Born a King. By FRANCES and MARY ARNOLD-FORSTER. (The Life of Alfonso XIII., the Boy King of Spain.) Illustrated. 1s.

Cassell's Pictorial Scrap Book. In Six Sectional Vols., paper boards, 3s. 6d. each.

Schoolroom and Home Theatricals. By ARTHUR WAUGH. Illustrated. 2s. 6d.

Magic at Home. By Prof. HOFFMAN. Illustrated. Cloth gilt, 5s.

Little Mother Bunch. By Mrs. MOLESWORTH. Illustrated. Cloth, 3s. 6d.

Pictures of School Life and Boyhood. Selected from the best Authors. Edited by PERCY FITZGERALD, M.A. 2s. 6d.

Heroes of Every-day Life. By LAURA LANE. With about 20 Full-page Illustrations. Cloth. 2s. 6d.

Books for Young People. Illustrated. Cloth gilt, 5s. each.

The Champion of Odin; or, Viking Life in the Days of Old. By J. Fred. Hodgetts.	Bound by a Spell; or, The Hunted Witch of the Forest. By the Hon. Mrs. Greene.

Under Bayard's Banner. By Henry Frith.

Books for Young People. Illustrated. 3s. 6d. each.

*The White House at Inch Gow. By Mrs. Pitt.	*Polly: A New-Fashioned Girl. By L. T. Meade.
*A Sweet Girl Graduate. By L. T. Meade.	"Follow My Leader." By Talbot Baines Reed.
*The King's Command: A Story for Girls. By Maggie Symington.	*The Cost of a Mistake. By Sarah Pitt.
Lost in Samoa. A Tale of Adventure in the Navigator Islands. By Edward S. Ellis.	*A World of Girls: The Story of a School. By L. T. Meade.
Tad; or, "Getting Even" with Him. By Edward S. Ellis.	Lost among White Africans. By David Ker.
*The Palace Beautiful. By L. T. Meade.	For Fortune and Glory: A Story of the Soudan War. By Lewis Hough.

* Also procurable in superior binding, 5s. each.

Crown 8vo Library. *Cheap Editions.* Gilt edges, 2s. 6d. each.

Rambles Round London. By C. L. Matéaux. Illustrated.	Wild Adventures in Wild Places. By Dr. Gordon Stables, R.N. Illustrated.
Around and About Old England. By C. L. Matéaux. Illustrated.	Modern Explorers. By Thomas Frost. Illustrated. *New and Cheap Edition.*
Paws and Claws. By one of the Authors of "Poems written for a Child." Illustrated.	Early Explorers. By Thomas Frost.
Decisive Events in History. By Thomas Archer. With Original Illustrations.	Home Chat with our Young Folks. Illustrated throughout.
The True Robinson Crusoes. Cloth gilt.	Jungle, Peak, and Plain. Illustrated throughout.
Peeps Abroad for Folks at Home. Illustrated throughout.	The England of Shakespeare. By E. Goadby. With Full-page Illustrations.

The "Cross and Crown" Series. Illustrated. 2s. 6d. each.

Freedom's Sword: A Story of the Days of Wallace and Bruce. By Annie S. Swan.

Strong to Suffer: A Story of the Jews. By E. Wynne.

Heroes of the Indian Empire; or, Stories of Valour and Victory. By Ernest Foster.

In Letters of Flame: A Story of the Waldenses. By C. L. Matéaux.

Through Trial to Triumph. By Madeline B. Hunt.

By Fire and Sword: A Story of the Huguenots. By Thomas Archer.

Adam Hepburn's Vow: A Tale of Kirk and Covenant. By Annie S. Swan.

No. XIII.; or, The Story of the Lost Vestal. A Tale of Early Christian Days. By Emma Marshall.

"Golden Mottoes" Series, The. Each Book containing 208 pages, with Four full-page Original Illustrations. Crown 8vo, cloth gilt, 2s. each.

"Nil Desperandum." By the Rev. F. Langbridge, M.A.

"Bear and Forbear." By Sarah Pitt.

"Foremost if I Can." By Helen Atteridge.

"Honour is my Guide." By Jeanie Hering (Mrs. Adams-Acton).

"Aim at a Sure End." By Emily Searchfield.

"He Conquers who Endures." By the Author of "May Cunningham's Trial," &c.

Cassell's Picture Story Books. Each containing about Sixty Pages of Pictures and Stories, &c. 6d. each.

Little Talks.
Bright Stars.
Nursery Toys.
Pet's Posy.
Tiny Tales.

Daisy's Story Book.
Dot's Story Book.
A Nest of Stories.
Good-Night Stories.
Chats for Small Chatterers.

Auntie's Stories.
Birdie's Story Book.
Little Chimes.
A Sheaf of Tales.
Dewdrop Stories.

Cassell's Sixpenny Story Books. All Illustrated, and containing Interesting Stories by well-known writers.

The Smuggler's Cave.
Little Lizzie.
Little Bird, Life and Adventures of.
Luke Barnicott.

The Boat Club.
Little Pickles.
The Elchester College Boys.
My First Cruise.
The Little Peacemaker.

The Delft Jug.

Cassell's Shilling Story Books. All Illustrated, and containing Interesting Stories.

Bunty and the Boys.
The Heir of Elmdale.
The Mystery at Shoncliff School.
Claimed at Last, and Roy's Reward.
Thorns and Tangles.
The Cuckoo in the Robin's Nest.
John's Mistake.
The History of Five Little Pitchers.
Diamonds in the Sand.

Surly Bob.
The Giant's Cradle.
Shag and Doll.
Aunt Lucia's Locket.
The Magic Mirror.
The Cost of Revenge.
Clever Frank.
Among the Redskins.
The Ferryman of Brill.
Harry Maxwell.
A Banished Monarch.
Seventeen Cats.

Illustrated Books for the Little Ones. Containing interesting Stories All Illustrated. 1s. each; cloth gilt, 1s. 6d.

Firelight Stories.
Sunlight and Shade.
Rub-a-Dub Tales.
Fine Feathers and Fluffy Fur.
Scrambles and Scrapes.
Tittle Tattle Tales.
Up and Down the Garden.
All Sorts of Adventures.
Our Sunday Stories.
Our Holiday Hours.

Indoors and Out.
Some Farm Friends.
Wandering Ways.
Dumb Friends.
Those Golden Sands.
Little Mothers & their Children.
Our Pretty Pets.
Our Schoolday Hours.
Creatures Tame.
Creatures Wild.

Albums for Children. 3s. 6d. each.

The Album for Home, School, and Play. Containing Stories by Popular Authors. Illustrated.
My Own Album of Animals. With Full-page Illustrations.

Picture Album of All Sorts. With Full-page Illustrations.
The Chit-Chat Album. Illustrated throughout.

"Wanted—a King" Series. Illustrated. 3s. 6d. each.

Great Grandmamma. By Georgina M. Synge.
Robin's Ride. By Ellinor Davenport Adams.
Wanted—a King; or, How Merle set the Nursery Rhymes to Rights.
By Maggie Browne. With Original Designs by Harry Furniss.

The World's Workers. A Series of New and Original Volumes.
With Portraits printed on a tint as Frontispiece. 1s. each.

Charles Haddon Spurgeon. By G. HOLDEN PIKE.
Dr. Arnold of Rugby. By Rose E. Selfe.
The Earl of Shaftesbury. By Henry Frith.
Sarah Robinson, Agnes Weston, and Mrs. Meredith. By E. M. Tomkinson.
Thomas A. Edison and Samuel F. B. Morse. By Dr. Denslow and J. Marsh Parker.
Mrs. Somerville and Mary Carpenter. By Phyllis Browne.
General Gordon. By the Rev. S. A. Swaine.
Charles Dickens. By his Eldest Daughter.
Sir Titus Salt and George Moore. By J. Burnley.

Florence Nightingale, Catherine Marsh, Frances Ridley Havergal, Mrs. Ranyard ("L. N. R."). By Lizzie Alldridge.
Dr. Guthrie, Father Mathew, Elihu Burritt, George Livesey. By John W. Kirton, LL.D.
Sir Henry Havelock and Colin Campbell Lord Clyde. By E. C. Phillips.
Abraham Lincoln. By Ernest Foster.
George Müller and Andrew Reed. By E. R. Pitman.
Richard Cobden. By R. Gowing.
Benjamin Franklin. By E. M. Tomkinson.
Handel. By Eliza Clarke. [Swaine.
Turner the Artist. By the Rev. S. A.
George and Robert Stephenson. By C. L. Matéaux.

David Livingstone. By Robert Smiles.

. *The above Works (excluding* RICHARD COBDEN *and* CHARLES HADDON SPURGEON) *can also be had Three in One Vol., cloth, gilt edges, 3s.*

Library of Wonders. Illustrated Gift-books for Boys. Paper, 1s. cloth, 1s. 6d.

Wonderful Adventures.
Wonderful Escapes.

Wonders of Bodily Strength and Skill

Cassell's Eighteenpenny Story Books. Illustrated.

Wee Willie Winkie.
Ups and Downs of a Donkey's Life.
Three Wee Ulster Lassies.
Up the Ladder.
Dick's Hero: and other Stories.
The Chip Boy.
Raggles, Baggles, and the Emperor.
Roses from Thorns.

Faith's Father.
By Land and Sea.
The Young Berringtons.
Jeff and Leff.
Tom Morris's Error.
Worth more than Gold.
"Through Flood—Through Fire;" and other Stories.
The Girl with the Golden Locks.
Stories of the Olden Time.

Gift Books for Young People. By Popular Authors. With Four
Original Illustrations in each. Cloth gilt, 1s. 6d. each.

The Boy Hunters of Kentucky. By Edward S. Ellis.
Red Feather: a Tale of the American Frontier. By Edward S. Ellis.
Seeking a City.
Rhoda's Reward; or, "If Wishes were Horses."
Jack Marston's Anchor.
Frank's Life-Battle; or, The Three Friends.
Fritters. By Sarah Pitt.
The Two Hardcastles. By Madeline Bonavia Hunt.

Major Monk's Motto. By the Rev. F. Langbridge.
Trixy. By Maggie Symington.
Rags and Rainbows: A Story of Thanksgiving.
Uncle William's Charges; or, The Broken Trust.
Pretty Pink's Purpose; or, The Little Street Merchants.
Tim Thomson's Trial. By George Weatherly.
Ursula's Stumbling-Block. By Julia Goddard.
Ruth's Life-Work. By the Rev. Joseph Johnson.

Cassell's Two-Shilling Story Books. Illustrated.

Stories of the Tower.
Mr. Burke's Nieces.
May Cunningham's Trial.
The Top of the Ladder: How to Reach it.
Little Flotsam.
Madge and Her Friends.
The Children of the Court.
Maid Marjory.
Peggy, and other Tales.

The Four Cats of the Tippertons.
Marion's Two Homes.
Little Folks' Sunday Book.
Two Fourpenny Bits.
Poor Nelly.
Tom Heriot.
Through Peril to Fortune.
Aunt Tabitha's Waifs.
In Mischief Again.

Cheap Editions of Popular Volumes for Young People. Bound in cloth, gilt edges, 2s. 6d. each.

In Quest of Gold; or, Under the Whanga Falls.
On Board the *Esmeralda*; or, Martin Leigh's Log.
The Romance of Invention: Vignettes from the Annals of Industry and Science.

For Queen and King.
Esther West.
Three Homes.
Working to Win.
Perils Afloat and Brigands Ashore.

The "Deerfoot" Series. By EDWARD S. ELLIS. With Four full-page Illustrations in each Book. Cloth, bevelled boards, 2s. 6d. each.

The Hunters of the Ozark. | The Camp in the Mountains.
The Last War Trail.

The "Log Cabin" Series. By EDWARD S. ELLIS. With Four Full-page Illustrations in each. Crown 8vo, cloth, 2s. 6d. each.

The Lost Trail. | Camp-Fire and Wigwam.
Footprints in the Forest.

The "Great River" Series. By EDWARD S. ELLIS. Illustrated. Crown 8vo, cloth, bevelled boards, 2s. 6d. each.

Down the Mississippi. | Lost in the Wilds.
Up the Tapajos; or, Adventures in Brazil.

The "Boy Pioneer" Series. By EDWARD S. ELLIS. With Four Full-page Illustrations in each Book. Crown 8vo, cloth, 2s. 6d. each.

Ned in the Woods. A Tale of Early Days in the West.
Ned in the Block House. A Story of Pioneer Life in Kentucky.
Ned on the River. A Tale of Indian River Warfare.

The "World in Pictures." Illustrated throughout. 2s. 6d. each.

A Ramble Round France.
All the Russias.
Chats about Germany.
The Land of the Pyramids (Egypt).

The Eastern Wonderland (Japan).
Glimpses of South America.
Round Africa.
The Land of Temples (India).
The Isles of the Pacific.
Peeps into China.

Half-Crown Story Books.

Little Hinges.
Margaret's Enemy.
Pen's Perplexities.
Notable Shipwrecks.
Golden Days.
Wonders of Common Things.

Truth will Out.
Soldier and Patriot (George Washington).
The Young Man in the Battle of Life. By the Rev. Dr. Landels.
At the South Pole.

Books for the Little Ones.

Rhymes for the Young Folk. By William Allingham. Beautifully Illustrated. 3s. 6d.

The History Scrap Book. With nearly 1,000 Engravings. Cloth, 7s. 6d.

My Diary. With 12 Coloured Plates and 366 Woodcuts. 1s.
The Sunday Scrap Book. With Several Hundred Illustrations. Paper boards, 3s. 6d.; cloth, gilt edges, 5s.
The Old Fairy Tales. With Original Illustrations. Boards, 1s.; cloth, 1s. 6d.

Cassell & Company's Complete Catalogue *will be sent post free on application to*

CASSELL & COMPANY, LIMITED, *Ludgate Hill, London.*